CIRCLE OF STRANGERS

ESTELLE H. RAUCH, LCSW, CGP

PublishAmerica
Baltimore

ISBN: 1-4241-1357-1
PUBLISHED BY PUBLISHAMERICA, LLLP
www.publishamerica.com
Baltimore

Printed in the United States of America

CHAPTER 1

Jenny was very disturbed by husband Adam's irritable responses to her attempts to engage him in conversation. He much preferred being glued to his computer, where he was intent on creating an itinerary for the most marvelous trip. Shouting, "I'm trying to concentrate, for God's sake!," Adam rose from his desk, heading for the kitchen.

"I know you're all caught up in the Galapagos trip, but that's months off, and I'm asking you about our lives today. I need your input in planning the fundraiser—it's in our house, and involves both of us."

"Look, I just retired. I'm sick of dancing to somebody else's tune. If you want this, go ahead, but don't drag me into it." With this, Adam buttered a bagel, and then became pleasantly distracted by their cats' imaginative play with the sunlight streaming in from the open door leading to the deck. Lazily watching them, his thoughts drifted to ideas he had nurtured for spending his retirement: maybe he'd go back to college for writing, or he'd dive into the travel business full force and open up his own place. Or, maybe he'd just hang out in their cabin in the Berkshires, and travel cheaply to places he'd always dreamed about.

Jenny convinced herself that Adam's distance was only natural because he's caught up in his new life. "I can't let myself be angry...we'll certainly be fine once he's settled."

The telephone rang continually in this house. For one thing, Jenny had her psychotherapy practice in a home office, and frequently got calls at times her clients knew she might be free. And, Jenny knew so many people, from her longstanding involvement in the profession, to family members no matter how distant, to friends dating back to kindergarten.

Warm, friendly, at times funny, she was able to laugh at herself and to confide intimately in others, which most everyone seemed to appreciate. Jenny looked and dressed like a 53 year old hippie. Not ever blending in with her elegant North Shore neighbors was part of her charm. They valued her friendship, sought advice about decorating and child-rearing, shared problems, and didn't seem to notice the messiness in this attractive, if unpretentious home. There was always fresh coffee and tempting snacks around, and a sense that Jenny was waiting just for them to drop by. On this day, daughter Dana, 31, did come by with 2 year old Amy, much to Jenny's delight and Adam's irritation. Just then her stockbroker called to ask Jenny if she was interested in shifting some of her cash to buy stock in Chico's, a hot chain of clothing stores. Never able to make any sense out of investing, Jenny turned the call over to Adam, who was delighted to handle it.

While Jenny played with Amy, trying to keep her from grabbing one of the cat's tails, Dana, tall, shapely, pretty, stylish but harried- looking, began her typical complaints: they'd never have enough money to get out of their crummy apartment in their sleazy neighborhood. She didn't plan to work even when she could earn big bucks; she couldn't bear to leave Amy like Jenny left her when she was a child—and husband Mel will never amount to anything as a roofer and handyman! It was hard for Dana to remember why she found her gorgeous hunk of a husband so fabulous now that gorgeous wouldn't cut it.

Shifting gears suddenly, Dana mentioned that she had finally heard from Carole. Friends from college tennis competition, the girls had stayed in touch over the years when Carole was in New Haven. Dana had been thrilled when Carole moved to New York three years ago, but the girls didn't see much of each other; Dana lived far out into Suffolk County, and Carole worked very long hours. Carole's moving in with her boss hadn't helped matters as Doug and Mel had nothing in common. Neither of the girls had much free time to meet by themselves. Dana was hoping that would change with Amy in nursery school, and Carole possibly more interested in "girl time."

"Carole seemed very troubled; she wants to get together, so we set up a noon appointment next Saturday at MOMA, so I need you to baby sit Amy. You remember that Mel works Saturday; we can't afford to pass up the money." Jenny whispered that Adam would be furious if she missed going hiking with him to care for Amy...could Mel's Mom do it? Her face registering anger, Dana roughly picked up her daughter and halfway to the door turned, barking her contempt: "You're a lackey to Adam! I won't let Mel ever push me around like that. And I remember plenty of times when Daddy treated you like dirt. Now it's Adam's turn!" This, in spite of the fact that

Dana actually liked Adam, and loved doing sports with him.

Unusual for her, Jenny felt quite depressed after Dana left. Adam had finished his call and was back at the computer. She felt restless, irritable, very like what her clients described, having an impulse to do some thing nutty. Jenny wanted so much to surprise Adam with her own creativity and initiative. She remembered when they were first in love, then he really admired her. Now all he admired was the big bucks she earned, that allowed them to buy their second home and to travel wherever. Jenny was even more disturbed, this time with herself, for the unending battles with Dana. She called her big sister to ventilate, and felt somewhat better afterward.

CHAPTER 2

Stephen dropped in on his mother, partly to show off his new red Corvette, which he leased "...at a great price...I know, Mom, you think I shouldn't have, but then again you never were able to give yourself anything fabulous." He had recently bought a condo, which Jenny had seen and approved of...but could she help with furnishing it? She had already bought towels, linens, silverware and dishes, and had given him $500.

toward window treatments. Feeling she was being manipulated again, Jenny turned him down. Then they shared a quick breakfast and some laughs after which Stephen left in good spirits.

Jenny had familiar guilt pangs: 'I've so much, why not help a little?' Because Adam didn't approve, she could do it sub rosa...his kids didn't need help, and anyway grew up in a pretty normal family. All they expected from Adam was staying up in their cabin with him, going fishing, hiking or skiing. Their father hadn't been murdered!

Jenny answered some client calls, and went into her office to begin her workday. It was downstairs from the living quarters, warmly furnished in browns, oranges and yellows, with big fluffy pillows and a comfortable couch facing a large window only partially covered by sheer drapes. Before her next appointment, Jenny called her supervisor, Marianne, to report on the psych consult completed on Joy Robbins. They had a friendly personal chat first, did their business, and confirmed an appointment to drive into Manhattan together for a group therapy committee meeting and dinner afterwards on Friday.

Larry, 45, white, Jewish, of average height but forty pounds overweight, seemed almost surprised when Jenny came into the waiting room to invite him in. He had been engaged in a good read, porno, no doubt, Jenny thought.

Larry's marriage was in big trouble, partly because he played around periodically, but mostly because his drinking had gotten way out of hand. He had actually turned up at Friday temple services obviously drunk...had driven himself there, and argued loudly with Bev when she refused to let him take the kids home in his car later. Bev had had enough! Larry would either call for a therapy appointment, or she would take the kids and move back to her home town.

Larry had proved himself to be quite a fencer up to now, dodging any attempt from Jenny to elicit information about his background, his current family life, or even his genuine feelings. This week would be different! In consultation with Marianne, Jenny decided to confront Larry with his in-therapy behavior and how much it was costing him to bullshit her.

By the end of the session, Larry grudgingly admitted that he had been "a substance abuser" since early adolescence, that it "has screwed up my life," but he had never really faced just how much...he didn't want to give it up, but Larry finally understood that he could lose his family; he had also noticed how after a drinking binge he was nasty the next day with employees and with his family, and he didn't like it. This admission, to an experienced Jenny, was the first inkling that Larry might not terminate therapy soon. He went on to tell her that he had been mean to his 3 year old son, "when Josh was only being a kid." Then, when his favorite, 9 year old Stephanie, told Dad off, he yelled at her, setting off tears and "I hate you!" Her reaction left him disgusted with himself. After apologizing to both children, and consulting with Bev, Larry made his first call to Jenny. On his departure this day, Larry said he was glad he came and he appreciated how Jenny "didn't let me get away with bullshit." Jenny thought to herself, 'I wish I could be that way in my private life.'

Ten hours, eight individuals patients and a therapy group later, an exhausted but exhilarated Jenny walked upstairs. She grabbed a container of yogurt, then a banana, some pretzels, topped by a strawberry frozen fruit bar, then wondered just how many calories were in such a bizarre "dinner" at 10 pm. 'I am going to change how I eat...I must work less, and take off time to eat...but how can I stop my work with some of these people?' Resolving not to commit to new evening appointments when these clients finished, maybe two years from now, Jenny already felt lighter.

Adam was exuberant! "I finished work on the trip; Galapagos here we come!" Grabbing Jenny for a quick hug, Adam invited her for a walk.

It was a gorgeous late Spring evening and she hadn't been out since early morning. Though exhausted, Jenny joined him, agreeing that the walk energized her. The couple then started to "fool around," went into the shower together, and ended up making love. Adam was really a terrific lover; he could excite Jenny, even overcoming her exhaustion, the hot flashed and the vaginal dryness.

At 4 am the Levines were shocked by the ringing of their bedside phones...it was Stephen. He had gotten arrested for cocaine possession and needed them to come immediately to bail him out. Also, "get me a good lawyer; if I'm convicted of a felony, I'll lose my broker's license, my condo, everything." Like the little kid he once was, Stephen sought his mommy to make it all better. Jenny wanted to go immediately, but ended up staying home till morning, arguing with Adam about her impulse to cover for Stephen yet again.

The following article appeared in Newsday on page three: "North Merrick resident, Stephen Roth, 33, a mortgage broker at Fitch & Laroy, was arraigned under the federal rico statute on possession with intent to sell cocaine and marijuana, in the US District Court for the Southern District of New York. Mr. Roth's bail was set at $250,000., which he was unable to meet. Mr. Roth has no prior criminal record. As yet, no trial date has been set."

CHAPTER 3

Naturally Jenny did ask her lawyer to represent Stephen at the arraignment, and was devastated at the high bail set. Naturally Dana was furious, feeling mother couldn't say no to him, but easily did so to her. Jenny had to cancel out the nice day she had planned with Marianne, feigning illness rather than telling the truth this time. It was one thing to share details of her own behavior, but quite another to let anyone know that Stephen had "dabbled" with cocaine.

On the Saturday following Carole's trip to the west coast, she and Dana were able to meet as planned because Jenny did not go away, and so offered to babysit Amy. The girls met in front of the museum, and agreed to bypass the exhibits for lunch in the sculpture garden on this glorious early June day. They looked so very different from each other: Dana fair, rounded, dressed casually in the Gap's best, while Carole was dramatically sunburned, had long, dark hair, and was in Ellen Tracy. On her shoulder was a burnt orange bag Dana could kill for…With all the contrast, there was real affection and trust, so that they were able to get past the long separation and jump pretty quickly into the real meat of their lives.

Carole did take time to swear Dana to secrecy, then began telling her friend that she had done something terrible…she felt horribly guilty, but first needed to go over events leading up to it. "After two perfect years with Doug, the last few months have been a nightmare. On Valentine's Day, he asked me to marry him, a real shocker to me. All along he had said he'd never remarry, never subject his daughter to that and himself to another failure. Then he did it! Since we were meeting Jill within the hour, we never really talked much about it that day. And in fact we didn't touch on the subject again until early May, if you could believe that. Right after we finished a great doubles match with the DiMartinis', over dinner Vito told Doug that if he didn't marry me

9

immediately he was a damned fool! Since Vito and Angela are so happy together after eight years of marriage and three kids, they feel able to jump in and push Doug, etc. Doug seemed queasy at first; then he turned to me, saying that he had already proposed but got no answer. Maybe I had enough time over the past three months to consider it! Glaring at me.

"When we got back to the apartment, Doug took King for a long walk. I went to bed and pretended to be asleep when they returned, but he got me up, demanding in his prosecutorial manner that I explain myself. He was furious, scared me. I had never seen him like this personally, except when he was consciously attempting to intimidate a defendant. He seemed to forget who I am and that he loves me. Though I felt on the verge of crying, knowing how much contempt he has for weak women stopped me, and I blew up instead. Of course, nothing was solved. He let me sleep on the couch.

"After a miserable week, each of us decided we just had to visit our families, on separate weekends, Doug first to his mom in Naples, then me to California this past weekend. Neither of us called for the first time since we've been together, though I thought of it. When I was in San Francisco with my whole family last weekend, (with my mother away on a mercy trip somewhere,) I began to think about moving back there. My sister Leslie was thrilled that I'd even consider such a plan, and pushed me to call an old Stanford boyfriend of mine who's a big shot in the local real estate market." Then, "let's have a drink...I need it." The young women took a half-hour break before Carole resumed.

"'Now to the terrible part: I slept with Nick.. .no, I didn't exactly sleep with him, I had sex with him, twice!" Evidencing self-disgust, Carole went on to say that she and Doug hadn't been intimate since the fight weeks before.

"If he ever knew about Nick, he'd kick me out!" Carole wasn't sure what she wanted, to be free or to leave. Tearful by now, she shared how much she loves Doug, but needs to break away because "I can never marry a man who refuses to have children. Being with my niece underscored how much I want children of my own, and would never agree to not having them. And Doug has been adamant on this point!" But Carole can't seem to do the leaving, so she thinks that her secret, trashy behavior was probably her way of sabotaging. Dana was stunned; she had heard only terrific things about Carole's and Doug's relationship up until this day. The "affair," if it could be called that, was so out of keeping with Carole's morals. It was hard for Dana to know what to say, how to help here. Her own troubles seemed trivial for a change.

Carole had shared some of Doug's history to explain his personality, how he grew up as an only child in the Bronx, that his father hated and had contempt for his mother, and how Doug despised it when his mother allowed all this abuse. "In fact, though she knew that her husband had girlfriends, even after he left to go live with one of them, his mother slept with him whenever he came over. And, according to Doug his father said a hundred times that he'd never have stayed with her even this long if it wasn't for his son. Naturally Doug associates having children with being trapped. Then his own miserable brief marriage, and having to stay connected with that bitch forever and ever because of their daughter."

By the time the women went their separate ways, Carole did feel better. Doug will never know what had occurred, and maybe they could go on as before once he recovered from being hurt over the marriage business. She'd be very loving and would tell him that she feels too young to make such a commitment. Anyway, Carole couldn't leave him now; first she must find a new job, one that would support her. She'd make calls to headhunters tomorrow!

CHAPTER 4

Before leaving for Florida and a visit to his mother, Doug called Jill. It was 6:30 am, and he found her just up, sleepy and annoyed with him. She knew he'd be away this weekend and that he expected her to spend the following weekend with him. After hanging up, Doug acknowledged to himself that the atmosphere in his place was not terrific for Jill right now; she'd had enough of Doug's and her mother's hostility.

After landing and picking up a rental, Doug headed south on 75 bound for Naples. He automatically found the music station 101.1 that Carole had discovered when she joined him in Florida last winter. 'Last year Carole really wanted to go with me, saying it was about time she met my mother. The two of them really got along very well...Carole is terrific at drawing out quiet, even withdrawn people and got mom to talk about how life is here in Florida these past four years after living most of her life in the Bronx.' Suddenly hearing Vic Damone sing "Our Love is Here to Stay."

Doug found himself tearing, and shut the radio off. He never had patience for people who fell apart over endings and this was no exception. 'I might love Carole...she's become very important to me, but I'll be damned if I'm going to let myself go to pieces over her. I don't understand what's behind her not wanting to marry me. I don't think there could be anybody else. We seemed so close 'til...the hell with her! Working so closely with her was a mistake I can fix, and soon. Then whatever happens, I'll roll with it."

Pulling into the parking lot of the shockingly yellow two story residence, Doug began to feel calmer. He grabbed two cokes, then remembered his mother was a diabetic and bought another sugar-free drink before signing in. The aide, a very plump pretty middle-aged black woman escorted Doug to his mother's room, down a long, immaculate hallway. On the way, she talked about his mother, the activities she participated in, her food preferences and friends, in short left nothing to the imagination.

Mary Malone was sitting on a chair near the window, but not facing it; she had a magazine on her lap, but was not reading it. Still pretty with some red left in the hair she once was proud of, Mary looked quite healthy and younger than her 67 years. When her guests arrived, she seemed to take a few seconds to recognize her son, but then hugged him delightedly. "Where's Carole? Don't tell me you came down without her!" Ignoring the question, Doug engaged his mother in conversation about her granddaughter Jill, his job, and the weather in New York. Before leaving, he assured her that he'd pick her up at noon the next day.

On Saturday Doug accompanied his mother on a visit to her sister Belle and brother-in-law Arthur, who lived in a high rise overlooking the Gulf. He had not expected to have his family history resurrected on this day, but Aunt Belle could not be stopped from talking about his father in excruciating detail. All the man's failures, his womanizing, withholding support, hitting his wife, and eventual disappearance came under renewed scrutiny. For the first time ever, Mary listened without defending her late husband. She even seemed to get some satisfaction from the stories, and added a detail or two as they went along. Doug got up several times to refill his scotch, to find a bathroom, and finally to say he'd had enough, let's go! Returning his mother to her residence, Doug felt unusually sad.

This time, an old favorite by Frank Sinatra, "I Think I'm Going Out of My Mind," started a powerful urge to call Carole, but Doug stifled it. Instead, he went to a local bar, had a few more drinks, and slept it all off until hunger called. The next morning, waking up with a disgusting taste in his mouth, he was conscious of having used alcohol to run away from feeling upset. He was kidding himself...he didn't want Carole to leave and hoped they'd be okay. For the first time in his memory, Doug admitted he needed someone; maybe they could use help to make it work. It was not a comforting idea, but at least it was a plan, and not at all anything his father would have done. On the way to the airport early on Monday, Doug began to call Carole,, decided against it, then called his Mom, apologizing for his abruptness. She always forgave him.

CHAPTER 5

Doug had to guest-teach a class at his old law school, this in handling a hostile witness. The instructor introducing him described Doug's work as a supervising assistant U.S. attorney working as one of three Deputy Chiefs of the Criminal Division. "Mr. Malone's area of responsibility is organized crime and terrorism, typically involving labor racketeering, kidnapping and murder. Many of the cases also involve drugs, though there is a separate unit for international drug smuggling." Students were then invited to ask questions, most of these beginning with, "how hard is it to land a job there?" Doug laughed, telling them "get all A's, make law review, go on to clerk for a federal magistrate, then work for a top law firm for big bucks so you can afford to come work for us for nothing!"

That brought general laughter, and comments about huge indebtedness from undergraduate and law school, before they went on to address the topic of the day.

Doug's office is in a nondescript federal building in lower Manhattan where the only ambience is a rather majestic view looking toward the Brooklyn Bridge. It's a large room with very modest, worn leather chairs and couches, and a conference-sized mahogany desk. For someone with responsibility for the supervision of so many cases, Doug's desk is remarkably uncluttered. He doesn't notice the view or the state of the furnishings, but has gotten furious if files are left around, or if he couldn't lay his hands on something he needs. He and secretary Barbara Bates are like an old cranky married couple, working well together, complaining about each other under their breath, but never, ever thinking about splitting up.

Today finds Doug and his boss arguing good-naturedly about the up-coming election; Lily admires George Bush and Co., while Doug calls Bush "our Texas cowboy" and his likely cabinet, "the President's hands."

Neither of them had had much respect for Bill Clinton, who they both viewed as soft on terrorism. They disagreed on the seriousness of his sexual behavior, but both were furious at how much the nation's priorities were diverted by the focus on such trivia.

Shifting gears, Lily brought Doug up to date on a new case: it involved drug-trafficking, to be handled in the federal courts because there was emerging evidence of a connection with a known mobster. Right now the FBI was also investigating the attempted murder of a federal judge, and the bribery of a sitting juror in another drug-related case. Though the defendant, just indicted by a federal grand jury, had no prior record, he was spotted having dinner with Marco Da Silva, suspected in the more serious crimes. The NYPD was involved because the guy had been picked up locally with large amounts of cocaine and marijuana.

Clearly, he intended it for local sale. The cops had been trying to flip him, but so far the guy's denying any knowledge. Lily felt Doug was the perfect ingredient: "you'll scare the shit out of him! Either that, or send Carole to seduce him!" Lily, who suspected something was going on between Doug and Carole but didn't want to know details, often threw out these cracks, and loved the stony silence that followed them.

When Carole walked into her boss' office, not having been told that Lily would be there, she apologized and offered to leave, but sat down at their invitation. Details of the case shared, she was sent to scout some information and to set up an interview with Stephen Roth and his attorney. Today's meeting was the first between Carole and Doug since their separate trips to families. His smile and pleasant greeting gave her no clue as to how he really felt, and she wouldn't know for many hours. He was never, ever personal during the work day.

CHAPTER 6

Carole, haircut accomplished, cancelled an appointment this evening to rush home, not having seen Doug except in passing all day at work. His huge brown Doberman greeted her enthusiastically, after which she discovered Doug in front of an open, nearly empty refrigerator. "I missed you so much, honey." Carole hugged him hard, and found him immediately responsive. They kissed, at first tentatively, then with growing passion, soon shifting to the living room to complete lovemaking. King, not used to this venue for their athleticism, nearly interrupted matters, but finally got the message!

Afterward feeling very close, Doug spoke: "We love each other, we definitely want to stay together, don't we? Things have been so strained for weeks. Please tell me why my proposing was so upsetting to you."

When Carole responded with "I'm not really sure, but I probably don't feel ready for marriage," Doug naturally wanted to know why. He got nowhere, even with gentle questioning. Eventually frustrated, he suggested they see a therapist together. "We need help to talk about this."

"I've always done pretty well without therapy…why should we need an outside person?"

"you can't talk to me about whatever bothers you, and remember, Carole, for all your great skill in relationships, it seems that whenever a guy got serious, you took off. Is that what's going to happen to us?"

"Don't psychoanalyze me! You accusing me of running from commitment? Ha!! Maybe I'm just not ready at 29 to give up the freedom of being single. Maybe I want to commit to my career, switch to a fancy corporate law firm for a huge salary and a partnership track. You've had time for the big career. Why can't you understand that I can love you and still not want to get married, do the whole nine yards." To herself, Carole acknowledged feeling scared: 'how can I ever discuss that mess in San Francisco with Doug, or even with a counselor?' Then, "why can't we go on as we have?"

"Something about this doesn't make sense. It scares me...and if you think it's easy for me to admit being scared...please let's try this therapy business. You know that I've usually had contempt for most therapists on the stand, so maybe after one session I'll feel the same way and give up on it. But I'm asking you to come with me that once."

The next day, with Carole's consent, Doug called for an appointment with Marianne Rand, a name she had gotten from Dana, who said her mother thought the world of her. He also called Jill, and arranged for them to spend Saturday together.

Marianne believed in seeing couples together for an initial appointment. Looking at this couple, she begins by remarking on the fact that Doug arranged this meeting. "Would you like to begin?"

"This isn't easy for me...or for us. We've been together over two years, dating for eight months, then living together. We're very close and I thought ready for the next step. That was on Valentine's Day. Carole has done a disappearing act ever since."

"You mean she left? Or emotionally abandoned you?"

"We're still under one roof, if that's what you mean. Just not allowed to talk about the "M" word. She also kept away from me sexually, but we're okay in that department again. It's not that I'm obsessed about getting married, but now it's become something that I'm mystified about. And I don't like mysteries!"

"So Carole, can you shed light on any of this? What did Doug's proposal on Valentine's Day set off for you, if you know...and would you be willing to say?"

"I didn't want to come today. Doug can be very forceful, and I do love him so I'm here. But I'm not sure that I can speak freely, in front of him and with you, a stranger."

"Certainly I'm a stranger, and I appreciate how much you must care for Doug if you pushed through your dislike for this kind of thing and came anyway. We can take it slowly, and in fact I want to meet individually with each of you next week, so that we won't stay strangers for long. How about both of you tell me about how you met, what you love about each other, and a little about your backgrounds today."

The balance of today's session was almost pleasant, as the

couplereminisced about their first working together, how he fought against his own impulse to date her for months before giving in, and how she knew way before he said anything what was going on. Marianne concluded by noting that Doug must have felt a powerful pull toward Carole to overcome his professional obligation to avoid intimacy with a supervisee, and that Carole was obviously flattered, and an astute observer. (Marianne reminded herself that she must not pre-judge Doug for this transgression.) Separate appointments were scheduled for each, and at Marianne's insistence, the couple agreed to split the fee. Carole had gotten used to Doug paying for most things, so was shocked at this request but went along for now.

Carole dressed carefully for her next private appointment. Asking herself why she was so nervous, and reassuring herself that she doesn't have to tell her anything she doesn't want to, Carole managed to show up on time. Then she remembered she had left her checkbook home, so couldn't pay for her own appointment today.

"Hello, Carole…you got here! Frankly I wasn't sure you would, but am pleased you did."

"You don't know Doug. He'd have the whole NYPD investigating me if I didn't come, so suspicious would he be! I'm just kidding, but you don't say no to him and easily get away with it."

"So you have been pressured, and violated your own judgment tocome here?"

"Not really. If we are going on as a couple, we have to do this, much as I hate to admit it. But can I ask you about your credentials? Dana recommended you via her mother Jenny Levine, but I don't really know anything about you."

Understanding that Carole was stalling for time, Marianne never the less answered her questions, then told her that "coming clean" in this private place could actually make Carole's life easier. Whatever she thinks she has to hide, given what she has already said about Doug, will inevitably destroy the relationship if not dealt with, at least within herself.

Taking a deep breath, shifting nervously in her chair, Carole begins telling Marianne how she can never marry Doug. "I love him, but sooner rather than later I've got to leave. He doesn't want children, and even if I could force him into it, who wants to undertake something so important that way?"

"What makes you so certain that Doug still holds hard to that position? Have you discussed it with him since he proposed?"

"I know. No, we haven't…I guess because he doesn't know it's such an issue for me, or because he may be afraid to touch it also. My fear was once he said it, then we'd have to break up immediately."

"You have a lot of 'have to's' in that sentence! In fact, it's usually what's not discussed that destroys relationships. Although there are thingsthat individuals may decide shouldn't be shared, would be too hurtful, and are unnecessary to share. Perhaps you are also dealing with something like that?"

Carole, shocked (is Marianne a mind reader?), was silenced momentarily. Then, "either you're brilliant or a good guesser—when I was very depressed after our terrible fight, I had a two day sexual encounter with an ex-boyfriend. If Doug ever knew…"

Marianne takes in Carole's extremely tense body language. "More important than you ever telling Doug is understanding why you were so vulnerable, why you would violate what obviously are your own moral standards in a relationship. What are your thoughts about this?" C a r o l e though tearful during the second half of today's session opened up about herself in a way she never had before. When Marianne said it was time to stop, it was a shock. She told Carole that the young woman might later feel regretful that she said so much; it was healthy that she did share, but not natural for her. Marianne hoped that Carole would call if she felt too upset after today's talk, and advised her to have some individual appointments before they undertook much in the way of couple work.

"I'll think about what you said, Marianne, but we can be sure that Doug will freak out if he thinks this work isn't for us to talk to each other.

He won't see you alone, I guarantee it. And I don't know how I can possibly come alone and with him because of the money." (Marianne privately wondered if Carole wanted to avoid paying for her own therapy, or get Marianne to cut her fee.) Marianne's session with Doug was very like a sparring match. When she joked with him about it, he freely acknowledged not wanting "to get too involved in this business," but did, in fact, go on to tell Marianne about himself.

"Doug, I don't know if Carole told you that I recommended she work with me alone for a period. I can't breach confidentiality, though she is free to tell you whatever she wishes…but I can tell you that her working on herself will eventually make for a far healthier relationship. That is, of course, true for all of us. While I'm seeing her individually, we should postpone the couple sessions. Of course, you and I also can meet by ourselves."

"Carole did tell me. She also told me that she thought I'd be upset and she's right! Neither of us came to you for therapy…we want joint counseling. I researched it on the Internet, and found that a lot of therapists believe separate therapy breaks up relationships. Are you sure you know what you're doing?" He spoke quietly, but the hostility and contempt were palpable.

"I know this isn't what you had in mind. When someone sees you professionally, doubtless they are surprised by what you suggest. That doesn't mean you don't know your business." Thinking she sounded and might in fact be defensive, Marianne added: "Of course you are free to consult with another therapist to check on my recommendations."

"Carole actually likes you. She won't switch, I asked her. So we'll try it your way for a while, say for a month, okay?"

"That's very reasonable. Let's set up our next appointment."

On the way home, Doug spoke to his daughter, who was doing a report on the U.S. Supreme Court; she had done her internet research, but naturally wanted her Dad's input, which he loved.

On June 23rd, Dana called Carole, close to hysterical, at her mother's request. Stephen's problem was far more serious than cocaine possession. "The cops are hounding him; they think he's involve somehow in trying to kill a judge. That's ridiculous! He may be a druggie, who knows maybe he even sold stuff to his friends to support his crazy, extravagant lifestyle, but he's no killer! I need your advice. My mother's desperate, she can't work. With all that she's gone through in life, this is the worse. Please help us!"

"Calm down. I'd love to be able to help, but frankly our office is handling the case, so I shouldn't really be talking to you. My best advice: get him a first-rate criminal defense attorney. They're expensive, but well worth it in a huge case like this. When judges are involved, believe me you're in over your head with anyone less experienced. Try RobertBarkley...I've seen him defend a half dozen clients in murder cases, and he knows his stuff. Even Doug has enormous respect for him."

"Where are we getting that kind of money? My mother is saying she has to sell the house. Did you know...I just learned that the house is in her name alone because Adam let his ex-wife keep their home and didn't put anything toward the down payment on their place. They own the little cabin together, but it isn't worth much and they have a mortgage on it.

Plus there's something about not selling it before a year's up to avoid big capital gains."

"Dana, I can't help your family figure out the mechanics, only can give you my best advice. We can't talk again while this case is ongoing, but please tell your mother how much I feel for her. And, by the way, Doug and I are both seeing Marianne and like her very much. Please thank your mom for us."

CHAPTER 7

Marianne called Jenny to thank her for the referral, but when she found her friend and colleague so distraught, shifted to a more personal approach. "What's wrong?" At this, Jenny burst out crying, and then decided to drive over to see Marianne, saying she was too frantic to talk on the phone. Marianne stopped her: "I'll come to you, you're in no state to drive this distance." Once together, Jenny spilled everything, leaving her friend very worried. At the same time, after hearing some of the facts aboutStephen's trouble, Marianne realized that she had a conflict. Clearly Jenny didn't know whom she had referred to Marianne, and what the potential professional problems were. Probably Dana did know, but hadn't filled her mother in.

Jenny informed Marianne that her marriage was probably over because she had decided to sell her house to pay for the high-powered defense attorney recommended by Dana's lawyer friend. Robert Barkley charged $650. an hour! He had already met with Stephen and agreed to take the case, even reassuring the Levines that Stephen was being set up, that he was probably innocent of everything but being a jerk!

After Marianne left, Jenny thought over their time together and felt cheated; her friend had continually changed the subject when Jenny desperately wanted some help with how she could deal with her son.

The next morning, having cancelled her appointments for the third day in a row, explaining to clients that there was a family emergency, Jenny called in an ad for her three story Long Island home. Afterward, intensely anxious, confused and lonely, she took a nap. Adam woke her, worried that she might be ill, and finally after their talk grasped that she needed his support, not his criticism of her "over-nurturing".

That was Thursday. By the end of the weekend, Jenny had accepted a full-price bid on their home, $750,000! Her intention was to buy an apartment in Manhattan for $450,000., leaving the balance to pay the lawyer. Adam was on board, even excited at the prospect of living in the city, closer to good schools, museums and theatre. Jenny was just relieved.

Several times over the next weeks, the two traveled between Long Island and Manhattan. In the city, they saw dozens of dreary, tiny, expensive apartments. Jenny often dropped in on Stephen, who was struggling with serious depression. The young man had been given Zoloft but there was little evidence of its impact as yet.

The Levines' excitement about living in town faded within a month. By July's end, with nothing decent available for under $650,000. and legal bills mounting rapidly, they started to panic. Using their funky log cabin as a base, Jenny rented an office on Long Island and moved all their furniture out of what was about to become someone else's house. Things were stored, the balance was either brought to the cabin or given to her kids.

The couple saw themselves being like squatters, in family's or friends' homes, living out of suitcases. They felt foolish, inept. Ultimately, in this state of mind they bid on a place neither liked, won it, then had to pay $35,000. to get out of the contract. Jenny told Marianne that it was a miracle that she and Adam survived the summer. but remarkably, they hadn't turned on each other, and actually seemed unified to those close enough to observe.

There was some other painful news: Dana initiated a separation from Mel, and had taken a job away from her home. She told Jenny that while she still loved Mel his lack of ambition left her perpetually angry and critical. So for everyone's sake, this separation was best. Dana would of course need some help from Mom, mostly with babysitting. "And, Mom, you don't have a clue about Stephen and how involved he's been with drugs."

CHAPTER 8

Carole and Doug went out for dinner at Elaine's, a real treat to celebrate a conviction. They were also in good spirits because both felt optimistic about their relationship. The place was packed on this Friday evening in early August. They had taken a vacation, two weeks at a rented house in Westhampton in July when the courts were closed. Afterward, they had flown up to Maine to visit Jill at camp. The girl told them that next year when she'd be thirteen she was definitely going on a teen tour. Her father started to object, thought the better of it so far in advance.

While at camp, the three played tennis, ran on the beautiful Atlantic beach, and did some rock climbing. Now home, they saw Marianne for two joint therapy sessions, after which she left for her month's vacation. "That's another reason to celebrate tonight, more money to spend on ourselves!"

Doug even gave Carole the go ahead on renovating their small kitchen.

Carole had not yet told Doug that she had contacted some headhunters to test the waters. When he went to the john she thought thateventually she'd have to tell him, if and when calls started to come in and interviews were set up. She didn't want to say anything just yet, hesitant to disturb their closeness.

After dinner, they strolled through Central Park headed for the West side and home, holding hands. Then, totally without warning, Carole threw up. Both assumed her dinner had been spoiled, or that she had had a little too much wine.

One month later, with no menstrual period in sight and nauseated nearly every day, Carole guessed she was pregnant; this confirmed, she called Dana: "Now I can use your help...I'm pregnant. Doug doesn't know and I'm not telling him, at least not yet. I'm pretty sure I want to get an abortion. But I really need to talk."

Dana came into Manhattan, a little crazed at her stressful schedule, and a little guilty at feeling almost happy that Carole's life wasn't so terrific after all. 'I'm not the only one whose relationship is falling apart.'   "I want to get an abortion…we never once slipped up with birth control…he absolutely wouldn't want a child, and I'm not about to do this alone." Tearful, but with some awareness of their being in a restaurant, Carole asked, "why did this happen to me, and just when things were going so well with Doug?"

Dana was shocked that Carole hadn't said a word to Doug. "You have to tell him. If he ever found out, he'd be furious and rightfully so! Since you want an abortion and are so sure he would too, why wouldn't you tell him?"

"Dana, you make everything sound so simple. Doug is Catholic, first of all, and I don't know how that would play into his reaction. Plus what if I blamed him afterward, whatever he thought? I know he strongly supports Roe v. Wade, but that's not the same as our terminating."

"I had two abortions, Carole, one in college and one when I got pregnant three months after Amy's birth. Be sure it's really what you want to do."

When Carole returned to their apartment, she felt as if she were seeing it for the last time. She noticed how graceful were antique carved oak shelf and matching mirror, and how the navy and dark red oriental runner made the eye move toward the large great room. Doug had welcomed her replacing his 'Salvation's Army's best' with her new furniture, two white leather couches, twin matching beige leather swivel chairs, and a modern glass coffee table. 'I'll leave these for him when I go.' Unable to afford nice artwork, Carole had gotten pleasure from the fine paintings Doug had accumulated over the years. One, of a very young Asian musician in native robe holding a large lute, particularly touched her. Now looking at the painting, Carole thought she knew why: 'she's so alone and confused, and can't ask for help.'

For all her sophisticated elegance, Carole at that moment felt like a little, scared child, She sat down on the sofa, and holding a soft pillow tightly against herself experienced momentary panic. Ignoring the ringing phone, Carole made her way into the smallest room in the apartment and sat down.

Jill's room is very small, really a maid's room from when many families had live-ins. But Doug had let his child do it over for her 10th birthday, and it was charming. For one thing, it has a Murphy bed, tucked in the wall with oak built-ins for books and cabinets for clothing. Jill was allowed to put up every poster imaginable with no adult input, and to bring her huge collection of stuffed animals. 'My mom never minded what I did with my room, but she also never helped me fix it up.'

Their master bedroom is large and neat. Doug didn't like her leaving her clothing and cosmetics around. He had to get used to sharing his space with a woman again after so many years. Their queen-sized bed has no headboard, and is flanked by two modest lamp tables; her one contribution here was a snazzy taupe and cranberry comforter with several matching pillows. For the nth time, Carole decided she would pay to have matching drapes made up. Then, nearly tearful, admitted to herself, 'I'm probably leaving within the week.'

Doug arrived home, took King for a good walk and returned with Chinese take-out; he then went looking for Carole, whose bag and keys were on the hall shelf. She hadn't felt well lately, and he was concerned, but she had told him that her doctor reassured her that nothing was wrong. Well, maybe the visit with Dana had helped, and they'd talk at Marianne's.

Within a few minutes of their coming together, Carole told Doug she was pregnant, and had decided against having an abortion. "Well, I guess you'll have to marry me now!," he joked. "Being a single parent sucks, I can tell you from my own experience." Carole, stunned, "What are you saying? I was so sure that you'd be upset, even angry. Are you implying that you actually want to have this baby?"

"Carole, I want you, and if we've gotten pregnant, of course I want our child. Are you telling me that you wouldn't have known that? Did you think I'd walk away from you, or force you to have an abortion?"

"I feel like I'm coming apart. One minute I want an abortion, then I don't...then I was sure you would want to terminate. Now I think that I hoped you would insist on an abortion. Maybe I don't want to take responsibility for it."

Doug took a call from his FBI friend Max, who filled him in on some new information in the Roth case. This was hardly the time to have this conversation, with Carole so upset, but Max told the prosecutor that he was headed out of town for surveillance, and wouldn't be easily available after tonight. Max seemed to think that Roth might not know much about the guy who looked like a good bet to be the boss, but there was some evidence that he did meet with him—and definitely did plan to traffic in narcotics. No sign of the gun involved in the judge's shooting, though ballistics had gotten a sharp image, and if the gun was found, could link it, and maybe even lead to progress in identifying the shooter. Doug agreed to prosecute on the solid drug evidence, and they'd see what else turned up. the two friends then spoke for a few minutes more about another case, then signed off with a promise to get together at Max's for billiards.

When Doug went into their bedroom, there was no sign of Carole.

He found a note on the kitchen table: "I'm going for a long walk." No signature, as if one were needed, but also no information as to when she would return, and her cell phone on charge on her night table. Feeling a mixture of guilt and anger, Doug ran two miles, had a scotch, then went to sleep.

Carole didn't come home and didn't go to work the next day. She did call, leaving a voice message that she'd be in later, that she "had an important errand to run, please tell the boss." When Doug heard it, he actually felt himself go pale. Secretary Barbara, who was used to Doug getting other people nervous, was stunned. She had certainly not been in the dark about his relationship with Carole, but now what was going on here? "If she calls, no matter who's in with me, you're to put her through!

Do not take no for an answer!" Barbara made the awful mistake of sayingthat she hoped nothing worrisome was going on with Carole, only to have Doug silently glare at her.

Doug managed to get a lot of work done, meeting with several litigators that afternoon to discuss cases he supervised, and also with some defense attorneys interested in exploring options. Barbara came in to say "goodnight," leaving, as she always did, at 5:30 sharp. That's when Doug realized that no one had heard from Carole again all day. He froze. Understanding that something was terribly wrong, Barbara left without a word.

Doug called several of their mutual friends, Carole's haircut and nail salons, even the tennis club, before leaving a message for her parents. As a last resort, he dialed Marianne's number.

In the subway, noticing a hugely pregnant, very young Hispanic woman probably also going home from work, Doug suddenly remembered a conversation he overheard between Carole and colleague Mark over a year ago. Mark had said that he's on pins and needles waiting to hear if his girlfriend of eight months was pregnant. Carole chided him, saying he should contact www.nokidding.com, a brand new website "for guys like you." Doug recalled Carole saying that young women resented having to be on the pill for years, and many would prefer their man taking care of it. Mark definitely had seemed surprised; he wanted kids someday, didn't Carole? She had shrugged.

Doug could not concentrate on reading, or on CNN reports of car bombings in Israel. He had yet to hear back from Carole's parents who tended to work very late, and only now actually left a message for Marianne. When she rang back, he didn't know where to start, and very unlike him, sounded shaky. She invited him in for an emergency appointment and was gratified by his ready acceptance.

Because he could not tolerate staying in the apartment for one more minute, Doug arrived twenty minutes early for the appointment. He spoke quickly, at first almost to himself, then slowed down, responding to his therapist's obvious caring.

"Doug, let's leave off speculating about just where Carole might have gone for now, though I appreciate your being preoccupied with it. How are you going to manage, not knowing? What are you telling yourself is your part in this?"

"When Carole told me she was pregnant, I actually joked about it, saying that now she'd have to marry me. Then I got annoyed with her for assuming that I wouldn't want our child...so we never really talked about what she eventually said. She wasn't sure she wanted it! I could kick myself that with her so distraught I took a long phone call. After I finished, she was gone. Clearly she felt I totally misunderstood her. And I did.

Carole always implied that she wanted kids someday, but she never said it outright."

In response to Marianne asking him what he meant by that, Doug referred to Carole's saying that her sister 'naturally' wants more children.

So he assumed she also felt that way.

"Doug, you are giving examples of indirect communication from Carole, which you stored; did you ever actually ask her where she stood on this issue?"

"No. I didn't want more children; I think she was pretty clear on this.

It occurred to me she might not tolerate that, might want to leave me."

"I don't think you are responsible for Carole's leaving because you took a phone call. But the amount of indirectness, of allusions between you, which we had begun to address in our joint sessions before my vacation, that style left both of you unclear and terribly insecure. And, it never encouraged either of you to fully investigate how you truly felt about such a crucial issue."

"In my work, I'm known as going for the jugular. With friends, guy friends, I probably can say anything. With other women I dated over the years, when I'd had it, I just stopped calling without explanation. If they called and asked, I'd be vague, I'm busy right now, until they got the message. With Carole, I actually thought until you told us otherwise that I had been

27

very straightforward."

"Well, that probably means that you have been your most honest with her, trusting her more than most women. But that also means youwere more invested in needing her to stay. It's pretty powerful to finally fall in love at age 40! You did say this was your first such experience?"

"Not quite true, but almost. I had a girlfriend from junior year in high school through lower sophomore semester college. Naively I thought we'd get married someday. But at Christmas break, she told me she found somebody else at Brandeis. Kate came from a pretty affluent family and was Jewish, while I was working class Catholic, a scholarship kid at NYU, with no money. I'm sure her parents had a part in her decision. But I got over it."

"Doug, I'm going to be as direct as you are in your work: you didn't get over it, which is why you never emotionally committed to a relationship even with your wife, until you really fell hard for Carole."

The silence spoke of just how on target that comment was. Because it was time to end the hour, Marianne told Doug that she'd be available as needed in this crisis. Doug asked her directly if she had any clue, given her private talks with Carole, as to where the young woman had gone.

Throwing aside confidentiality, Marianne replied that she hadn't actually seen Carole for private sessions since her own return from vacation. The couple had kept two joint appointments. Marianne's calls to Carole to clarify why she wasn't setting up individual times were not returned. Doug, obviously startled by this news, left saying he'd keep in touch, and he hoped Marianne would contact him should she hear from Carole.

CHAPTER 9

Alone in the cabin on this bright mid-September day, Adam returned his son's call. He was hoping to have some company for fishing and hiking. But the call was to tell Adam that his ex and her husband were moving to Sedona in early November, and that they had invited their children to stay for all of the Thanksgiving weekend. Since Dana was likely to be working, and Stephen could possibly be in jail, it looked like the Levines would be sans family over the holiday. Jenny would certainly find people to invite them over, no problem there, so why did just thinking about it make Adam feel empty? Why should he care about a lousy holiday?

Calling Jenny, who was home in Manhattan seeing clients all day in their co-op apartment, Adam left a message saying he was unexpectedly returning to the city and would be there by late afternoon. "Let's do dinner out. I'm sick of feeding myself."

Jenny returned his call, missing him, and left a message saying she was working 'til 6pm, "so stay away 'til then, and yes, we can go out, I'm exhausted and will be starved. How about Adolpho's? Also, is it okay for me to invite Dana? She came in for a gyn appointment and said she could stay for dinner."

Adolpho's was one of those Northern Italian restaurants New Yorkers love so much: dark, great bar, romantic booths, soft operatic music, moderate prices, and even on occasion good food. Jenny had discovered it in her single days after ending her second marriage. Then, having met Adam, she didn't dare venture there until after they were married four years ago.

Everyone ordered wine and antipasto while studying the menu, as if they didn't know it by heart. Once having ordered, conversation turned to Stephen, of course, much to Dana's disgust. "Can't we ever talk about anything else? Does anyone want to know about my job?" For some time, the three tried to stay in neutral territory. Then, a bombshell from the combative Dana: "Mom, how much money are you spending on Stephen's defense? Do you remember half of it is my inheritance?" For a moment, Jenny could not allow herself to trying grasp what her daughter just said.

Then, "I don't want to know you…you're so greedy, when did you get that way? Jenny shouted, very unlike her, and didn't at all respond to her husband's pleading for her to keep her voice down. "Damn it, I'll shout if I want to!"

Dana, on rising, yelled back: "There's the prosecutor who'll bury your precious son, sitting there alone. Why not ask him a few of the dozens of questions you've asked me?" With that, Dana walked by Doug's table, said hello, asked about Carole without getting a straight answer, and left the restaurant.

On her return from the bathroom Jenny did walk over to where Douglas Malone sat reading his NY Times and eating what looked like mussels marinara. A bottle of cabernet was half consumed, and he was, in fact, pouring himself more when she interrupted him.

"I'm Jennifer Levine, Stephen Roth's mother. My daughter Dana who just spoke to you is a friend of Carole's. May I sit down and talk to you?"

Surprised and annoyed at the second interruption, Doug nevertheless relented.

"But I can't tell you anything, Mrs. Levine, and you shouldn't be talking to me. So really there's no reason for us to be here together."

"All I want to tell you, Mr. Malone, is that Stephen is absolutely innocent of any plot to hurt anyone. By now I'm facing that he had been using cocaine and marijuana since high school, and even was selling it to friends, but only to friends, because he was always broke. It is ironic that I work with people who use, yet I couldn't see the pattern with my own. Maybe we're all blind to people we love so much."

Quickly ending the conversation, Doug left his dinner partially uneaten and went out into the chilly evening. 'I don't want to go home yet. I don't feel like being alone but I don't want to talk to anyone. I wish I could take a drive, yeah, right, after nearly a whole bottle of wine. I'll walk the forty blocks home.' Noticing every couple, their closeness or distance, feeling sorry for himself and intermittently upset with Carole, suddenly Doug stopped; 'Carole may not have left on her own steam…she left some pretty special things behind, like her Prada bag and the Mark Cross travel case I got her for her last birthday. She might leave me, but she'd never leave that!"

So instead of going home, just blocks away, Doug walked twelve blocks northwest and entered a very crowded NYPD station, uncomfortably warm even at this late hour.

While waiting to make a missing persons report, Doug called his boss. The two liked and respected each other, at times went to lunch but rarely talked outside of business hours. Their lives were so different, with the older woman married for thirty-odd years, having grown children and grandchildren. Lily joked about what she imagined was Doug's lifestyle, but never asked questions or contributed to the office gossip. Tonight's call was immediately understood by Lily to be important.

"Carole's missing, Lily. I guessed she had left because of some personal trouble between us; now I'm not so sure, in fact it's just possible that she's been abducted!" Doug then added that he's waiting to file a missing persons report. Disturbed by what she had been told, Lily replied: "You do that…in the meantime, I'll call Janet Frame at FBI. I hope to hell you're wrong, and this isn't connected to a case you've been working on together. And, Doug, I need to know just what is the 'personal trouble' you alluded to." Doug naturally filled her in.

The tall and very shapely young black officer who took Doug's re port introduced herself as Sergeant Melanie Cooke. Brisk and efficient, the sergeant went over dozens of questions from her report sheet, barely looking up as she wrote. Without seeming to be impressed by Doug's professional credentials, she inquired as to his relationship with Carole, demanding uncomfortable details. Reluctantly given, these included the reality that the pregnant young prosecutor might have left NYC to get an abortion away from his influence. Sgt. Cooke even said, at the end of their interview, that Carole would undoubtedly turn up, maybe not to see Doug, but perhaps at a friend's or at her parents'. That last comment infuriated Doug, who by now was convinced that Carole would never have left this way of her own volition.

CHAPTER 10

Lily contacted Doug on his cell, asking him to meet with her and Janet Frame at the local FBI office a-sap. Getting there by taxi, exhausted after the wine, the walking and the emotional stress, Doug nevertheless felt relief at having a team in place.

Janet Frame, plump, slightly disheveled, in her late 50's, seemed almost motherly. However, her sharp approach to questioning Doug and seemingly random but incisive a peculation quickly altered that impression.

She acknowledged that Carole probably had been intercepted on her walk and may be at present being held against her will somewhere nearby. Then, noticing Doug was devastated, she barked some orders at him:"This is not the time for you to think of her as your lover; you are a prosecutor, potentially going after some dangerous predator. Think! Who is likely to have reason for such an act?" The remainder of this meeting focused on this question. The meeting ended with a decision for the NYPD to be fully briefed; time was of the essence, and they know all the local players.

Of course, Doug's phone in the house and in the office would be tapped. Of course, there would be surveillance set up immediately. And, Doug was ordered to operate business as usual as far as work and his social life.

A call came through the next evening while Doug was in the apartment scrounging through the refrigerator. It was Vito: "Where the hell are you both? We're at the courts, it's Friday, remember?" In a less aggressive manner, Vito asked Doug if he and Carole "were pissed at us for pushing you around the marriage business." both he and Angela had noticed that Carole was not her usual self and they held themselves responsible.

Doug had completely forgotten about the standing tennis date, told Vito it had nothing to do with that conversation, but work pressure made playing just now impossible. Vito tried to argue him out of it to no avail.

So much for living life as usual.

After several calls from Carole's parents, the cleaning woman and from close friend Monica, Doug turned on the television, hoping to relax.

Instead, he was confronted with a Channel 4 report on "Federal assistant attorney, Carole Lewis, presumed abducted..." with several pictures from their many interviews after trials, a short bio, then commentary. NYPD and FBI were described as cooperating in the investigation and asking for the public to call in or go to fbi.gov with information. An upset, angry Doug put in calls to Janet Frame and to Lily. Neither was available.

Doug reached Jill on her cell phone. She was sleeping at a girlfriend's and studying for a big math test. Naturally, she was surprised at Dad's calling her so late, and he seemed unsure of what to say. "Jill, I have some disturbing news for you; it's all over TV. Carole's been abducted, the FBI's involved, of course, and they're very optimistic that they'll find her." the child gasped, briefly silent. "How could this happen, Daddy?

Why would anyone want to kidnap Carole?" After Doug tried his best to reassure her, and stressed that he wanted Jill to keep in close touch with him about all this, he said goodnight. Jill then asked him to pick her up at Noreen's. She wanted to go home with him, he must be so sad. But she was the one crying.

CHAPTER 11

With difficulty, Jenny returned to her practice. She was mostly working on Long Island, but had picked up a few clients in Manhattan on referrals from some other colleagues in the city. And, she had gotten oneof her late LI appointments to see her midday, since he worked in town.

Larry knew that his therapist shouldn't be seeing clients in her co-op; he was sophisticated in such matters, being someone who stretches the rules himself. He had announced the first time here that "I'll keep your secret," leaving Jenny troubled at what was being set up in their work.

Thinking she'd have to address it sooner or later, she elected for later; "I have enough to deal with in my own life right now."

Though he kept his appointments and paid his bills punctually, Larry showed no inclination to go to AA or to give up alcohol and pot "all the way." Instead, he now used sporadically, maybe once or twice a month, and brushed aside Jenny's statements that such an approach was destined to fall apart. She should have conferred with Marianne at this point, but was still angry with her, and besides, couldn't spend the money for supervision just now. So, she'd muddle through on her own. Stuck for ideas, Jenny just tried to stay focused with Larry, who began telling stories about people at work. Was this his way to keep her at bay, or was there something about these stories that had relevance to him? Wondering this, Jenny felt good by session's end when she actually posed that question to her client.

Joy Hope Robbins came in. She had been in Florida for a short vacation in a friend's new home. Looking bronzed and buoyant belying her always present depression, Joy told a few charming tales of her visitsouth. Because Jenny knew her long term, she waited until the real stuff came out. "My friend Ellen made no effort to make me comfortable. She knows I'm allergic to dogs but didn't even put her precious Sierra to board and barely had anything I like to eat. When we did go out, she took me to crappy restaurants!" Then, "I don't want to waste my good money talking about this. I need to tell you about something important." A rare silence ensued. From Jenny, "Maybe you're not so sure you actually want to tell me today?"

"Don't psych me, Jenny. Remember, I'm pretty shrewd, so I know what you're doing. Of course I want to tell you. I'm just not sure where to begin."

"I'm being audited by the IRS again, this time by the frauds division.

Me, who doesn't have a cent they go after, while al the corporate thieves who steal millions get away rich!" By now tearing, this 62 year old woman seemed like a little girl. Jenny had an urge to physically reach out, but of course contained it. "I can't afford to pay back anything. And what if they take away my real estate license, or if my malpractice carrier drops me?"

Privately thinking that Joy should have considered these possibilities all along, Jenny pushed that aside in her response: "You are of course afraid as none of this ever occurred to you as possibilities; you seem shocked."

"I'm beyond shocked. Maybe my bitch of a daughter-in-law turned me in. Why else would the IRS be interested in me? Before I found out about this mess, Ellen's husband, who is the squarest bore you ever met, said something to me about the way I manage money. At the time, all I thought was that he can afford to play straight, with all his money."

Jenny remembered close to the end of the session that she had planned to bring up Joy's getting two months behind in her therapy bills. With this crisis, she couldn't deal with it today. She was more than annoyed with herself for letting it go this far, especially knowing how Joy manipulated with money.

Marianne called Jenny for a lunch date, which they actually managed to squeeze in at a favorite local bistro. Sipping coffee while waiting for their food, the two old friends and colleagues seemed well past the previous mutual strain. Over lunch, Marianne spoke openly: "I know that I haven't been much of a friend to you lately. Let me tell you why. You remember a referral you made to me last Spring? That couple is professionally active in some aspect of your son's case. At the time, I couldn't figure out a way of telling you this and still maintain confidentiality; this past week I got permission to share with you what I just said, nothing more." It was a huge relief to both women. Jenny verbalized her gratitude for this…and, "It's been hell and it's not over. On top of that, my daughter is not talking to me. We had a terrible fight over her greediness, or jealousy as I see it, and probably over my insensitivity or favoring Stephen as she sees it. Adam, believe it or not, has really tried to help me here,speaking to her, even calling Mel. But she's adamant. She for a while was keeping me from seeing Amy, which killed me. I'm about to see a shrink myself." When Marianne responded, "That's a good idea," and Jenny, "Where's the money supposed to come from?," a certain pall came over the visit, and the two friends separated shortly thereafter.

CHAPTER 12

Stephen, out on bail, was being advised to plead guilty by his very experienced attorney, and mother agreed. Since it was his first offense, he would undoubtedly benefit under federal sentencing guidelines, which gave judges discretion to credit those who pleaded guilty and had little or no prior criminal history. But Stephen had contempt for the high-priced expert. "I wouldn't survive in jail, even for a year. Look at me, do you think someone who looks like me can handle himself with those animals?"

Though Bob Barkley strongly disagreed with his client and privately thought he was a fool, Barkley got nowhere even after assuring Stephen that he'd likely be in "a country club where you can practice your tennis."

Stephen had seen too many Hollywood films which made more of an impression on him than anything his lawyer said.

In June he'd been in jail for a few nights until his bail was reduced; it had been set ridiculously high for a first offense because someone had thought he was implicated in attempting to murder a judge! After Stephen's release, when mom came up with the lowered bail, he decided to stay with friend Ellie, who was clean and lived in a comfortable one bedroom in the Village. Because he was charged with a serious crime, a felony, Stephen was put on long term leave from his job. He couldn't even think of trying to get something else to do, though Ellie offered to help with that.

Instead, he took money from his mom, and felt pleased with himself when he was able to negotiate getting out of his car lease for her $3200.

Jenny had been making payments on his condo, and moved a few nice pieces of furniture from her large home to his place. Driving him to his home from Manhattan one afternoon, it seemed to Jenny that Stephen was unreachable. She vacillated between making small talk and respecting his need for silence. When they stopped for groceries, the atmosphere temporarily lightened.

Unfortunately, the neighbors knew all about Stephen's troubles from numerous Newsday articles, and they met up with several on this nicer than usual late October day. Those who seemed inclined to say hello were deflected by Stephen's demeanor. Jenny realized that he wasn't so much embarrassed as unrelated.

"Let's put your things away and talk." The place had been searched and left a mess, but Jenny had tried to straighten up. "This is not the time for you to crack up. You have no choice, you have to pull yourself together to participate in your own defense, since you are hell bent on opposing your own lawyer."

"I don't need you to yell at me! For all I care, I could be dead now.

Maybe I'll kill myself! What's my future like whatever happens? Who gives a shit?" Stephen went into the shower for what seemed an improbably long time.

Calling Adam from her cell phone, Jenny asked him to join them. She needed him. She was scared. Maybe she did the wrong thing in posting bail. Now he could kill himself. Stephen had refused to see a psychiatrist; pills couldn't help!

For a change, the usually slow-paced Adam made it over in record time. He was shocked at seeing Stephen; the younger man, usually fit and muscular from thrice weekly gym workouts had dropped thirty pounds.

Adam had only visited him once, at that point in jail, and hadn't fully taken in his wife's picture of her son. Now he got it.

When Jenny left for an hour "on some business," Adam tackled his assignment head on. "You've got to see a shrink; I can't have you driving your mother crazy with worry. You can't be a selfish bastard!" The shock treatment seemed to be working. After only half an hour, Stephen capitulated. He'd see someone. Adam pressed his luck: "we're calling now. My daughter-in-law likes a guy named Jerald Marcus in Baldwin. I got his number. Call him right now! And, I'm taking you to the appointment." Stephen seemed off kilter by this changed Adam, and followed his instructions without complaint.

On her return from eating a huge Hagan Daz sundae nearby, Jenny fought back tears of relief at learning of the already scheduled psychiatric appointment for the day after tomorrow. She would be eternally grateful to Adam for what he accomplished today.

CHAPTER 13

Carole had decided to go for a walk alone at such a late hour because she was thoroughly shaken; not yet ready to push through her own confusion, she did grasp one fact: she was the one who felt unready to be a parent. 'Doug won't let me get an abortion even if I insist I want one…and I know that I'm nowhere ready to be a mother! I'm trapped between two horrible choices: he'll never forgive me if I leave, but if I stay, what then?

At Broadway, realizing that her light jacket was far from warm enough, Carole briefly considered going back home. Then, while standing in front of her favorite Thai restaurant, a couple she hadn't noticed before addressed her: "You're Carole Lewis; we know you from TV. You are the ADA standing next to that Douglas Malone they're always interviewing, right?" Later, Carole attacked herself for her naiveté, but just then she acknowledged their observations, a bit flattered. 'Blondy' then hooked her arm through Carole's, startling her, while the tall, muscular man did the TV bad-guy thing, putting a gun in her side. Quickly taken to a nearby Ford Taurus, with the woman at the wheel while Carole and the guy werein the back seat, they headed over the Triborough Bridge toward the Bronx. Carole decided to be friendly, not to give in to her rising panic.

"Are we headed for Yankee Stadium? I'd love to see a playoff game, if you've extra tickets." No comment from either of them, as they continued their journey west on the Cross County, and then north on the Saw Mill River Parkway.

By now Carole was clear she was being abducted, and probably by professionals. 'What do they want? After all, I have no money, so if they are pros, they have to know that.' Her mind flooded, going from one possibility to another, landing nowhere that made any sense to her. The driver then pulled off the parkway onto a narrow dark local road, and then into a driveway leading to a modest split level house. Since they had not made any attempt to keep her from noticing where they exited, and they certainly knew she was no dope, Carole faced that they are likely planning to kill her. 'Why me? Why not?' The man identified himself as John, almost certainly an alias. He told Carole she could use the bathroom under the woman's supervision, showed her where she would sleep (clean, at least), and offered her some Frito's and coke for a snack. These were 'nice' kidnappers! The quiet blond woman posed a different threat. She seemed jealous of Carole, or at least of the attention "John" was paying her.

At midnight, "Maggie" insisted that Carole drink her coke, and whenshe refused, got a little rough. At that point, Carole was pretty sure they had given her a sleeping pill so they could sleep. Waking up in the late morning with Maggie standing over her, she discovered how right she'd been. At the same time, Carole felt calmer, why she didn't know. Here she was, alone with two gangsters, no one knew where she was or with whom, they showed every evidence of possibly killing her, and she felt in control. How bizarre!

For the next three days, the routine was followed perfectly. They fed her, allowed her to use the bathroom, but never once asked her any questions or gave her any information. She even tried a little flirting with "John" when "Maggie" wasn't around, but got nothing out of him. Her days were spent alone in the starkly empty master bedroom of this 50's rather dilapidated house. Carole thought it funny, noticing in the midst of her calamity that she was aware of the ugly pink and green tile in the "master"

bath, and the filthy institutional green carpeting. She spent her time obsessively going over cases for clues, or more peacefully, thinking back over pleasurable times in her life. Then, on Sunday, her abductors disappeared without warning, and after careful scrutiny, she pulled off an easy escape.

Once outside the house, Carole, in silk blouse and lightweight wool pantsuit was chilly. She also experienced mild nausea, and forgetting she was pregnant attributed it to the sleeping pills. A U.S. mail carrier had stopped for a special delivery, saw the young woman's wave, and agreed strictly against policy to give her a ride to local police headquarters.

Before even talking to the desk sergeant, Carole asked to use the telephone, having identified herself as an assistant federal attorney. She tried Doug on his cell, and getting no answer, left a rather hysterical message on their home phone: "I'm in Dobbs Ferry—that's Westchester County—

they're taking information from me, but I want to go home. Call me here, please!" Then, nearly hanging up without leaving a number where she could be reached, Carole pulled herself together.

Because the criminals had operated in his domain, the Captain insisted on questioning her, before giving Carole a police escort to her Manhattan home. He also alerted the FBI; their case officer said someone would meet Carole there.

Carole had spent an hour answering questions, and did succeed in getting a copy of her signed complaint to take with her. Arriving at her building, she got an affectionate greeting from the doorman and the elevator operator. but in the apartment there was no sign of Doug or King.

The answering machine had her recent message still on it, so obviously Doug hadn't been home. Just at the point where she was beginning to panic, the bell rang. It was the FBI supervisor, Janet Frame, accompanied by Lily, who had also been notified of Carole's release.

"I can't concentrate on what you're saying to me, on your questions.I feel very lightheaded, detached, not here with you, almost as if I were watching a movie." When Doug appeared shortly thereafter, he took her in his arms, disdainful of the others' presence. "They'll leave now. They can finished up with you later." Neither Mrs. Frame nor Lily had the heart to contradict him, as Carole's demeanor made clear just now vulnerable she was just now, but they'd have to return shortly. In the meanwhile, the information they had already obtained was communicated to FBI headquarters, and to the NYPD precinct captain.

Once alone, Carole insisted that Doug lay down with her. "I need to tell you what happened. I didn't plan to leave you...you must have thought I did. I was so upset with you about that call you took, but more upset with myself. Please forgive me."

Doug apologized profusely; it was beyond understandable that he should have even picked up the phone when she was hurting so.." Sometimes I can't let go of the work...you know it's important to me, but you're more important. If I had only stayed with you, this would never have happened! Did they hurt you?"

"Doug, I don't understand why they took me, or why they let me go. How crazy is that! Why me, what did they want from me? They never called you, did they? They made me leave a message for you at work, but at 6am so no one would be there."

After a shower and a short nap, Carole ate tomato soup and a half bagel, feeding King the other half. The dog didn't seem to want to leave her side; he put his large head on her lap, and they kissed each other repeatedly. Watching this, Doug nearly started crying himself. He talked to Carole about how he felt when he thought he had lost her, now not trying to hold back his tears. Carole at some point seemed to come back to herself, and she hugged him tightly in response to his obvious pain. "We'll be okay, Doug. We are okay."

Carole tackled the necessary calls to parents, sister Leslie and brother Richard, then to Doug's mother. Out of respect for her ordeal, everyone kept the calls brief. It was very disturbing to Carole that her mother didn't seem at all sympathetic when the girl described her painful struggle over the unplanned pregnancy. In contrast, Dad was caring and asked her to visit when she was up to it.

Mrs. Frame was accompanied by another agent, who took prodigious notes the whole time. Doug seemed mostly to watch Carole for signs of distress, but finding nothing to trouble him, kept silent.

"John, or whatever his name is, could be described as an Hispanic man in his mid-30's, olive complexion, slim, with a largish nose and very dark eyes. He speaks perfect English, with a hint of an accent. Maggie is slutty-looking, blond, plump, aggressive with an irregular walk. She has hazel eyes, probably wears contacts. The house, a small very modest 50's style ranch, was just off the Saw Mill River. It was completely emptyexcept for the cot I slept on, as far as I could tell. The electricity was off, so they used large portable lanterns and gave me several blankets. John wanted to make sure I was comfortable! They didn't converse in my presence, but during the day one of them always came when I called. I'm not sure if they stayed in the house at night.

In response to Mrs. Frame's questioning regarding her escape, Carole said that she had awakened that day to discover that she was not tied up, this a first. And no one came when she called. She had waited for quite a while, afraid to start trouble should they return. But when they didn't, she began pushing against the door and saw immediately that it wasn't firmly locked; it had an outside hook and eye which she was able to dislodge using a paper cup. "If you can imagine this, I was actually scared to leave the house. But as I got to the front walk, I saw the mailman returning to his truck, so I forgot about my nerves and just ran to him."

CHAPTER 14

The FBI had rapidly discovered the hideaway and naturally did all the investigative work on site. What they found was that the house had been advertised as part of an estate sale; it had been described as "available for immediate occupancy," code for empty. Undoubtedly the kidnappers had seen this ad, and correctly guessed that they might easily make use of it. It had been thoroughly wiped clean of their fingerprints, strongly suggesting that the kidnappers were professionals. The FBI learned that the blue Taurus Carole had described had been stolen from an elderly woman in Riverdale who rarely used it and therefore hadn't reported it as missing. It too offered no obvious help.

On the other hand, Carole's precise description of both kidnappers was extremely valuable, and they had her going over pictures of possible candidates.

While Carole seemed on the surface to be her old self, she showed extreme volatility when it came to responding to the many calls and even near assaults by the media. At times she was fairly understanding: "they just have to do their job," while at others, she became enraged, hanging up with "you bastards, just leave me alone!" Doug tried to run interference whenever possible, but of course he wasn't always there. He was also struck by Carole's clinging to him; it was perfectly understandable, given her traumatic experience, but it too, was unpredictable. She never got angry with Doug, and not once referred to her pregnancy.

In spite of the incredible workload which burdened his smart and highly effective staff, Doug decided to follow through on his promise to the Lewis family to accompany Carole to California. Their arrival in San Francisco's airport was naturally known by the media, who greeted them en masse. Carole repeatedly stressed that she couldn't say anything because of the ongoing investigation, but it took Doug's strongly stated, "You're not getting anything more from us," to end the assault. Carole's dad was there waiting to drive them to his home.

Once in her parents' modern, white, sprawling ranch house with its separate guest wing and huge pool deck, Carole seemed like her old self.

She even had a return of appetite, fairly gobbling down the tex-mex late lunch Leslie had brought. It seemed strange to Doug that Carole's mom sat throughout the meal not interacting very much, letting Leslie or Dad carry the conversation.

Carole had been disappointed that her niece, now in pre-school, hadn't come by. Brother Richard and family were flying in and would be there in time for a late dinner, which he was hosting at Carole's favorite steakhouse. In short, they couldn't do enough for her, but seemed to Doug to be a bit awkward too. He sensed their hesitancy to ask too much yet of course, they must be dying to know.

Just before Carole went to nap, (for her it was late afternoon and she was exhausted,) Dad finally got her alone. He hugged her again, asked how she really felt, and then asked her if she and Doug were planning to marry. Before Carole could even reply, he apologized for asking, "putting you on the spot," implying he didn't have that right. While Carole appreciated his getting her off the hook, she chose to answer: "Doug and I have begun to discuss things. We love each other and plan to marry. I'm surprised that you and Mom never asked me before about marriage or the pregnancy. How come you're both so hesitant to ask me about my life?" From saying he "always respected my children's privacy," Dad went on to convey that he was delighted by her news and that he "will naturally tell your mother, if that's okay with you."

To Carole's description of her conversation with Dad as "so formal, he could be a stranger," Doug queried, "Is that so different from how it always was? You gave me the impression that they typically were out of the loop." Upset by Doug's on-target observations, Carole found herself again seeking comfort in sleep in this chilly, antiseptic guest bedroom.

The couple later joined the rest of her family, including Richard, his wife, their teen-aged sons, and Leslie and Stuart, whom Carole liked a lot. It was fascinating to Doug that Richard and his wife confined their conversation to what their boys were doing, professional activities or world affairs. Leslie seemed to withdraw in Richard's presence, and Carole's parents were pretty quiet. The liveliest one was her brother-in-law Stuart, who spontaneously hugged and kissed her, chatting easily.

Doug had known her parents, having seen them briefly over the last three years, usually in connection with her physician parents conferencing in New York, or when he and Carole were on a trip out west. Anxious to understand Carole better, with all her contradictions, Doug took a rare backseat in the conversation. He then was very amused when her Dad, close to the end of dinner, asked Doug if he were feeling all right, he'd been so quiet!

They spent warm lazy Fall days hanging around the pool, taking calls from the office or the FBI, and evenings with a few of Carole's good friends. Most of these friends were married with children. They had met Doug before, but had no relationship with him because of the infrequent contact. Doug remained in the background, allowing Carole to reconnect with her friends. His picture of Carole as a teenager and young adult was shaping up. At one point, her then closest friend, Nancy, reminded Carole that she'd always gotten her way! Doug couldn't resist his, "tell me more about that!" which amused Carole no end. (Both knew where that question came from!) What Nancy really meant was that Carole was a star; as an outstanding student, on the tennis teams, and with guys. Nancy added that with Carole's parents rarely being home, she had had pretty much free reign to do what she wanted. Her brother had been out of the house for years, and Leslie had either tagged along or went off with her own friends. There had been a housekeeper, of course, but the Korean woman was very quiet, and wouldn't challenge Carole; that wasn't her job.

Nancy thought this was the "perfect family"—nothing like hers where her mother "was always around to drive us kids crazy, and my father constantly lectured us about every conceivable subject."

On the afternoon before they left, the women organized a tennis game followed by a barbecue at Leslie's. It was quite an operation, involving four toddlers and infants, two nannies and six little dogs racing around the two acre grounds.

The animals stole the show; unbeknownst to Carole, the barbecue was really a doggie welcome home to Rags, a Kerry Blue male puppy.

Doggie treats were offered in brightly colored "happy birthday" cups; hats balloons and dog toys were everywhere. Naturally the toddlers ran after the dogs, and the tiniest dogs ran faster!

The only other memorable event came when one guy lit up a joint.

Doug signaled Carole who asked him to put it out; she reminded the jerk that kids were present, and that two federal prosecutors could not stay where drugs were being used. Afterward, Bob reminded Carole of the times when she was "one of the girls," who joined in that type of fun.

Carole may have been very sad when their visit was over. She didn't say that, but seemed quite preoccupied on the way back to N.Y. A disappointed Doug had expected to talk with her in flight because they had had no alone time in San Francisco, and work pressures plus the ongoing FBI inquiry promised to keep them apart on their return. 'I don't want to pressure her about marrying me or about having the baby. But we can't just ignore it. I wish I knew the best way to deal with this.' The taxi stopped at his ex-wife's to pick Jill up so that she could have an overnight with them. Usually flamboyant, Jill was quiet, maybe even sad, asking no questions of either of them. They bought a pizza and a gorgonzola salad on the way home to a very excited King.

Before heading for a late bedtime, Jill kissed Carole and told her she loved her and was so glad she was safe at home. Both gals were very emotional,so Doug went into his study to hide. He fell asleep after checking his email and phone messages, only to be awakened by Jill, who came in to kiss him goodnight. "So are you and Carole going to get married, Daddy?" Though exhausted, Doug did talk to his daughter for a while, alert to any upset the youngster might feel. Jill denied worrying about having less access to Dad; she loves Carole.

CHAPTER 15

Adam had been going to the Great Neck office of Merrill Lynch for years to follow the ticker tape whenever he had days off or was having a meeting with their broker. But since retiring he had been hanging out there on a much more regular basis and loved it. There were always a dozen or so like-minded people, usually more guys, and mostly older than himself. But for the past several weeks, a fortyish woman, a slim, beguiling redhead, stylishly dressed and with an educated interest in finance, was a marvelous addition. The third week there together, Adam and she gravitated to the exit around the same time, talked on their way to the parking lot, and discovered they were both headed for Bruce's, their favorite local luncheonette.

The two lingered over lunch, having no particular errand or timeconstraint. They discovered a lot of mutual interests, like history and politics, as well as the obvious investing. Laurie was divorced, and as the only child of very wealthy parents, she was quite free to travel extensively.

A PhD in political science, Laurie had once taught for a five years' stint at CCNY. For the past ten years she had been unemployed by choice. She did not have children, and told Adam that it was just as well, given her friends' trouble with their adult children. This gave Adam an entry to talk about his current struggles with both of Jenny's adult children. He found Laurie extremely understanding and supportive of his position.

Their meetings occurred nearly every day now, lasting well past lunch except on Thursdays when he took a course in Manhattan. Adam began to daydream about Laurie, wondering how life would be if he were married to her. He then felt guilty, at least until the next argument with Jenny, which was inevitable. He was not a disloyal man, but the combination of feeling quite neglected while Jenny divided her time between dealing with her demanding son and nasty Dana had left Adam very frustrated.

He thought it was all right to daydream, and certainly couldn't imagine initiating any sexual liaison with Laurie!

The night after one of his warmest times with Laurie, Adam had a dream and woke up with a hard-on. He was a little taken aback as he had felt his own sex drive diminishing since Jenny's loss of interest in sex. Aroused and not inclined to masturbate, Adam woke Jenny up and convinced her. The sex was not terribly gratifying beyond the physical release.

Adam skipped Merrill Lynch that Wednesday, was at school Thursday, and then with Jenny drove up to the Berkshires for a long weekend.

The days were cold and rainy, leaving both of them mildly irritable, noshing on junk food since either had planned for any indoor cooking. When their friends cancelled out on them for Saturday night the Levines had more alone time than they could tolerate, and drove home early.

On Tuesday, Laurie invited Adam up to her stylish Great Neck apartment and he accepted, nervous but very excited. They drank some really terrific wine, and gradually shifted from talking to touching,, ending in oral sex. Adam had wanted more, but Laurie said she had her period, was turned off to intercourse at such times. It was extremely difficult for them to part when Adam insisted he needed to go home. In fact, he knew that Jenny wouldn't be finished with work for hours, but Adam was now very anxious. Stopping off on his way home, he splurged, buying Jenny some pink and white tulips, and then on impulse, added a box of her favorite milk chocolates.

That night, clueless about events, Jenny was gratified when her husband not only gave her the flowers and chocolate but most especially when he seemed interested in her day, and was uncharacteristically not annoyed or preoccupied when she told him of Stephen's latest troubles.

CHAPTER 16

Carole and Doug were relieved to hear that the FBI had identified the couple involved in her disappearance. Their real names known, and also much about them and their usual habits, it was still disturbing to have them free. But neither Doug nor Carole seemed to be excessively worried about her safety. They returned to working long hours, began playing tennis again, and booked the Tavern on the Green for an early January mid-week wedding. Doug's friend, a civil court judge, was to officiate, and invitations would be sent out just before the Thanksgiving weekend.

Carole's pregnancy was showing. The early months' exhaustion and nausea passed so she didn't even seem to mind it. Doug's concern that Carole would resent temporarily losing her figure seemed without merit. Still worrisome was her saying "jokingly" that she didn't mind being pregnant, but having a kid, that was something else again! On the other ' hand, she definitely seemed to get a huge kick out of Jill's excited interest in the pregnancy, and appreciated the youngster's volunteering to paint and otherwise decorate the baby's room. He was due April 2nd.

Doug had surprised Carole with a trip to meet a highly respected jeweler in the 47th Street diamond district. In the leisurely process of their selecting a lovely diamond engagement ring, the 72 year old orthodox Jewish Hungarian-born jeweler shared memories of his escape from the Nazis: "I was in a forced labor camp and luckily got work for a very nice Catholic farm couple. They treated me well, fed me and gave me warm clothing. Because I trusted them, when I felt the need to escape to rescue my parents, I told them, and they didn't report me. To this day I feel grateful, and so sad that I never tried to contact them after the war." It was Carole's and Doug's first intimate contact with a Holocaust survivor, and they were profoundly moved by his story.

The couple worked very hard leading up to their ski trip to Killington over the long Thanksgiving weekend. Staying with good friends, Doug would ski, while Carole probably would hang out.

During that Vermont visit, Carole had an unsettling dream which she, out of character, described to Doug. So upset was she, she even tried to call Marianne, but hung up before the machine picked up. "In my dream, I was very little, maybe four years old, and left alone in a strange house with my two year old sister. We were both very frightened. I saw myself struggling to change Leslie's diaper, but I didn't do a good enough job, so it kept falling off. Even though the house seemed to be in California, it was so very cold there, so it must have been somewhere else. No one ever came to help me, and then I woke up." Carole was ashen.

Doug had of late been asked about his own dreams, which he never recalls, so, moved by Carole's painful recital, he knew enough to inquire as to what Carole made of the dream. After several hours wherein she insisted on going back to sleep, then to breakfast and some quick runs, she finally allowed Doug to join her in their room. It was the only place the couple had any privacy in this packed ski house. She was definitely ready, even anxious to talk.

At first calmly, Carole started to "associate" to the dream. "I think that I often felt alone when I was little. Not that I was alone. The housekeeper was always there. But wait a minute, she didn't come until I was five or so.

I can't exactly recall who took care of us before her. I do remember some sitters, but they didn't live with us. It's funny, I can hardly remember either Richard or my mother. My father used to take us for bagels on Sundays, and I remember him taking all three of us to the circus once. And he took us to his barber for haircuts, and to the club.

"That house is not at all familiar. I think it had bedrooms upstairs. We never lived in a place like that. Or at least I can't recall it. I'm going to ask them. It's funny how protective I was of Leslie, almost like I was her mother." Beginning to tear up, Carole asked, "So who protected me?" Doug held her hand for a moment, then she continued: "Is it even remotely possible that we were actually left alone? Of course not! My parents would never do anything like that. The scene is just a metaphor for what it felt like. Leslie has always said that our mother never wanted us …and when I mentioned the abortion mom spoke about before Richard was born, Leslie said that she was pretty sure mom had an abortion after his birth as well. I didn't tell you that because I absolutely don't believe it."

Carole wanted the conversation to end here, but Doug encouraged her to continue. He felt that Carole's own confusion about being a mother came from this stuff. It definitely did not surprise him that Dr. Lewis wasn't mother of the year then or now, but he agreed with Carole that the dream was unlikely to be based on her really being left alone. Doug was gratified when Carole told him that she and Marianne were talking about her mother, and that the young woman was planning to bring this dream into her therapy. Carole was no longer resistant to going for therapy, able to use the cover reason that she had recently been traumatized by the abduction.

Very close to bedtime on their last night in Vermont, Carole had a memory that totally threw her. "My mother had driven to her friend's ski house in Park City, Utah, with Leslie and me just around the time when I was about four and Leslie two years old. My father was somewhere else, I don't remember where. We kids were put to bed upstairs in what I think was probably a loft…far from the lively, drinking, laughing adults whom we could hear. At some point, I had to go to the bathroom and wanted my mother to 'take me potty' as I called it. But there didn't seem to be anyone in the house with us. We were so scared. So we fell asleep downstairs, and when I woke in the morning, we were back in the bedroom. Mother told me that I had imagined the whole thing! Of course, Leslie didn't know anything. I guess that I totally forgot about it 'til now, being here in a skihouse and everything. Do you think it's possible that she really would have left us alone?" Carole's earlier certainty about her mother's behavior was shaken.

Doug didn't want to add to his fiancée's distress by saying that maybe her mother did leave her toddlers alone, but he was by now open to considering it. Instead, he said that the two women might have walked out the front door momentarily to see the stars, etc. Then, another surprise from Carole: "There were also two men, I guess friends of Aunt Janet's.

She's not my real aunt, just a very good friend of my mom's. They were at UCLA together, they roomed together, and were in each other's wedding parties. But Aunt Janet got divorced very soon, and she never had children. Mom and she sometimes traveled together; even now they go on nature trips, like to Costa Rica, or on a photographic safari to Africa, when my father wouldn't go." Carole withdrew in silence for what seemed like minutes, and Doug didn't interrupt. She was clearly thinking hard. A range of feelings showed on her lovely face, her green eyes filmed with tears. She didn't want to be touched just then, so Doug controlled his impulse to reach for her.

Just prior to leaving for home, Doug made several calls and retrieved his messages. Two were important: the FBI requested he call back immediately, and Carole's mom reiterated her earlier response to their wedding plans: "of course we'll be there, though the date conflicts with aprior commitment of ours, and is a workday." He was floored by the woman's attitude, but elected not to hurt Carole by reporting such a cryptic message. What Doug did not know is that Carole had received a note from her mother shortly after their return from California. In it mother suggested that Carole marry quickly before she "was too pregnant to make a pretty bride," and that she "forgo the big wedding given the reality of your situation."

The FBI agent he was to reach was not available, so Doug again left him his cell number. After that call, he actually became suspicious…why hadn't he tried to reach him on the cell, or call Carole, who could also be easily reached at any time? Maybe it was sheer incompetence.

He had been very disappointed when Janet Frame, whom he respected, reassigned the case to a junior case officer, once Carole was known to be safe. And Max, his good friend, had been assigned to another higher-profile case. Doug would have really appreciated his being around even just as a friend these days.

The weekend had been a mixed bag, mostly pleasant, but also stressful. But the drive home was sensational, with bright sunshine and cool, crisp air on their two stops en route. Traffic was surprisingly light; that fact, and their comfort in being quiet together made this a specially relaxing trip. Just as they exited the West Side Highway, Doug's phone rang. It was agent Philip Bice to alert them to the kidnappers' arrest inGeorgia en route to the Florida panhandle, where the man apparently had relatives. They were picked up driving a brand new Ford Explorer which they had apparently just leased in Maryland, where the woman lived. Naturally both denied knowing anything about Carole Lewis' abduction. The man had a long record of petty theft, drugs, and DUI, but nothing involving violence or kidnapping. Connection with organized crime had been suspected but never confirmed. The woman had been in prison for a scheme involving her pretending to be pregnant; she sold the "baby" several times before being arrested. She had also plea bargained a charge that she used a customer's credit card when she worked at Macy's. Here again, no crimes involving assault or kidnapping.

CHAPTER 17

Jerald Marcus MD is a psycho-pharmacologist He sees sixty, maybe seventy patients a week, with two mornings devoted to fuller evaluations of new patients. This morning, Stephen Roth came in for his intake. It was obvious, once the young man told his story, that he was depressed. He seemed to have no remorse for his behavior, but plenty of anger toward the police. Appeared to Dr. Marcus to be dependent and manipulative.

The drugs were a factor to be explored more, but Dr. Marcus was not convinced that Stephen was an addict. He seemed more inclined to use coke recreationally, or maybe when he was down, but had used pot regularly since high school. Alcohol wasn't a significant part of the picture. Marcus was also struck by the absence of close friends, or of relationships with women which went beyond their doing things for him.

In writing up his report later on, Dr. Marcus diagnosed his new patient as having an Adjustment Disorder with Mixed Emotional Features, in addition to Depressive Disorder NOS and Dependent Personality Disorder. He added on Axis I: drug abuse: marijuana, cocaine.

Dr. Marcus informed his secretary about the new patient's issues and when he rescheduled him, adding that he was quite unhappy to take cases where there is high probability of court involvement. He couldn't get out of this because he's doing a favor for a friend. From his considerable experience with psychiatric patients and with substance abusers he put Stephen on small doses of two anti-depressants, one of which had an anti-anxiety component. He would not use tranquilizers with users, and also was alerted to possible, if remote suicidal. He strongly advised the young man to stop the marijuana use. Stephen denied using since being arrested, but Dr. Marcus was too sophisticated to believe him.

Stephen had liked Dr. Marcus and was okay with the medication, though doubtful it would do much good. But he was very grateful to Adam and felt close to him for the first time. Adam had always judged Stephen harshly, he felt, and unfairly too! Stephen was determined to have Adam get to know him in a fuller way. Maybe they could even be friends, like Adam seemed to be with Dana. Stephen could not understand why

Adam's kids ignored him at family gatherings. That could change too; but how? Stephen would be in jail! That one dinner he had been proud to attend with a bunch of wealthy people included this big shot, Marco Da Silva. He didn't know the much older man. He had barely exchanged ten sentences with him…now he knows who Da Silva is, and the FBI thinks Stephen is part of the mob!

Instead of heading into the drug store to fill his new prescriptions, Stephen bought himself expensive sneakers and a camel-colored turtleneck.

A telephone message from his lawyer's secretary said that a trial date had been set for Feb. 26th, more than two months off; it would probably be postponed, she said, but Stephen must get in touch with the office immediately. Some new information required that he be interviewed again.

And, would he and/or his mother take care of the bill sent two weeks ago. the office appreciated prompt payment, and there was a $9000. arrearage.

It was pretty rare that Stephen would call his sister's house but today he hoped he'd catch his mother there. Mom was so caught up in Dana's life, couldn't do enough for her, when his problems were so much more serious. Dana thought he sounded like a cranky kid when she heard his "hello," and said as much. He had never taken the role of protective big brother. On the contrary, she felt older, more mature, especially since Amy and though irritable that mother didn't give her as much as she gaveStephen, Dana was actually proud of herself for solving her own problems.

Jenny had just left but Stephen seemed anxious to talk. It wasn't a real conversation. Stephen talked nonstop, Dana mostly listening. Then: "I think you'd better listen to your lawyer and at least meet with the US attorney. Why are you being so stubborn? I'm sure mommy thinks this too. You'll end up with a long jail term. Then what?" Stephen was very irritated with his sister: "What do you know about this stuff? And how can you possible know what it would be like for me in jail?" Before ending the conversation, Stephen did accept his sister's invitation to come over on the weekend; his niece should get to know her uncle.

Two hours later, relaxing in his own place for a change, Stephen got another, much more disturbing piece of news from his attorney's office. The FBI was at this moment planning to execute another warrant to search his premises and those of his friend Ellie. He should expect them momentarily and he must keep out of their way. He wasn't told what they were looking for. Stephen tried again to call his mother; unable to reach her, he lay down on the couch immobilized.

CHAPTER 18

I feel best at work these days, not so focused on myself and what's happening next. I'm okay being pregnant, but it's very hard for me to imagine being a mother. Why can't I be like most women? My sister has had two miscarriages since my niece was born, and she's frantic, dying to have another child. Doug did not find me amusing when I said, as a joke, that maybe we could give the baby to Leslie!" Carole looked away from her therapist, glancing several times at her watch, then at the titles on Marianne's crowded bookcase.

"Carole, in our recent sessions you've been talking a lot about you and your mother. Today you're giving me the impression that you're very aware of the connection between how you were mothered and your hesitancy to take on that job. So what are we to make of your wanting to be out of here right now?"

"You know me pretty well...I hate having to think about all this. Doug has become your greatest fan! You couldn't make this up. He enjoys his bi-monthly individual sessions with you and never says a word to me about them. I don't ask, of course. He does wonder when we're resuming joint sessions."

"Are you wondering that? If we did resume couple work, are you thinking we'd stop our private appointments?"

"Marianne, I actually feel ready for the couple therapy because I have nothing to hide from Doug, except the San Francisco debacle, which will never come out. You agree with that, don't you?" ('And maybe these private sessions have become too hard for me!')

"It's a difficult call for you. I can see that such a revelation would be devastating to your relationship; it might never recover. On the other hand is there anyone who would be inclined to tell Doug what occurred? You need

56

to consider that."

"You're beginning to sound like me...first one thought, then another cancel ling out the first! but I understand that you can't tell me how to handle my life. I've made my own decisions for what seems like forever, so that's nothing new 1"

"Carole, you seem angry with me. Perhaps you feel I'm letting you down, very like your mother did. She left you struggling with hard choices.

Since you are so intelligent, you made some great choices when it came to your career. But for most of us the emotional choices are much tougher."

"You said too much! Do you want me to answer your first question, or talk about my mother? I could let you off the hook by focusing on her again, but I'm not going to. I am frustrated with you, not really angry. All you therapists are probably the same, no answers, only questions or 'observations'. I think it is time for me to stop these individual sessions and just come with Doug. Even the money is really getting to be difficult."

"Your idea of stopping our individual work at this point, when you are frustrated with me and at the very end of our session, is too important for us to decide today. Let's postpone this decision for a while. But I do agree that we can begin couple sessions right after the New Year.

Carole returned to the office on this freezing December 20th, only to learn that Doug was meeting with an FBI agent, and they wanted her to join them immediately. "In searching Stephen Roth's condo late yesterday, a 9 mm Smith & Wesson was found hidden in back of his linen closet in a laundry bag. As we speak, the gun is at the lab for ballistics.

We suspect it may be the same gun that was fired at Judge Reid."

NYPD Detective Ivan Brown joined the group meeting. A member of the organized crime task force working with FBI, he contributed some nuanced interpretations of the emerging evidence. Doug asked questions of both men, while Carole basically looked on and took a few notes. She was disturbed by the new turn of events because of her affection for Dana, and her gratitude for Jenny Levine's help finding Marianne. With these complications, should she bow out of the case? It might be an option; another assistant could definitely be tapped and they'd enjoy working with Doug.

Once alone with him, Carole threw out the possibility of her being replaced. "I don't like it, Carole. You've kept your distance from Roth's whole family and they seem to respect that. I think you should finish what you started. It'll take someone else too long to get on board." It amazed Carole that Doug treated her in such an impersonal way when they were at work.

What he expected of anyone else, he demanded of her, more!

She certainly wasn't going to challenge him on this.

Doug left the office early and blended in with the tourists visiting the Christmas tree at Rockefeller Center. He got much pleasure from watching the graceful (and not so graceful) skaters while he snacked in the restaurant facing the ice. After admiring the gorgeous holiday window displays, he went shopping.

CHAPTER 19

Doug failed to get to his cell phone in time, so burdened was he with the beautifully wrapped gifts for his four special ladies. Finally muscling himself into a crowded, screeching uptown subway, he discovered that Bob Barkley wanted to meet as soon as possible. Doug was very aware of the reason for this. If ballistics showed a match, finding the gun would be powerful circumstantial evidence against Roth, and definitely infer a longstanding connection to the drug cartel.

Barkley must have forced his client to face the likelihood of conviction, and the strong possibility of his receiving a life sentence on the more serious charge, so now Roth might be willing to consider pleading guilty to potentially reduce his sentence, at the judge's discretion.

The next morning Doug, Lily and Carole all met with Bob Barkley and Roth. The young man, with bail revoked because of the ballistics evidence, looked like hell. Doug took over the show: "What do you have to say?" He wanted to scare the guy and noticed that Roth's lawyer didn't seem inclined to interfere. Lily, on the other hand, was playing the niceone, and her approach temporarily seemed more effective.

"Look, I only met this Da Silva guy once, at that dinner. I got there by knowing one of his workers for around five-six years. That guy sold me drugs, always a little pot, sometimes coke, nothing very much. It was for me and my friends. But I got in a hole the last year or so. My firm sucks as far as paying my commissions on time. Maybe I shouldn't have leased the Corvette, I had to put thousands on the down payment, and I wiped myself out on the condo before that. So I used credit cards for everything, even at the supermarket, for haircuts, for everything."

"Roth, stop bullshitting us, get to the point!"

"Okay, okay, you don't have to attack me." Stephen Roth was by now sweating, his face red, his breathing labored. He appeared to be close to a panic attack. Doug wanted to push, but he had to respect Lily's lead. Continuing, Stephen acknowledged that he told Frenchie, his contact, to arrange a bigger buy, this time to sell. He needed the money. It partly was his mother's fault; she wouldn't stand up to her husband and give him more! The 'peanuts' she doled out hadn't helped at all. By this point his audience was nauseated by Roth's performance.

Stephen suddenly seemed to see Carole in the room, and something clicked. "You're a friend of my sister's, aren't you? Can you help me here?" Startled to be pulled in after being ignored for an hour, Carole remained silent. Doug responded: "Look at me! I'm the one you have to answer to! And I'm not at all satisfied with what you're giving me."

Barkley tried to help his rapidly deteriorating client focus on the facts, and did get some more information out of him. However, no one was able to get Roth to give anything at all on the gun. He totally denied knowledge of how it got into his condo, admitting however that only he and his mother had the keys and that it is a guarded community. Repeating himself, "anyone could do it," and "you didn't find prints, did you?" Stephen seemed to vacillate between panicky understanding of the seriousness of his situation and hostile contempt of his interviewers.

After the meeting, which accomplished very little for either side, Carole complained to Doug about his hostile approach to Roth. Doug was disgusted with her...he was sure the guy did try to kill the judge for money from the drug cartel, and here she wanted Doug to treat him with kid gloves...just because he's a friend's brother. They went their separate ways for lunch.

CHAPTER 20

Adam was unnerved by what was happening with Laurie; it almost seemed like that Michael Douglas picture where the girlfriend becomes obsessed with him and gets to be dangerous. When Adam wanted out after their one sexual encounter, she began calling him. Not often at first, but too often by his standards. He finally decided to meet the situation head on.

"Laurie, this is Adam, in case you can't tell. I'd like to talk to you. Can we meet at the Chocolate Factory around one today?" Since she wasn't home, Adam also asked for her to confirm the meeting by calling him on his cell phone. Jenny was in and out of their apartment, so he certainly didn't want Laurie to call there. She did unfortunately know that number too, having gotten it from information. Adam thought again that Jenny was far too comfortable with everyone having access to her home telephone number; after all, she saw disturbed people, didn't she? But he knew that not one of them ever used their private line, so his adventure was the real risk.

The lunch date confirmed, both adults showed up at the Westbury restaurant, next to Fortunoff's and Off Fifth. Often Adam had visited this mall to shop for clothes. He rarely had eaten out during the day before meeting Laurie. Retirement could be dangerous! Adam had already decided on what he would say to Laurie, that he absolutely must break it off today.

A very elegant Laurie warmly greeted him. She was done up in black, the dress in a tasteful clingy fabric, touched off by simple pearl earrings with a coordinating broach. Capping the picture were Laurie's extremely high heels. She had told Adam that her short stature demanded heels, and he couldn't help noticing how lovely her legs looked encased in sheer black stockings.

At Laurie's suggestion, they ordered drinks and lunch before talking about anything significant. Then, "I bet you asked me here today to gently break it off, Adam. Am I right?" A little thrown by such a direct approach, Adam replied: "My marriage is very shaky. I can't do anything to risk it. My wife's having a terrible time right now with her son's situation worsening by the hour. You and I really need to cool it." He wanted to leave Laurie with the impression, partly true, that he found her very attractive, but now wouldn't work. Maybe if she thought that at some future date he'd be open to it, she'd agree.

Laurie kept her composure, staying sweetly understanding. When they said goodbye, Adam felt very relieved, that is until he remembered that she hadn't actually committed to an ending.

There was a hellish amount of traffic on the parkway leading to the Triborough Bridge. Eventually exiting the FDR on 96th Street, Adam was in no mood for the total standstill. He pulled into an illegal spot next to a hydrant, left a message for Jenny that he was held up, and grabbed a nap.

Jenny focused on straightening up their small apartment, not making impressive progress, as there was no room to put her many treasures.

Under the best of circumstances she wasn't the most organized person, and today was the worst. Apparently Adam had a girlfriend! Jenny had become suspicious of late, but had decided it was ridiculous. But today someone named Laurie had called, probably not expecting his wife toanswer—or maybe she did! the two women spoke for just a moment, with nothing specific exchanged, but when it was over, so was Jenny's peace. She desperately needed to talk to someone, but who? Her sister was on a trip to Hawaii, her best friend's in the hospital for hip replacement, and certainly she could not call Marianne these days.

Adam walked into the apartment's tiny kitchen right off the small entryway, grabbing a beer. He thought it might calm his nerves or settle his stomach. Where was Jenny? It took about ten seconds more to determine that she wasn't home. But it was also clear that she had recently been there, what with TV and lights on in the bedroom and her makeup open on the bathroom sink.

'She knows…she knows people. She might have become suspicious. Or maybe Laurie did call.' For once, in this hot Manhattan apartment Adam began to shiver. It might be the 23rd of December but in here it usually felt like summer. Not today. 'Please come home! I can explain.

But can I? What can I tell Jenny to make her understand? And understand what? That her husband is a cheat and a liar? That I spent a hundred hours with this woman, made love to her. Should I pull a Bill Clinton, "I didn't have sex with that woman?" After all, we also didn't have intercourse.'

Jenny came home around ten, finding Adam asleep on the couch with the TV blasting. The cats were meowing, so he had not given themtheir dinner. She took care of them first, thinking they're far more lovable than most people she knows. "Wake up, Adam. We have to talk!" Instantly he grasped that she knew…and wasn't going to beat around the bush. Wow, two direct women in one day, what a fate. They then talked for hours, each shifting from defensiveness to the offense, before agreeing that they really needed some outside help if this marriage was to continue.

CHAPTER 21

Christmas season was always very special to both Doug and Carole, but this year was more special. Together they had decided not to splurge on expensive gifts for each other; after all, they had a wedding coming up, with a baby to follow. And, Carole had already "spent a fortune on therapy." She and Marianne had taken a break over the holidays, but did agree to meet twice before the wedding, once with Doug.

Mary Malone had made a very surprising decision for someone her age, and especially for a Floridian. She was coming up to New York early for the mid-January wedding, in fact, would arrive December 28th, and planned to stay with a nephew in Scarsdale, rather than in their apartment. She didn't want to push Jill out of her room. While both Carole and Doug tried to dissuade Mary, her plans were set. Doug joked with his mom that she was getting tough in her old age, and she chided him, "so who's old?"

The couple normally gave one huge open house over the holidays, to make up for all the invitations they got all year. But this year, their big event would be the wedding reception. Even though Carole's father had insisted on paying for it, and for all the extras associated with her getting married, Carole was very nervous about money. Her fiancé was amused by her newfound caution. He had been tolerant of her self-indulgence because it was balanced with real generosity. And he loved giving her things, loved that she was used to the best and expected it. His mother never had anything, never expected anything.

Carole made one extravagant exception. She treated Doug's mom to a very special occasion, a full day of beauty in Elizabeth Arden's salon.

the older woman had never had a pedicure or a facial or a massage. This day she'd have it all and more. To make it that much more special, Carole joined her mother-in-law to-be, and also treated Jill to a half-day. The three delighted females seemed almost like peers. Mrs. Malone even accepted a glass of white wine with lunch, getting a little tipsy and apologizing for her silliness. She was charming. At day's end, the ladies were made up—eyes, lips, cheeks, rouge and shadow everywhere. When Doug came by around 5:30 pm for their trip to Scarsdale, he cracked up: "you all look like clowns or stage actors. Our hosts won't recognize anyone but me!"

After the unending personal and professional stress of the past months, this levity felt terrific. But Carole and Doug both understood thatsome issues were temporarily tabled.

Early on the morning of December 31st, Carole got a surprising call; it was her mother. the young woman's first thought was that mom hadn't expected her to be home, didn't know the federal courts were closed that day for the holiday, because most often her mother called when she knew Carole wouldn't be available to talk. At this thought, Carole was sad; she had never been so conscious of her mother's motives before therapy. It was not pleasant or comforting to face some of this. 'And for this I pay good money!' Dr. Lewis, for that's how she thought of herself and typically introduced herself, wished Carole and Doug "Happy New Year," but that wasn't why she had called. 'She had a helluva time getting around to it." Leslie had told her mother that mother had no choice, she had to be willing to honestly talk to both daughters about a lot of things when they got together in New York for the wedding. Mother was asking Carole what that was all about, and thought the timing wasn't right, whatever it was. Did she agree? Carole felt her mother didn't really want to know what Leslie had in mind, and she didn't volunteer, but did strongly emphasize her unity with Leslie. Then, in a striking departure from her normal passive stance with mother, Carole said she expected them to have this conversation in the days immediately after the wedding, since the newlyweds wouldn't be leaving New York until the following weekend. Mother "had not plannedon staying in New York." Carole essentially demanded that she stay, "you owe it to me, to us." The women's conversation abruptly ended on this note.

This New Year's Eve was going to be different too. Every year in recent memory, Doug had gone to a big party, and since being with Carole, she naturally joined him. there was usually a lot of drinking, beginning late and ending very late. January first was typically a lost day. This year, with Doug's mother in town, the couple decided to stay in with her and have an elegant dinner sent in from Claudine's. Mary loved great Italian food, but never had anything the likes of this. After each had one glass of excellent champagne, Mary looked around with open joy. "I'm so thrilled that you'll be my daughter, Carole. I always wanted a daughter and here I have you without all the sleepless nights! I don't know if Doug remembers, but I had a miscarriage when he was five years old. His father would never agree to another pregnancy, and made me tie my tubes.

Doug was stunned. Not about the miscarriage. "How the hell did he get you to cooperate with that? Why did you always give in to him no matter what he did?" Carole interrupted him, but Doug brushed her aside with, "keep out of it!"

"Douglas, you sounded just like your father when you spoke so sharply to. Carole. How can you criticize him when at times you sound so like him?" To Carole: "Douglas adored his father. The man was a rotten husband, but he was crazy about his son, took him everywhere, bought him everything, bragged about him to anyone who'd listen. Douglas was miserable when his father left, but he never, ever said a word about it."

Mary struggled to stay awake until midnight's toast to 2001. Doug and Carole seemed unsettled, not wanting to go to bed, not wanting to talk. He took King for an exceptionally long walk. She changed into off-white pj's, played some jazz CD's and ate pistachio ice cream. When Doug returned, he persuaded her to dance. that way, they were close, but in their private places.

CHAPTER 22

After the long holiday weekend, Carole heard from Janet Frame with an update on the couple who abducted her. When weeks of interrogation elicited nothing of value from the couple, Bice decided to change tactics with the woman, based on something Carole told the FBI when first questioned. Carole had noticed the woman was very jealous whenever her man seemed to pay attention to her. So the agent warned her that Frenchie would be with another woman soon, while her broken probation (on the baby scheme) would put her away 'til she was old and ugly!

This was certainly not a novel tactic, but in the hands of Bice seemed to be effective. Furious, the woman blew her top, and eventually made a deal. She was prepared to turn against her man and testify about everything.

Carole's biggest question had to do with why they had selected her, then released her...she now learned that on orders from "higher-ups" her capture was supposed to distract Doug into looking away from any connection between Da Silva and the judge's shooting. The woman claimed Frenchie was told "to get rid of that woman," but he just couldn't do it.

Marcy Kidd had never met Da Silva, so any use of her testimony to support the older man's connection with the abduction would be challenged successfully. She quoted Frenchie: "the boss said, when the gun turned up, that we should have done that first; it would have made the kidnapping unnecessary."

Doug went to interview Marcy Kidd and decided not to take Carole along, though she asked to go. He was inclined to be protective of her, so went accompanied by another assistant. After about an hour with Kidd, Doug was prepared to proceed against Da Silva. His plan was to convene a grand jury to investigate the connection and to get an indictment.

At this point, Doug was fairly convinced that the Roth guy did not do the shooting, and that the gun was planted in his condo. But how?

From the January 4th meeting with Marcy Kidd to just a day before his wedding Doug hardly left his office before 10 pm. On the other hand, Carole was out of the office often during each day, with numerous last-minute errands having nothing to do with work. She joked that Doug'sformer boss, Giuliani, reduced crime so much in New York City that she wasn't needed; he even scared away the mobsters! The joke was lost on Doug, but privately he was delighted that Carole was so obviously caught up in their wedding preparations.

One exception to his working so late was the evening when he and Carole together met with Marianne. She congratulated them on their upcoming nuptials, just a week away, and found them quite excited at the prospect of a committee life together. But she also noticed that neither had mentioned a baby! The child, definitely a boy, was due in three months, and neither parent seemed particularly inclined to talk about him.

Marianne struggled privately with whether she should address the issue at this time, since they were taking such a huge step, and would be away from any sessions for several weeks. She decided to put it to them.

"Would you like to talk with me tonight about another upcoming event, namely the birth of your son?" Doug, as usual, responded quickly: "Just because I haven't said anything about him tonight doesn't mean I'm not as excited as hell! We have the room mostly completed, thanks to our 12 yr. old painter/decorator, and my mother took Carole for the layette just last week."

"What's all this activity like for you, Carole? You didn't actually say anything about the layette, though you did mention Jill's doing over Doug's home office."

"What should I say? The baby's certainly coming, look at me! I'm huge. Think what a sexy bride I'm going to make next week. Doug insists that I'll look terrific in my wedding suit, but believe me..."

"I certainly can appreciate that if you had your way, you'd be getting married before any pregnancy. But I didn't hear in your response any ideas about the baby per se."

"Please be direct with me, Marianne. What exactly do you want me to say? I know he'll be here before Easter, and I already put in for my maternity leave, so I'm not in denial, if that's what you're worried about!"

"Marianne, Carole thinks that she's going to get back to work after a three months' leave. We just discussed this, or at least I raised it. It's a touchy

68

subject because I feel infants should be with their mothers for at least a year, maybe with some help from a sitter, but Carole is thinking her career would be in jeopardy if she takes off so much time. I think we shouldn't make any firm plan beforehand because she can't possibly know how she's going to feel until he's actually here."

"You know, Doug, that makes a great deal of sense. My raising the whole issue of the baby and your plans for him may be premature. I can fully appreciate, Carole, if you're irritated with me for doing it."

"I think you believe I'll be a lousy mother!" With this, Carole began quiet crying, and shook her head when Doug moved to comfort her.

To Marianne's "who believes that," Carole covered her mouth, saying"I do. I'm scared to death that I'll be like my mother, neglectful, always running away from her kids, from her husband. How do I know that I won't be just like her?"

CHAPTER 23

Jenny and Adam went to see Mike Barbara, LCSW, Ph.D., who specializes in couple counseling. Neither of them knew him, except by reputation via a close friend who had trained under him. In addition to his private practice, Mike is also on part-time faculty at NYU, and a trainer at a psychoanalytic institute.

Jenny had insisted that Adam call for their appointment, and that he tell Mike "the truth about the mess you put us in."

The first session was awful as far as Jenny was concerned. Mike seemed very interested in hearing Adam's story, which was defensive of his actions. Adam depicted himself as "abandoned by my wife for months, so I was at loose ends and did something I am ashamed of. We should have come before this, when Jenny first vanished." Adam went on to describe Jenny as totally wrapped up in her kids; "let's be clear about this: she was obsessed with Stephen way before his trouble, almost like she had another boyfriend." Mike was intrigued by Adam's perception, but didn't say much, just nodded.

Jenny spewed out her rage. She was "disgusted with him. I work so hard, I thought we talk about everything, and he even seemed more caring about my situation. And all along that was an act, to put me off the scent!"

Subsequent meetings were less confrontational, as Mike tried to help the couple identify their struggle to stay close. It had, in fact, well predated the current crisis, and they both had sensed that. Mike felt it was crucial for them to investigate when their difficulties began, and what was happening at that point in their relationship. "You are married around five years; how were those first two years?" The couple agreed that those years were "wonderful," and "close."

"The best relationship I ever had," said Adam. Jenny gave some history:

this was her third marriage, with her first ending traumatically when her husband was murdered, and with her second brief marriage ending when she initiated a divorce. In retrospect, Jenny felt she had not gotten over the death of her children's father, and shouldn't have remarried when she did. "That guy and the children hated each other even before we married, so the handwriting was on the wall. Neither of us regretted its ending. But this is different. I love Adam, even my kids love Adam. He has a great relationship with my daughter and her husband, and with their daughter. And he has been nicer to Stephen recently, very supportive of me at last. Is that all an act? How can I ever trust him again?"

Mike saw each of them separately for two sessions before bringing them back in together for the ongoing work.

"Jenny, how about telling me about your first marriage, and what happened to Paul."

"I got married at nineteen, only finished a year of college. Paul was just out of the navy, maybe about a year. He was twenty-six and so handsome. We got serious very fast, but neither of us had any steady work, so we both lived at home with our parents. My mother disliked him; she felt he was flippant and immature, that he didn't really think like a man. Everybody failed to measure up against my father. Though my family didn't have a lot of money, whatever we had came from hard work, with both parents working. My father was an electrician, my mother a bookkeeper for the Board of Ed. We lived in a garden apartment in Queens where there were lots of kids for my sister and me to play with. She's three years my senior.

"Anyway, Paul and I were absolutely determined to get married. I think that was because I refused to have sex with him 'til we did, and we were both very passionate. So his father rescued us. He set Paul up in a convenience store in Sheepshead Bay. It was a pretty good neighborhood, mostly Jewish with some Italian families. Paul hated the trip on the Belt Parkway, all that traffic, and complained bitterly about the rotten hours.

He literally worked seven days a week, but when he opened, someone else closed, etc. Sometimes I went there to keep him company, but once our son was born, naturally I couldn't. For all the complaining, Paul made really good money. Much better than I ever thought such a small place could do. In three years we bought a house, Paul hired more help so he could be home at least one day on the weekend, and we were happy. He even got me a used station wagon, my first car, I was so excited!"

Mike listened, not saying a word, as Jenny seemed almost to be talking to herself, reminiscing. He noted that she wasn't at all emotional in the telling. It was a long time ago, but even so her demeanor seemed a little off.

"When Dana was born, Paul thought we should get a bigger house, one closer to the water, and in a district where there were better schools.

I was shocked that he wanted to move to Long Island because that meant more of a trip for him, but he insisted. My mother was resentful of this, I can tell you. She also was very suspicious, the only one, and I hated her for it. She was always asking, "where's all this money coming from?" and I once told her she was jealous of me for living so well. My father kept out of it. Well, she was so right...am I naive or something?"

Mike told Jenny that she had used this expression about two other situations in the short time he knows her: that she ignored Stephen's drug use from high school on, and with her not picking up on the problems in her current marriage. "What I don't want to see, I don't see. It's so strange, with clients, I'm on top of things. In my family, I wear blinders."

Jenny continued in her next individual session to describe how Paulseemed more and more stressed and irritable; this was in 1980, when the kids were around 13 and 11. "I had already graduated from college and was thinking of going for my masters; Paul had only a high school diploma, so I attributed his moods to jealousy or insecurity. But the phone calls...he got them at all hours, and never would tell me what was going on. I even accused him of having an affair. When I knew what the real story was, didn't I wish that were true!

"He had gotten involved with the mob, with serious drugs. The store which had started out legit had become a front, and even the cops knew about it. He paid them off. Paul told me this after I badgered him about his hours, the calls and affairs. Mind you, he was so frustrated by my accusing him of infidelity, he admitted to major crimes. The worst news was that my father-in-law, whom I had been crazy about, made the contacts for Paul."

Jenny stopped her recital at this point. It was clear that she was finally feeling something. "It was my fault that Paul was murdered. I demanded that he get out from under or I would take the kids and leave a-sap.

He argued with me, tried to tell me that it wasn't really an option to just walk away, but I thought he was conning me. It turned out that he wasn't."

Sobbing nearly uncontrollably, Jenny accepted the tissues Mike offered, and said she'd had enough for today. Mike respected that, but did ask her if she had ever discussed all of this with Adam and with her kids.

After Paul's murder in his convenience store, naturally the news was everywhere so Jenny had to talk to the children. Since he was depicted as mob-connected and as a drug kingpin, ridiculous, said Jenny, she had to be pretty straight with them. Dana was openly devastated, while 13 year old Stephen kept playing football outside with his friends and never would talk with her about his dad. She took them to a family therapist, but he refused to go after a couple of sessions, and Jenny didn't push it.

Because the money was illegally obtained, nearly every penny in the bank was confiscated. She got to keep her house and the car. So the kids lost her too, as she had to work fulltime for the first time in their lives, and all hell broke loose. Stephen screwed up in school, was fresh to her and very nasty when he had to baby sit his kid sister. Dana was angry with her mother because the girl couldn't go anywhere like her friends did. It never got better until they both left home. Jenny depicted her second marriage as her attempt to bring a man into the family to help with the mess and with the money problems; it only made matters much worse. "Everything I did turned out wrong!"

"You asked me if Adam knew. I told him in bits and pieces after we got married, but since Stephen got into serious trouble with drugs, everything came out. It felt to me that my son was mimicking his father, you know, following in his footsteps. I'm sick about it. Adam has a very hard time being understanding because his kids are terrific, straight-shooters, alwaysdoing the right thing. He's also resentful of all the money I've spent on my kids. We've had plenty of fights about that."

"What you haven't said, Jenny, is whether Paul's killer was ever identified and convicted."

"Never. The case was open for years, and they kept coming to interview me, as if I knew something. Believe me, I was scared to death. I thought whoever killed him was coming after me, after my kids, but thank God that never happened."

CHAPTER 24

Stephen, you'll either come clean with me so that I can properly represent you, or we're quits. Know this: I am smarter than you, this is my territory, and you are a jerk to think you can put one over on me! To say nothing about trying to snow the FBI and Douglas Malone & Company.

Stephen's body hurt all over from constant tension. He had just been diagnosed with irritable bowel syndrome, and in addition to not being able to eat almost anything he liked, he hadn't slept through the night in months. Right now, he didn't have the strength to control his tears.

"Pull yourself together. You'll have plenty to cry about if you don't tell me everything. Believe it, I'm not staying the course with you. And it's extremely unlikely that the Magistrate will grant much of a continuance if I step down."

Stephen was done with fighting. "Frenchie blackmailed me after I made that first big buy...not the one I was caught with. He told me that his boss wanted me to do him a favor, that's how he put it. Not to shoot anybody. They wouldn't use me, I never touched a gun in my life! But to approach a young woman juror who was sitting on a drug case. Over the three months of the trial, I was pretty much everywhere she was, in the supermarket, in the gym, which by the way wasn't far from my house, and even on a movie line. They knew how this worked, so they kind of supervised me. Believe it or not, at first it was fun. Was I a jerk? I know you think so anyway. Okay, she wasn't bad looking and she was single, and around my age. So we hooked up. For a while I actually forgot why I was there. But Frenchie contacted me, reminded me...so gradually I started to mention my own drug use. The idea was not to talk about the case she was on, she'd get suspicious and she had sworn not to do that.

Instead, I'd tell her about my father's trouble (not the murder), and my own fondness for cocaine and pot, just a little recreationally. They thought if she was sympathetic to me, understood that drugs were just a commodity that ordinary, nice people enjoyed, she wouldn't be so inclined to come down hard on the defendant.

"Since I was always broke and they didn't want me to get caught with anything, they actually gave me stash and money. Not a lot...just enough to take the girl out a little here and there. She's a smart girl...a translator at the U.N. no less...but never married and a little uptight aboutsex. We did have sex, and it wasn't half bad.

"When the case was near closing arguments, I was told to raise the ante, that is to throw in some direct comments, like how the government unfairly makes laws to stop people from doing everything, like using pot, but allows other substances, which are worse, like tobacco, then prosecutes innocent people, etc. Amazing that such a smart girl never even got suspicious! But the funny thing was, someone on the jury, a guy nobody tried to turn, actually voted for acquittal. My gal must have been acting more confused in the deliberations because someone said something to the judge's clerk. Of all things, she was interviewed by the judge, denied any violation, of course, but she was replaced by an alternate.

"Frenchie said his boss was furious. That guy on trial was a very close friend of his son's. Da Silva had promised his son that he'd take care of it. Of course at that time no one knew that there'd be a hung jury because of this other juror. Frankie told me that I should be very worried; it was a big mistake to get his boss pissed with me. I asked him why he picked me to begin with, since I'm not exactly a prime candidate to do this stuff. That's when Frenchie really shocked the hell out of me!"

Stephen looked around as if he expected someone to jump out at him. He was pale, sickly-looking, openly shaking. After a short silence, he continued at Bob's insistence.

"Frenchie invited me to that dinner everybody is so interested in,where I finally met Da Silva. He seemed like a nice guy, fatherly you know.

Of course, I knew who he was, no tender father to me, but when we first met, he seemed very warm and friendly. After we talked a while, he reassured me that he wasn't mad about the girl being replaced, it wasn't my fault. Then he said he had known my father! I couldn't believe it. That was twenty years ago. Of course this Da Silva is in his 60's, same as my dad would be if he were alive. And I knew my father was heavy into drugs, not using ever, just selling.

But I never made the connection, why would I?"

Bob asked a bunch of questions: who else was at the dinner; did he overhear other conversations, and did Da Silva say anything specific about the judge's shooting? But Stephen wanted to continue talking about Da Silva and his father.

"Da Silva was about to leave me hanging, so before he did, I wanted to ask him something: do you know anything about why my father was murdered? Frenchie nearly dropped dead! He shut me up, actually told me that I should leave sleeping dogs lie or some such crap. Frenchie is not much older than me, so I knew he didn't have anything to do with it. He probably didn't know anything but Da Silva, that's another matter. Why shouldn't I ask him? He didn't look angry, just smiled and said he didn't know everything."

"Was there any talk about Carole Lewis' abduction?"

"I never heard anything. But remember, this meeting was before Iwas arrested, about two weeks before. Now I'm wondering, maybe they set me up? Frenchie had acted nice as usual, even nicer since he gave me stuff on credit, which was unusual. When I got caught, I was more scared about not being able to pay them than I was about the cops. Little did I know where this was all going."

"Did they try to contact you since your arrest? Anything at all which would suggest an interest?"

"No. but wait a minute. I did wonder if an old guy working at the jail was trying to tell me something. When I was released on bail, this guy told me to 'keep calm, nerves can kill you, and so can ratting on anyone else.' At the time I didn't even think twice about what he said, but later on...then when Frenchie and his girlfriend Marcy got picked up for grabbing Lewis, I got plenty scared. It seems to me they're everywhere. Than the gun magically appears in my condo. Believe me, Bob, no way did I ever see that gun in my life! I knew they were setting me up. Do you believe me?"

Barkley called Malone immediately, with his client's permission, and filled him in. The two men actually did believe Stephen, but getting solid proof was another story, if the powerful circumstantial evidence was to be invalidated. Barkley also told Malone that Roth's money was going fast, making the continued use of private detectives for their team very difficult.

Malone told Barkley that an investigator from his office has been looking into the matter, and he'd share whatever materialized.

CHAPTER 25

The maternity wedding suit had been made up for Carole by Marcy.

It was shockingly expensive, but Carole, in her fitting before the wedding, felt beautiful. Cleverly the dress was designed to highlight Carole's lovely neck and shoulders while deemphasizing her abdomen; the long, fitted matching coat with its high oriental collar completed the picture. With her simple veil, and high heeled dyed-to-match stunning sandals, she would make a gorgeous bride.

Doug had not seen the outfit. Following tradition, Carole would be dressed with sister Leslie's help in their parents' hotel suite. Both girls' hair and make-up had been done by Henri, a favorite of Broadway stars.

Leslie's husband had a contact. Their mother had insisted on having her hair done at the hotel salon and doing her own simple make-up. Dad just sat on the sidelines, amazed at just how much went into this getting ready business, and how much it cost. But he was very moved by this event and by how lovely his ladies looked.

At five o'clock on this Wednesday evening a limousine picked up Carole and her entourage, taking them through Central Park to the Tavern on the Green. Richard and family were staying with friends locally, and would come separately. The groom was accompanied by his very excited mother, and elegantly attired daughter Jill. The twelve year old girl wanted to wear a strapless gown, vetoed by Dad; she looked like a princess in pale blue tulle with its slim bodice and wide skirt. Jill and Leslie were to be maid and matron of honor; there were no bridesmaids in this "simple" wedding. But five year old Elizabeth, Carole's precious niece, was flower girl. Richard's boys would have been given a role, but firmly declined.

"That's for girls!" Doug's best man was also his closest friend from their

Bronx childhood.

Even the most sophisticated people are impressed by this landmark with its breathtaking setting and the hundreds of lights creating a powerful imagery. Entering the main restaurant, guests are only then escorted down a long hall to a party room, stunningly decorated at Carole's direction in white and silver. Everyone is milling around, some drinking coffee, others just chatting. There are dozens of friends and family from California, Boston and Florida, as well as the couple's local friends and colleagues.

The wedding ceremony was officiated by Judge Jay Bevin, an old friend of Doug's from Columbia Law, where the older man had Doug as a student, then mentored him in his career. Guests for the most part stand up during the short ceremony.

When her audience has their first glimpse of Carole, they are shocked: her dress is a deep red brocade! Doug, waiting for his bride but facing away, hears the ahs, and turns to get a peek, grinning at her impudence; nothing retiring about her! Accompanied down the short aisle by her father, Carole joins the waiting Doug, himself starkly handsome in welltailored Versace. A few of their closest friends spoke quietly to each other about just how hard the couple had worked to arrive at this day.

Dana commented to Leslie about Carole: "Her abduction was a life-changing event. Afterward, she was not at all conflicted about marrying Doug, or about having their child. What I'd give for some help in figuring out my confusion over Mel." This allowed Leslie to confide that she and Stuart were struggling with their own dilemma: "to keep trying to conceive and hopefully have our biological child, or to adopt. We're stuck."

Before their parents left to return to their hotel, Leslie and Carole literally grabbed mother, reminding her of tomorrow's meeting. Mother laughed, saying they're acting as if she would run away, at which Leslie cracked, "that would be nothing new!" Their dad was not amused by Leslie and didn't hide his irritation.

Doug and Carole had decided to sleep at their own apartment and had insisted that his mother and Jill do so as well. They would be taking a four day trip beginning Saturday, staying in gorgeous, costly resorts, so there was no need for splurging in their own city. King would be staying with Mrs. Cohen and Melissa; if Carole had it her way, he would have been an honored guest at their wedding and would accompany them to Key West.

The Malones slept very late and were exhausted even at that. After brunch, presided over by a proud Jill, Carole finally got dressed and tookthe longest route possible to the Waldorf. As the time approached, she felt apprehensive. 'Could Mom tolerate honest discussion? Can I handle whatever her response would be?'

On entering the suite, Carole nearly bumped into her father, who was leaving. "I'm not hanging around for this meeting, gal. And don't be too hard on your mother," his usual admonition. It always irritated Carole that he protected her mother no matter what, but she knew that would never change.

Shelly or Rochelle Lewis is a good-looking woman, but not particularly pretty at first glance. Then people realize that she has very good features, but there's a hardness about her, and a definite aloofness. Outside of her profession, people are not normally drawn to her. Yet she has very good and close friends, most dating back to her college or medical school years. Maybe she was more fun then, it's hard to know. These friends, mostly but not exclusively women in science or medicine, are very devoted. Carole and Leslie cannot remember the last recent acquaintance allowed to enter this private club.

Dad is a very different type…gregarious and handsome, he draws people to him and they always invite him, and his wife, to play golf and bridge, go on vacations, or just go out to dinner. These invitations are generally turned down, though Greg Lewis does play both golf and bridge at the club with his own group of friends. When the children were living at home, they spent wonderful days and nights there, with their mother sometimes joining them for dinner. The Lewis' also use the club for entertaining colleagues, and for fund-raising events on behalf of their favorite charities.

Shelly greeted Carole by telling her she looked tired today. "How's a woman six months' pregnant who got married yesterday supposed to look?" Lately, that's how it went with them. But mother never responded to the hostile tone, leaving Carole feeling invalidated. Leslie joined them and the three women went into the sitting room. It was enormous, very tastefully decorated in pale greens and gold with hints of turquoise. Leslie had made sure there was coffee and cookies, as well as milk and soft drinks in the small refrigerator.

Five year old Elizabeth had been taken by her dad to Rockefeller Center to watch the skaters and possibly find the courage to ice skate herself today. Stuart was told to return by five o'clock so that Aunt Carole could spend some time with her niece. The child had loved being a part of the wedding, but had naturally fallen asleep shortly after the ceremony and dinner, and then was taken back to their hotel early by Stuart.

So nothing was in the way of mother and daughters having an intimate talk…nothing but their lifelong style of keeping away from anything too personal, too unpleasant, too revealing. Counteracting that would take enormous strength to push through personal resistance to change, as well as to challenge a very powerful mother who was determined to keep the status quo.

Shelly Lewis fixed herself some coffee and leaned back in the armchair, looking the picture of relaxation. But both daughters knew better. She turned to Carole: "Well, I ask my patients' parents 'what brings you' so that'll have to do for a start."

Carole was always stunned by her mother's formality, but this time it wouldn't deter or depress her. "Mother, we have some questions about our childhood, especially where you fit into it. My confusion about becoming a mother, even Leslie's obsession with being a mother, point to our relationship with you. Did you plan for Richard, and for both of us? And why did you wait seven years after Richard to have me? Were there any pregnancies between us?"

"My God, Carole, you overwhelm me! Of course you all were planned. And you know why we didn't have children right after Richard; I was in back-to-back residencies in pediatrics and pediatric surgery, then a fellowship in facial reconstructive surgery at Boston's Children's Hospital.

A lovely woman took care of Richard, with your Dad's help, of course. I was there weekends. He was a delightful infant and a very good boy. By the time you were born, Richard was in second grade, launched. He hardly needed any of our attention, so independent was he!"

From Leslie: "What, independent at seven? Are you kidding? Mom,what was Carole like as a baby, who took care of her?"

"Carole was a gorgeous baby, the apple of your father's eye. She was born perfect after an easy pregnancy and she still is gorgeous, isn't she? Maria was there living with us. I was working at Mt. Sinai Hospital, usually operating 2-3 days a week, so in very early, but the rest of the week after my checking on patients I got home pretty early, around 4 -5pm.

Your father never worked Fridays. He played golf in the mornings, then devoted himself to you girls. You were lovely, too, Leslie, and a particularly good baby, rarely crying. The one problem with you was later, when you wouldn't toilet train. Richard and Carole had both been trained at 2, but you were closer to 3 1/2, and wet the bed even later than that."

From Leslie: "Did you ever wonder about that? After all, you are a trained pediatrician, though you never practiced."

"We investigated it from a physical standpoint. You were fine. I know that you're implying that there were emotional problems; there was no sign of any such thing. You were both very happy children!"

From Carole: "What was my relationship with Leslie like? And what about Maria? When did she leave us, and why?"

"You and Leslie were always together. Leslie went to you for her bottle, according to Maria.. I don't know how you did it, but early on you picked her up when she cried. Dad was scared to let you do things for her, but I thought it was safe. And I was obviously right!" "Now about Maria. She was an Ecuadorian and had left her own three children with her mother in Quito. I have no idea if she had a husband, none of my business, but I did know she was here illegally and so couldn't go back and forth. One day, I clearly remember it was a Thursday in February when you were four and a half, she announced that she was leaving us the next day. Your father and I were stunned, very upset. He was headed to San Diego to present at a medical conference, and I was going skiing with Aunt Janet in Park City. So I had to take you both with me."

"Where was Richard? Don't tell me you left him alone at age 11?"

"You're impossible! Of course he stayed with your Aunt Ellen and her boys. He always loved being with them, so he very often stayed on weekends. That had been the plan before the mess with Maria's leaving."

From Leslie: "Carole must have had a reaction to her leaving. I have no memory of her at all."

"Carole was very upset. She cried and cried. I tried to explain about Maria's wanting to be with her own children, but Carole, you couldn't be consoled. I guess I gave up on that. We flew up to Utah, and you acted like you were mad at me. What did I have to do with her leaving?

Maybe it was unrealistic for me to believe you'd understand something like that. But you never talked about Maria again, so I thought you got over it."

"Mother, I guess you never did a psych rotation…you seem clueless about the emotional side of things. Didn't it strike you as strange that I didn't talk about Maria if I had been so attached to her? Maybe even four year olds know when their mother doesn't want them to bring up a subject." ('Running, just like me!')   "Now that's ridiculous. I never told either of you not to talk about Maria. You were always a very intelligent child. Is it possible that you were angry with her for leaving without saying goodbye?"

"You mean she didn't even tell me she was going, she didn't say goodbye? Next subject! What was that ski week like for us? I had a dream about it. Could you give us details?"

"You both were in ski school all day and loved it. Even Leslie was zipping down the slopes without fear. They had a class of about ten little ones from 10am to 12 noon, then we picked you up for lunch, and a nap at least for Leslie, and back you went at around 2 to about 4. I had two little skiers at the end of that trip. I remember calling your Dad, and he was so proud of you. Carole, you had been on the slopes one other time with Dad when he took you and Richard to a nearby resort when I was out of town. Leslie had been a baby, so was at home with Maria."

"Who took care of us after Maria left? I have no memory of any particular person until we got Li when I was six or so."

"We had several people, some live-ins, but it was hard. One woman did stay for nearly a year, maybe nine months; you girls didn't like her.

Christine, that was her name. She was a great cook and kept the house clean but I don't think she liked children very much. When she left, without even telling us, she stole things of mine and some money. We never contacted the police, which was a mistake. You didn't care about her leaving."

"When did you start to travel so much? How could you go away for weeks at a time and leave three small children?" Leslie started to tear up asking this…

"First of all, Leslie, Richard was not small. He was 14 years old the first time I went to Africa with Doctors Without Borders. And you girls were 7 and 5 years old, both in school full days. And you had a very capable nanny, plus Dad. Until you were older, I only went for three weeks at a time; not until Carole was in middle school did I take 6-8 weeks away."

"Didn't you think we'd be upset? I just don't get it! Will you admit that you didn't enjoy being with us? And what about your marriage? How did Dad feel about these excursions? Weren't you worried about that?"

"You didn't seem upset. I brought you wonderful African-made toys and books, had terrific pictures and good stories to tell; Carole, you were particularly fascinated by them, so I was sure you'd become a doctor yourself. Later you never showed much interest. Leslie, you did talk about going to med school and you got in easily, but now you're un-ambitious. I worry about you. About Dad: of course he didn't object. He was proud of me and knew you girls would be fine. He always supported anything I wanted to do, that's probably why we have such a solid relationship."

During the first hour of their conversation, both Carole and Leslie experienced a full range of emotions: anger, sadness, disbelief, while their mother seemed cool and in control. The young women both suggested a break before launching into heavier stuff.

FBI Supervisor Janet Frame had been advised that the couple who had abducted Carole Lewis turned against each other and were each trying to negotiate. The federal prosecutor was prepared to accept her confession; Frenchie stuck to denial of any connection between Da Silva, Lewis' kidnapping, and the attempted assassination of the judge, in short gave them nothing. Janet Frame sent confidential emails to Doug's secure work computer, unaware that he and Carole were at this moment on a flight to Miami.

Included in this honeymoon were Jill and Mary Malone, and they were headed to the Ocean Key Resort in Key West. Doug and Jill would scuba dive, while Carole and Mary would sunbathe, take walks on the beach, and visit the Hemingway and Truman houses in town. Doug had not been in Key West in twenty years, the others never. They all enjoyed the brightly colored sea shanties, numerous lively bars, each with blaring "music"; Mary was shocked by the openly affectionate gay and lesbiancouples, while Jill was thrilled at her step-mom's generosity offering her sips of pina colada and buying her great swimwear. When Carole joked with Doug, "You're getting more attention from guys than I am, so I know why you picked this place," Jill asked her Dad "How come she can say anything to you and you laugh?; if Mom said that, you'd bite her head off.

I know, don't tell me, you hate Mom!"

Mary went to bed early most nights in the room she shared with Jill, feeling so lucky with her new life. The "honeymooners" got a kick out of how they were spending this week. Because of the action-packed days, most nights they were too tired to make love. But when they did, there was new tenderness mixed in with their passion. Much freer with "I love you," able not to touch each other all day unselfconsciously, the couple drifted from being sexual partners to committed lovers and close friends.

Stretched out on a beach lounge with a fabulous crab and lobster salad and an iced strawberry daiquiri, Carole watched her new husband emerge with Jill from the Atlantic. the two were laughing, but also seeking out the others. Mary, fearful of too much sun, had left the beach. Jill followed to shower and change in the room she shared with her grandmother.

Doug bent down to kiss Carole gently, but she was already aroused by the sun, and the smell and feel of his body. She pulled him on top of her, all the while kissing and licking him until she felt him harden against her. "Let's go upstairs; give me a town." but Carole responded, "I'd loveto fuck right here…I'm all wet. Touch me and see. He obliged briefly, covering them with the scanty beach towel. Both were very aroused but Doug insisted they go to their beach condo. They walked the twenty yards touching all the while. Inside, Doug took off her maternity bathing suit, exploring her much fuller breasts and growing belly with his hands and mouth. Carole then took his engorged penis in her mouth, sucking gently until Doug came close to climaxing. They rested for a moment, then he entered her, slowly at first, teasing them both. When he couldn't hold back, and she was ready, Doug thrust hard and they climaxed together.

Awakening a little later after a brief nap, Carole pulled Doug's hand to her already engorged clitoris, where he slowly masturbated her, until by the end she took over with her own sure hand, reaching satiation violently. "Pregnancy becomes you…you're wilder, freer, you know that?"

Carole responded, "I could make love ten times a day. You'd better be ready!" Doug laughed, then remarked that it's all for him. He's not quite sure he's up to the challenge, "but I'm sure as hell willing to try!"

After dropping Jill at Miami International Airport and driving Mary across Alligator Alley to her group home, the couple was to enjoy three days' stay at the Naples Ritz Carlton on the beach. Instead, once Doug retrieved his messages, work took over. Stephen Roth had attempted suicide in his cell and had been transferred to the Bellevue Hospital psychiatric unit. And, the mobster's henchman wasn't saying anything to link DaSilva with Carole's abduction; he must be terrified at what would await him in jail if he ever talked.

84

CHAPTER 26

In my whole life I never thought I'd be going to see my brother in Bellevue psychiatric, or in jail, and here I'm doing both.' Dana was appalled, furious, but also scared and sympathetic. 'I resent having to do everything...now a single mom with a three year old. I did it, but it's so hard, I have no life! But I'm so upset about what's happening with Mom and Adam...what if he disappears from my life, from Amy's? Mom would say that this isn't all about me. How come she and I can tackle all the shit that comes our way, and the men, they fall apart?'

Entering Bellevue Hospital, a huge, old, institutionally smelly building with no amenities for visitors, Dana gagged; she had to wait to see her brother, and was nervous being seen here. 'The media had even found us in Holbrook...soon they'll be visiting Amy's nursery. I despise the reporters, they're like vultures trespassing in our lives. And once the trial starts, it'll be a circus. Maybe they'll even dig up stuff about our father!' Horrified at this thought, Dana attacked the shackled Stephen: "Why the hell did you pull that suicide shit? And, do you think the papers will find out about daddy?" Dana never said a word to Stephen about her own marital problems...she was so unsure where she and Mel were headed, and besides, 'Stephen couldn't care less about anybody but himself.'

For the duration of the visit the two siblings discussed their memories of father, and then Stephen's idea that Da Silva might be implicated in his murder. Stephen was convinced after talking to his lawyer that there was something fishy about why Frenchie was given the go-ahead to pull him into that bribery mess. "I was just an ordinary customer, peanuts for them, so why give me stuff on credit unless they wanted me to get in a hole and play me?' After this conversation, Dana emailed her mother asking for more information about her father's mob connection; she could not bear to discuss it on the telephone, and wasn't planning to visit this week. And, she emailed Carole, asking her to get Doug to read her brother's letter. For the first time in memory, she let herself wonder about just what happened to her father.

Stephen did write to Douglas Malone outlining his findings from all the conversations he had had with all parties, and he pleaded with him to "seriously consider my innocence, other than the drug buy and the juror tampering; also please look into the possibility that Da Silva had my father murdered twenty years ago." He referred to his late grandfather's long friendship with Da Silva's father, which allowed him to set up the convenience store as a front for drugs. Stephen even made a list of several of his father's friends and their likely whereabouts, thinking that they might know something, even though they had been contacted at the time of theoriginal investigation twenty years ago. And, as a last resort, he urged Malone to interview his mother, who might remember things she had overlooked then, now was a mature, much more confident adult.

After reading the letter, Doug met with Bob Barkley over dinner at Spark's Steakhouse near his office. The two men who had been adversaries on numerous occasions respected and liked each other. But this time was unique, because they both were of one mind: Stephen had been set up, was a schnook whose extravagant lifestyle got him into trouble, but he was no mobster and definitely not a hit man. (The very thought of this got both men laughing heartily.) By dessert, they had an agreement: assuming they could clear Stephen of the gun charge, the federal rico charges could be dropped; then the case could be tried in NYS criminal court where Stephen would likely get a lower jail sentence pleading on the original drug charge and the juror tampering. This would naturally depend on Stephen's willingness to plead guilty, and on the NY district attorney going along.

Barkley did meet with Stephen, insisting that Jenny be present, to finalize their agreement before bring assistant district attorney Young on board. Stephen would have to state in open court what he had actually done as part of any plea agreement.

CHAPTER 27

Jenny was tremendously relieved that Stephen, after being suicidally depressed, was now active on his own behalf. And Stephen had agreed to accept a plea, if and when the state accepted the change in jurisdiction.

So many 'ifs'.

On February 16th, Dana announced to Jenny that she and Mel had decided to get back together. He had really been trying, changed jobs for one that paid better. She had also come to recognize that she wanted him to be someone he wasn't...and it markedly reduced her anger. Dana did increase her work hours, enjoying her job as events planner for the Jets, which put her in touch with all kinds of interesting people, and paid well to boot. However, this job required that Jenny baby sit more, which she took on, reducing her time at home with Adam.

Adam and Jenny were making some headway in their relationship, with their therapist's help, but Adam seemed depressed. "I took early retirement. It sounded terrific and I had some great ideas about what I'd like to do. Now look at me! I'm not doing anything, no school, no traveling, nothing! While you're working thirty hours a week and aren't free to do a damn thing with me!"

Jenny was too busy to ask herself how she felt. "This is definitely not the time for you to whine like a kid. I've no patience for anyone else's neediness." Then, regretting her harshness, "Look, Adam, I know you're strung out over everything that's happened and that you've really been a terrific support for me these past few months. Please find something to do, not another girlfriend, of course!" She could laugh now that it was understood how little that woman meant to him.

In the midst of all this, Jenny continued to see clients, and actually began to take on more work in Manhattan. She hoped eventually to end her Long Island practice, which had become more trouble than it was worth because of the commuting. She needed to keep her income up…the debt to Barkley was terrifying and regularly confronted her on elegant stationery the first of each month.

A new patient was referred by her Long Island physician in mid-March. The woman, Naomi Parker, said she wanted a Manhattan therapist because she was moving into the city in late Spring. On the telephone she stated that she had been widowed two months before, her husband having died of lung cancer after a short illness. She was depressed, but mostly emphasized her need for help in refocusing her life. Jenny was pleased to set up an appointment, as this seemed like it could be a time-limited case, and there was no managed care problem.

Naomi Parker proved to be a 50ish woman with long black hair, wearing a heavy black wool coat she kept on throughout the session. "I am always cold…it's freezing in New York. My husband and I always went south for the winter, but this year I couldn't handle leaving home."

Very logical to Jenny, who listened intently as her new client spoke about her situation. But simultaneously, the woman was looking around taking in the apartment, and then asked pointed personal questions: "You probably live here with your husband. Does he stay in the bedroom while you work? I guess it's hard to afford this place and an office, too, huh? He's probably retired while you're still working. So many of my friends are in that situation. My husband was retired…but I have always been home, pampered, I guess."

The session was at a point where Jenny normally pulled together what she had heard, suggested a focus for going forward, talked about her fee, cancellation policy, etc. Suddenly, Naomi jumped up, took a small caliber gun from her coat pocket, and shot Jenny twice before she left the apartment and the building.

CHAPTER 28

Doug had a ton of work and two of his top assistants were out. Carole was close to her delivery date, and would be on maternity leave for three months. When the call came in that Jenny Levine had been shot, then taken to Roosevelt Hospital with two shoulder wounds in stable condition, Doug naturally wondered if this was payback from Da Silva. After all, Stephen had given the office enough for Doug to proceed with a grand jury indictment of Da Silva, but Stephen himself was in a protected environment in prison. So the next best target might be his mother.

Carole had to be told…she was Dana's friend, and had met with the young woman at least twice since Dana's marital troubles.

When he called her on the intercom, "hey, babe, if you're not busy, I need to discuss something with you," his light tone left her quizzical. She had begun to have pre-labor contractions meaning nothing yet, but she was feeling some physical discomfort mixed with anxiety. Carole took in Doug's information, much relieved that Jenny was going to be all right.

Hearing Doug paraphrasing Jenny's description of her shooter, Carole interrupted Doug: "that's not Da Silva; I bet it's the woman Jenny's husband had the affair with. Dana described her as in her late 40's, stunning, petite." This was news to Doug. He'd have to confer with the NYPD detectives working on the case.

Conveniently the following Saturday morning, Carole went into labor. This was new for Doug as well, as his first wife had been with her second husband when she had delivered Jill. Surprised at how anxious he felt, Doug nevertheless keep his cool, and noticed that Carole seemed in control of things. She had packed her Mark Cross with nice lingerie, make-up, hair stuff, etc., and only when he reminded her, added an outfit for their son's homecoming. Leslie had sent a white fleece one-piece winter bunting, along with a pale blue blanket and matching sleeper.

After thirteen hours of labor, with Doug at her side, their son Daniel Carl Malone, just under eight pounds, was born. Carole was in a private room in Guggenheim Pavilion, Mt. Sinai Hospital. The FBI insisted on the privacy because they still did not know why she had been abducted, and if the person who ordered it had lost interest.

Everything, including the initiation of breast feeding, had gone well.

Doug took off the week to help.

CHAPTER 29

Adam was horrified at having to face that his brief fling with Laurie had led to that woman's attempt to kill Jenny. Appropriately guilty, Adam was enormously relieved that his wife seemed fine, and that Laurie was quickly apprehended. Laurie had wanted to plead temporary insanity, and initially it appeared that she was willing to go to trial. However, sometime later she and her attorney decided that such a defense was farfetched and unlikely to succeed; thus she accepted a plea bargain on a lesser charge, receiving a 2-6 years jail sentence.

After a months' recuperation but emotionally exhausted, Jenny joined Adam on the Galapagos trip planned so many months ago. They flew to Quito, Ecuador, then onward to Baltra, gateway to the Galapagos.

There they were met by the young guide from the ship Traveler. The tiny cruise ship had only eight passenger cabins and a crew of seven headed by the Captain and by naturalist/guide Juan Marcos. Jenny looked forward to stimulating interactions with the other guests, while Adam was anxious to eyeball the remarkable wildlife he had seen on a National Geographic special. the physically recovered Jenny hiked over rock-filled terrain to view sea lions and tortoises, and snorkeled the chilly and at timesturbulent Pacific flanked by tiny penguins and harmless sharks. Adam generally stayed close to his wife and tried to be as social as possible, including with those in whom he had no interest.

Some of the passengers were intriguing to Jenny, and even Adam had to acknowledge their uniqueness. One such couple, professors of entomology and biology at a prominent southern university, were always going off by themselves, "out of bounds" as it were, to study the bird and animal life in a way no one else could fathom. Another couple, the youngest on the ship, was physically very attractive, though quite a contrast to each other; he was tall, heavily muscled, powerful and dark, while she was petite, very slim and blond. the 44 year old man was in law enforcement with his state's fish and wildlife service. He entertained everyone with details of how his unit supported the coast guard in protecting the northern Florida waters from illegal immigrants and drug smugglers who perpetually attempted, against all odds, to get into this country. While Randy described some of his close calls at sea, his wife Ellen seemed mesmerized.

Jenny wrote a long letter to her friend Marianne: "And I met Myra, a well-traveled, probably affluent rag picker! Short, with unkempt grey hair, heavyset, generally unattractive, Myra is traveling alone and doesn't seem to interest people. Nor does she care about interacting. Which is why I'm intrigued and did reach out to her. She said that two years ago she moved to Los Angeles from her hometown in Connecticut; she lives very frugally, but goes to theatre several nights a week and volunteers at the local zoo. Maybe she prefers animals to people, or at least is more comfortable with them. did I say that Myra also looks incredibly clumsy, but actually managed the challenging cliffs remarkably well. She never passed up an opportunity to snorkel or to do an extra hike. You and I are always talking about writing a novel; believe me, this character should be in it!"

The Levines avoided loaded topics. They even managed to make love several times on the ridiculously narrow cabin beds. Little did Adam know that while lovemaking with him, Jenny fantasized about Juan Marcos, their young, handsome guide.

When the cruise ship reached Puerto Ayora, Jenny finally found time to shop, buying a charming hand woven fish mobile for Amy, a wallet for Dana, and a watch for son Stephen. Normally disturbed by her extravagance with family gifts, Adam was pleased by her frugality. He never wrote postcards and certainly never shopped for himself or for anyone else. But this time he made an exception, buying his wife a beige suede pocketbook with matching wallet, to be given after they arrived home.

Following their cruise and return to Quito, the couple, much calmer and friendlier to each other, hired a guide to take them north of the capital to Ecuador's craft center. Though the weather was cold and rainy, and the food not at all to their liking, the Levines agreed that it added much to their overall pleasure in the trip.

CHAPTER 30

Adam had asked for his own private session with Mike, to get some help with figuring out why he couldn't make a plan for his life. "I'm sick of blaming everybody for being miserable. First it was Jenny. She was too busy with her kids to be with me. Then it was my own kids; they were too busy with their own families. Then I obsessed about money. Even with Jenny earning plenty and my having a very good pension, what's going out is way exceeding what's coming in. Now I'm facing reality: I'm stuck, immobilized!"

Mike was very pleased to hear Adam speak this way and said as much: "Only when you face that can you really begin to plan for yourself.

Any ideas about why you might avoid committing to something?"

"Before I went into sales, I wanted to go to law school, but I thought it might be too hard. Why should I have thought that way? I aced college, 3.7 and magna. I took the easy way out, and spent twenty-two years being bored to death, hating work."

"You probably have some clues about why you were afraid of competition. How about sharing them."

"My father was smart and ambitious. He dropped dead at age 53. My mother always said the pressure killed him. He came from a poor, uneducated family, was the youngest, the only one to go to college. As a Jewish engineer, he experienced plenty of prejudice. And he supported his parents, helped with his grandparents, and anyone else in the family who needed money. No wonder he dropped dead! I was 17."

"So you traded success for longevity?" Adam didn't respond quickly to this inquiry. Ultimately, he told Mike that in college he had many physical symptoms which weren't real, while pushing himself for high grades. He was tortured by chest pains, headaches, stomach stuff, the works. On a number of occasions Adam actually visited hospital emergency, thinking he was having a heart attack. Then he was diagnosed with panic attacks.

All of that went away after he decided against law school and got an easier degree in accounting and business.

"And now, if I'm honest with myself, what I'd like to do would be a stretch; I want to get a Ph.D. in political science and maybe teach on a college level, write, something like that. But maybe I'm too old. By the time I'd finish, I'll be past sixty! Who would ever hire anyone that age?

What makes me think that I can write well enough to get published? Am I really as smart as I like to think I am? These questions kill me!"

"Did it ever occur to you that you don't have to earn money even if you do get your Ph.D.? Who's the degree for anyway? Why not do something interesting that you might enjoy?"

"You mean there's something more in life than making big money?

From my family I should consider doing something just for pleasure? That certainly is a life changing idea! But seriously, I wonder if I could reallyabsorb that."

"Well, you could start something and hope for the best. If you began to feel guilty, then deal with me about it. You've got the right therapist, a real hedonist at times!"

"It's funny, Jenny's been telling me this stuff for years, but I haven't really listened. I pay you and I listen. What if I can't get into a good school like Columbia or NYU? Okay, I know, I should deal with that when the time comes."

"And Mike, I'm beginning to think that some of my frustration with my wife is because I'm jealous that she loves what she does. Sure, she earns good money at it, but she forced herself to struggle through school, got really in debt, and refused to give in when the obstacles were far greater than anything I ever encountered. Instead of admiring her, I've actually made fun of her. That she doesn't know about finances, that she's not interest in U.S. history, etc. I've been a bastard, putting her down at every opportunity. Maybe even the affair was about that?"

Leaving his therapist, Adam was hit with a troubling idea: 'When I began to think Laurie might be dangerous to Jenny, how come I never thought it through, why didn't I tell Jenny? Could I have felt that much hostility toward my own wife? I love her!' 'For the first time since I was a kid, I could see myself actually talking honestly to a friend, if I had one.'

CHAPTER 31

What a relief that Jenny didn't have to testify against Laurie at trial.

She almost felt sorry for that woman, who seemed pathetic in her desperation to connect with Adam, and thereby needed to get rid of Jenny.

When she told her kids and her friends how she felt, they were incredulous, but somehow Mike understood. The same qualities that made her a non judgmental therapist allowed Jenny to feel empathy toward such a damaged woman. "I know such narcissistic people, when they're panicky they can do crazy things. But am I too understanding? Maybe that's why I get set up so often."

About her son, Jenny felt more anger. While she sympathized with his difficult childhood after his father's death, Jenny felt that he had a better than good life up to age 13. Maybe her guilt had let him off the hook about a lot of things he should have been held accountable for…and besides guilt, she had to work so hard, maybe ignore some things just to survive those difficult years. 'Now Stephen is a felon, never able to work in his industry again. For the first time in his life, he'll have real challenges and maybe, just maybe that'll be the making of the man. Or not.'

Having dinner with Marianne, Jenny filled her in. "I'm freer than I've been since before Paul died. Nobody's getting away with anything with me anymore. Even Adam's noticed the change, and I'm not sure he likes it!" Marianne, who had often been disturbed observing family manipulate her friend, took great pleasure at the announcement. Jokingly, she advised Jenny: "Start with your cats; they boss you around and run you ragged!" Then Marianne asked for some "air time" herself; she needed to think through her very new thoughts about retiring. "I'm scared, but also excited. I want to do other things, write, play. Do I have the guts?"

Jenny called Stephen the very next day to tell him she was going to sell his condo. It would bring good money, so she could pay off the debt to Barkley, freeing her up to cut back on her grueling schedule. Stephen would have to find housing when he completed his prison term.

CHAPTER 32

Little Danny largely slept days and was up on and off all night. He was nursing well, gaining nicely, and when his tired mother found the energy to venture outdoors, he cooperated by sleeping through her hair appointment or a poetry lecture at the 92nd Street Y. Today she was bravely descending into the subway loaded down with baby stuff, all to honor Doug's request that his precious son be introduced to his office mates.

Carole arrived downtown precisely at noon, as planned, and though greeted warmly by everyone she met, security included, felt like an outsider. Barbara was thrilled to finally meet little Danny, but no other staff seemed free just then. Doug was in a meeting which had run over, so Carole changed her son's diaper in the ladies' bathroom.

On exiting, she was met with "SURPRISE" from all quarters! Quite shocked—'who gives a shower after the baby is born?'—then handing Danny over to whoever wanted him (only women, of course), Carole responded to questions: "How do you like being home? She looked gorgeous! "How did you get your figure back so soon? (from the women again) And from the men, "Does Doug get up with the baby at night?"

Then came the presents, cute clothing mostly for when Danny was bigger.

Plus toys, stuffed, plastic, big and little. Oh, my God, how would they ever get home? Doug reassured her that he had in fact driven to work together having known about this event.

Around two o'clock everyone was back to work except for Carole.

She felt irrelevant, and giving Doug a quick goodbye hug, left with Danny for home. but she didn't feel like going home just yet. Where else could she go? It was late April, but still quite chilly in spite of the bright sun.

Calling Mrs. Cohen to ask if Melissa could walk King, Carole went uptown to Cinema I, and almost without thinking entered the nearly empty theatre.

Doug purposely left work early, at least in part to avoid the brutal traffic he'd encounter driving home later. The doorman helped him up with the many packages, then in passing mentioned that "Ms. Lewis, I mean Mrs. Malone, isn't home yet. But Melissa took King out around an hour ago." The guy knew everything there was to know about everyone in the building. It was unnerving to Doug just how much he knew!

Entering the apartment, Doug immediately played back messages, none from Carole, then double checked his cell phone; nothing. 'It's five o'clock, she left the office around two, where the hell is she?' Vacillating between worry and irritation, Doug distracted himself by playing chess on line. Carole walked in at ten to six.

"Sorry, Doug, I really should have called. I went to a movie, believe it or not, and then I had to nurse Danny so I ran into a coffee shop near Bloomingdale's. I'm really sorry."

"You can't do this to me! You're not living alone, remember? Maybe if we didn't go through that nightmare I wouldn't be so upset...no, that's not even true. Responsible people call when they're going to be late!"

"You don't have to get nasty. I had a hard day. How do you think I felt about leaving the office? What do you think it's like for me hanging around all day watching Danny sleep, napping myself, even watching TV?

I'm not sure I can do this...two more months and I'll be nuts! Marianne thinks I should join a mothers' group...she says they're all professional women, some older moms with their first children."

"I'm not telling you that you have to stay home with Danny. You decided that you wanted to try this...it will be easier once he's up during the day and sleeping at night. Maybe you'd like to bring him to the office and do some work. I can really use the help right now. What do you think?"

Privately, Doug had been uncomfortable about Carole's staying home, why he didn't know. "I can't imagine you being like my mother; she drank, gained a hundred pounds and didn't put on real clothes for twenty years after having me!"

"Why do you think that happened, was she depressed?"

"She had plenty of reasons to be depressed. Before she and my father were married, she worked for the telephone company at a clerical job she loved. Afterward, he muscled her into quitting her job, some macho thing in those days that working wives imply husband are failures.

98

She actually fought with him and so did work until midway into her pregnancy, then she was ashamed, mind you, of how she looked on the train.

Once she stayed home, getting fatter and fatter, my lovely father began to call her a fat slob, a stupid pig. My God, he was such a bastard! When I was in elementary school, she hung around with Mrs. Connelly, the two of them drinking been on and off all day, wearing housedresses. I can still see her tent dress with its blue and yellow flowers. I can also remember her pleading with him for money to buy clothes. Do you know what he said? Lose a hundred pounds, then you can get my money!"

Carole was choked up. "Your mother's such a warm, loving person. How could anyone treat her so horribly? What did you feel living through all this?"

"I hated her! by the time I was in my teens I had contempt for her. My dad treated me like a crowned price; we were the smart ones, we werewell-built, we were out there doing stuff. Meanwhile, the genius was a truck driver. He had had big dreams but needed to leave college right away to help his family out after his father was hurt on the job, and afterward, got into his father's union. Besides driving, my dad's main pleasures were drinking and women. Oh, and torturing her. But he never managed to divorce her."

"It sounds like you became his partner in hurting her. I hate thinking of you like that."

"I did it all right. At least for a few years, till he left the summer before I went into my senior year in high school. He moved in with some woman, seemed to forget he had a son. If I ever pull that shit, Carole...In my junior year, I applied to several colleges, Like Notre Dame and Columbia, and to NYU as back-up. My father had promised that if I got into one of the top schools, he'd help me go. Well, I got in everywhere, and got scholarships, but NYUJ offered me full tuition. When he heard that, the others were out! We fought for hours, then he stormed out calling me a spoiled bastard. My mother wanted me to go to Notre Dame, and even called her sister, who agreed to co-sign loans. But at that point, with my father gone and my mother a basket case, I was scared to leave her. So I went to NYU. She lost most of the weight over the next ten years."

"Doug, when I try to talk to you about me getting a part time job in a few months, you're not happy about that either!"

"My father brainwashed me about women; marry one who can support herself, make sure she never stays home and gets to look like your mother! The women I've always been attracted to have been attractive and successful, not necessarily warm and cuddly. When you and I first met, naturally what I saw was the smart, successful, love-looking young woman, the outside person. Only over time have I come to know you. I like that you need me, that you want me to do things for you, to take care of you, and not because you can't do it yourself. But I also like to see you take care of Danny; he needs us both...and guess what, I also miss our working together. So it's very confusing for me, this business of your staying home full time or working, especially for someone else."

Carole decided to return to her job part time once she got some support from her friends and discovered her neighbor could baby sit two days a week. Doug was able to make it all happen by detouring the usual rules against having part time attorneys; another staffer was out with a complex fracture, so at least temporarily this would work.

CHAPTER 33

Carole's assignment was to interview Jenny about her recollections from the period leading up to her first husband's murder. Jenny said she had been totally involved in her two children's lives, so much so that she had been "out to lunch" about most things connected with Paul until the increase in late night phone calls spiked her suspicions. Most of her later information came from talks with her mother-in-law, who had "known plenty" and shared it after her husband was on the hot seat himself following Paul's murder. Following this conversation, Carole and Jenny flew to Wilmington, North Carolina, to meet with Paul's 90 year old mother, Sara.

Jenny had kept in touch with her mother-in-law regularly while her children were growing up, after Paul's untimely death; the older woman had contributed financially to her grandchildren's college fund, and regularly sent them cards on birthdays. She never forgave her husband, who was himself charged, but never convicted in the drug scandal that followed Paul's murder. When her husband died less than three years later, Sara moved to North Carolina to be near her younger sister and extended family.

Sara Roth was quite surprised by Jenny's call to arrange the visit, but at the same time was open to it. She was living in a group community, where residents had their own apartments but ate communally in an attractive dining room overlooking the beach. After getting clearance from the staff who expected them, Carole and Jenny joined Sara on the outside protected deck facing the then peaceful Atlantic Ocean. Both New Yorkers were excited at the prospect of all this sun after a chilly, damp Spring. At ninety, Sara was remarkably alert and healthy. She quickly told the younger women that her "secret" was daily exercise and careful diet, no alcohol or caffeine, and lot of work; to her this involved volunteering as a dog walker at the local pound! Jenny had of course known of her former mother-in-law's high energy as a younger senior, but Carole was astonished.

Having exchanged pleasantries, Jenny spelled out the reason for this trip: what, if anything, could Sara tell them about her late husband's involvement with Da Silva? The information might help keep Stephen from a much longer jail sentence. Of course, Sara wanted to help her grandson, though she was disappointed that both grandchildren failed to keep in touch, and Jenny had been no better. No pulling punches here! And she couldn't imagine how anything she had to say could be helpful so many years after Paul's murder.

At the outset, Sara claimed forgetfulness, but her detail-laden recital belied that claim. She spoke of her husband's and Da Silva's father meeting over handball at Manhattan Beach, (located in Brooklyn's Brighton Beach, in spite of its name). the older men, owning retail businesses in the area, actually introduced their teenage sons, but the boys didn't click. Unbeknownst to Paul's dad, the Da Silva kid, Ray, had entered into the family business, racketeering, before even graduating from his private school.

According to Sara, her husband had begun to be less than open with her about his income around the time their only child entered junior high. His small electronic store, good location notwithstanding, did not appear to be busy enough to support their pleasant lifestyle. However, Sara was not the kind of woman to ask too many questions in those days. She was occupied with home, with her son, and with a very ill mother. And she sometimes helped out at various volunteer activities in the Jewish community in which she lived. When Paul finished Abraham Lincoln High School, his father insisted they move to Queens, and purchased a small house in the Queens College area. both parents were terribly disappointed when Paul elected to drop out of college after two aborted semesters.

The young man tried several types of jobs, but never found his niche until he joined the navy at age twenty-two.

Sara insisted on a long break for her afternoon nap, during which Carole and Jenny changed to shorts and went for a walk on the inviting beach. They tried to figure out how to get Sara to move along with her story; she was a bit obsessive and couldn't easily be interrupted with questions from either of them. Ultimately Jenny suggested that they let her do it her way; she remembered Sara from years ago, and that was best!

"Come and meet all my friends. I told them you're a famous U.S. District Attorney so everyone wants to meet you!"

Carole smiled at the commentary, but didn't contradict the elderly woman. Her friends seemed decades younger, but some were more obviously physically impaired. Clearly Sara was a dominant force here, so Jenny and Carole participated with her scenario until signaled that their agenda could resume. This time, Sara led them into a small sitting roomand shut the door. Her affect changed; there was sadness and anxiety evident as she asked, "where shall we start?"

"We were so happy when Paul married you, Jenny, and were naturally thrilled when you had Stephen. I had no inkling at that time about Dad's putting Paul in touch with Da Silva's son, but after Paul was murdered so many years later, Dad told her everything. He had to...he was indicted by the grand jury, but they had trouble getting any evidence on him because your father-in-law was a lot smarter than his son. We never moved from the small house, we drove a five year old Dodge, he never bought me fancy jewelry, and Dad declared a modest income from his shop in keeping with this lifestyle. Paul, on the other hand, lived big. What Dad did with the money I never knew then, but later he told me he used cash for dinners out, theatre tickets, gifts, stuff like that which couldn't be tracked.

"Jenny, when you insisted that Paul get out of his involvement with the mob, Paul spoke to Dad. They were both very worried, scared. Dad warned Paul, but he ended up speaking with Da Silva, the father, who reassured him that it'd be okay. Later, after Paul's murder, he wouldn't speak to daddy, so dad knew...he feared they'd come after him or you, Jenny.

But as years passed and nothing like that happened, he relaxed. Dad sold the business and retired, but you remember he had a heart attack within the year and never was the same. I probably killed him. I held himresponsible for Paul's death, my only child. How is all this going to help Stephen?"

Carole conveyed her gratitude for Sara's honesty, and then asked a number of questions, most of which the elderly woman couldn't answer or never knew. She had not met Ray Da Silva, but had know his father from a few dinners together at Lundy's restaurant. According to Sara, her late husband's meetings with both father and son always took place there, on an outside deck overlooking the Sheepshead Bay boat basin, even in winter so they wouldn't be overheard. But Sara herself was never at any of these meetings, so it was all hearsay.

Carole took prodigious notes on their talks, then typed up a summary and asked Sara to sign it. The next morning, as they were leaving for the airport, Sara stopped them: "Daddy had a diary...I remembered it last night. Why I kept it, I'll never know, but it's in my safety deposit box.

Can you use it?" Delighted with this news, they accompanied Sara to the bank, got custody of the diary and signed attribution. On the late afternoon flight into LaGuardia, Jenny and Carole began reading the diary.

They didn't get very far, because Jenny was emotionally overwrought by events of this visit, and Carole felt responsible for the dredging up of such painful memories.

Barbara, Doug's secretary, couldn't get over the change in Carole's voice when the young woman called to confer with Doug. Afterward, she told her boss that he really needed to find a way of letting attorneys work part time.

On their return from Sara's, Carole and Jenny were confronted with two news articles. The first, in Newsday, dealt with Stephen's case, reiterating the drug charges, spelling out in excruciating detail his attempt to bribe a female juror via having an affair with her, and then discussing the finding of the 9 mm in his North Merrick condo. The story was accurate, but quite inflammatory. In the second article, this one in the New York Times, the writer went back in history, reviewing the murder of Paul Roth and the subsequent dropping of charges against Ray Da Silva. In describing the current legal problems of both Stephen Roth and Ray Da Silva, the writer inquired as to the possible relationship between the present and the past.

He made it clear that Stephen Roth was a child at that time, and that it had been established that his long-deceased father had a business relationship with Ray Da Silva. So why would Da Silva kill Paul Roth? In conclusion, this quite skilled investigative reporter noted that known mobsters are frequently assumed to be guilty, while others are overlooked.

CHAPTER 34

The Malones, including Jill and baby Danny, were headed out to Seaview, Fire Island, to find a July rental. Carole, Jill and the baby were planning to stay for a whole month, while Doug could only take the first two weeks. Jill signed on as "mother's helper," vetoing a return to camp.She showed no interest in the long ago discussed teen tour, which her dad wouldn't have agreed to anyway. What they quickly discovered was that they were welcome, but King was not...so they ventured to the busy community just west of this, Ocean Beach, for lunch and a day on the then lightly occupied beach.

Carole and Doug could be a little romantic together for a change, as Jill disappeared with Danny to the children's playground. At seven weeks old, Danny was making good eye contact, and laughed when a motion delighted him. He seemed particularly enamored of big sister Jill. Naturally his proud parents were pleased at their connection, but Doug was a little concerned at Jill's diminished involvement with her peers. Little did either adult know that Jill had already met a 14 year old boy who was babysitting his younger brother, and the two teens got something going. By visit's end, Jamie brought the Malones to his real estate agent dad, who promised to work on finding a doggie-friendly rental.

The family sat on dock benches facing the Great South Bay, taking in the picture postcard scene, while waiting for their ferry to return them to the mainland. A tall, re-haired and bearded young man, slim and muscular caught up with them, having tried unsuccessfully to get Carole's attention when she exited the real estate office. He totally startled her: "BOO!" Like a kid, shoeless and free-spirited Nick entered their lives. Because Carole was totally speechless, Nick took over. "I guess Carole never told you about me...I was her last boyfriend at Stanford. Madly in love we were, or at least

I thought we were…that is 'til graduation. We did see each other briefly last Spring, but then I guess life changed for you, Carole. Is he yours?" (pointing to Danny) Doug couldn't miss his wife's expression, which seemed to him to be a mixture of shock and anxiety. Nowhere was her usual delight in unexpectedly seeing an old friend. Since they had to rush to the ferry, Nick accompanying them all the way, nothing much was said beyond his telling the couple that he was now a partner in the real estate firm Summer's Joy.

He'd do everything possible to find them a rental.

"Doug, that was quite a surprise to me," Carole said on the car ride home. She knew he had noticed something odd about her response to Nick, and wanted to head off his questions. Thinking privately that it would be hard to talk normally and deal with the rush of feelings inside, Carole went on: "the last I saw him, Nick was running quite a big real estate office in San Francisco. In fact, my brother-in-law invested with him in a land deal which they were going to turn into a large upscale shopping center in San Jose. So when I flew out last May, Leslie hoped that I might relocate them, and urged me to meet with Nick to check out the rental market."

Doug didn't have much to say. He heard Carole going on and on.

'Different from her usual style,' he thought. He'd deal with it later, when Jill wasn't around. but when they arrived home after dropping Jill off at her mom's, for whatever reason neither touched the issue. It was handing over them and would stay there until they did.

Thank God the next day was work for Doug, who left home before Carole stirred. He was carefully going over the three volume diary she had brought him, most of it utterly useless, and the rest in a primitive type of code. Notations like "had lunch with my special friend today and we figured out how to manage unwelcome interest" or "Paul is very confused about how friendly to be with his colleagues these days. Says Jenny is jealous and wants him home." Knowing what he now knows about Paul's dad, Doug could of course arrive at a pretty good guess about who the "friend" or "colleagues" were. But how to connect the dots. 'And then, why so many years later would Da Silva look to get Stephen involved?

Was it happenstance, or a predetermined event? If I can't decide, how the devil can I convince a jury?' Doug needed more help from the NYPD detective; Brown could also canvass his colleagues on the drug squad to see if they could come up with anything more. 'Around and round we go.

Would I be pushing so hard if Roth wasn't Dana's brother?"

Doug spent the rest of Monday afternoon on cases he had a firmer handle on, and then turned to prepare one of these for litigation. Naturally he filled Lily in at their regular meeting.

Carole meanwhile had called her sister, frantic, wanting to get a handle on what Leslie might think about whether Nick was likely to sayanything to Doug. Or to anybody, maybe to his new partner on Fire Is.

So anxious she couldn't eat all day, so preoccupied she hardly noticed Danny's needing to be changed or fed. Just before Doug was to arrive home, for the first time since she began nursing, Carole made herself a stiff drink. Then, leaving the baby to nap, she went into the shower.

Doug brought home deli sandwiches, his task on Monday nights, since Carole had begun to attend a "mommy and me" group at the Y. Coming out of an already too warm subway, he looked forward to a cool shower and a cold beer. When he went into the bedroom and heard the shower running, Doug stripped, preparing to join his wife; she nearly jumped out of her skin. "You scared me!" 'Here again, so out of character.' She normally enjoyed showering together, and at times when Danny was napping, could experience that unhurried intimacy.

Fortunately for Carole, or so she thought, Danny woke up and needed feeding, after which Doug naturally paid some attention to his little guy. Then they were supposed to enjoy this great kosher deli...Doug did, but Carole seemed unable to eat a thing. She instead made a big production of how much "the girls" had consumed in the way of cake and coffee at the Y.

"Okay, what's going on? I haven't seen this from you in months. We are way past this. You're a nervous wreck, you're not telling me something! What is it?" Doug's tone was caring and worried, unlike months ago when he scared her.

"I'd like to make this go away. We're so happy. From my not wanting to be married, not wanting to have a baby, I love my life. I love You. I love Danny. .. but you're going to kill me...or at least this could totally wreck us." Carole began crying, softly at first, then near hysterics. She began to walk to their bedroom, but Doug stopped her physically.

"Look at me. I can't imagine what you think would make me so enraged with you. Trust me, please! And don't take another sip of that damned drink!" Outside, a siren shattered the quiet.

"Okay, I definitely should have told you this after we got back together. You remember when I went to San Francisco when we were close to breaking up? Remember I told you Nick showed me some possible rentals in case I might move back? Well, God, how can I say this? He said he loved me, I was very depressed and we had a lot to drink. We got involved, had sex. Of course I know nothing excuses what I did." She sat waiting for the explosion.

It was Doug's turn to be speechless. He wanted to erase what he had just heard. At this moment, he couldn't imagine ever again feeling the same toward Carole. It felt dangerous. "If I say what I feel or what I'm thinking, I'll never be able to take it back. Let's not talk right now. I've got to be by myself." with that, Doug walked into Jill's darkened room.

Carole couldn't sleep, so she tried cleaning, not her usual tranquilizer, and then was relieved when Danny needed her for his 3am feeding.

Nursing him, she began to consider her options more calmly. None of them involved leaving Doug. She was amazed at herself, with her history of "I'm outa here." After diapering her sleepy son and putting him back in his crib, Carole walked into Jill's room.

"Doug, please wake up." she nudged him gently but firmly. "We need to talk. I can't let you go to work tomorrow, or today, without our talking." He stirred, went out to the bathroom, and returned, still foggy.

"Maybe we should see Marianne together."

"Did she know about this liaison of yours?"

"Yes, I told her in our first private session. We talked about why I did it, and what I felt about tell you or not telling. She of course left it up to me."

"Well, so she's a snake in the grass, covering for you, never even clueing me in about what went down. Believe me, I've seen the last of her."

"Why blame Marianne? She couldn't breach confidentiality and tell you, you know that! If you want to hate someone, I'm it. And, say whatever you want to, but once we've talked we have to put it behind us. There's no way I can allow myself to be a pincushion indefinitely for some stupid thing I did."

"Stupid is it? You're far from taking responsibility for it. You violated every standard for decency in a relationship. You can't make the rules forhow we'll handle this. My father fucked everything in skirts and my mother swallowed it all. that's not a role I'm prepared to fall into."

"Doug, I'm not your father. Naturally you're more sensitive to what I did because of him…of course if I ever did it again I'd expect you to throw me out. But it won't ever happen again. We have so much together, too much to toss away. Don't walk out on us!" Doug swiftly left Jill's room. By now past 5:30am, he headed for their bedroom, Carole following closely behind. He'd dress, and go to Starbuck's for breakfast on the way into his office. Carole touched his arm. "Don't try to seduce me, you're good at that, but this time I'm not buying!"

Doug felt very alone. Carole was the one he always turned to, his confidante. He has friends to play tennis and pool with, to go to ballgames or out drinking together. It would never occur to Doug to talk to a friend anyway, or to his mother, and now he certainly wouldn't call Marianne.

Dressed for work, before leaving Doug stopped off in Danny's room. In watching his sleeping infant son he began sobbing uncontrollably. Doug hadn't really allowed himself to cry this way since his father left for good.

When Carole heard and came in to console him, Doug let her.

CHAPTER 35

Jenny was extremely gratified at Larry's progress; after months of vacillating between drinking "just a little once in a while," Larry had decided it wasn't for him. this was not his therapist's doing, but instead his oldest child's; she had asked him if he was an alcoholic! And, the biggest surprise for both Larry and Jenny was his decision to stay in therapy even after attaining sobriety, as he faced that he had only begun to do the necessary work to be healthy.

On the other hand, it seemed that Joy Robbins was getting nowhere.

Frequently panic-stricken over her struggle to meet basic expenses and unable to take any more money out of her house, Joy nevertheless spent money recklessly. She had survived the IRS audit miraculously, but in spite of her good intelligence did not see it as an opportunity to make changes. The agents were "stupid, too lazy to really find anything, thank God,"—when Jenny told her client that she was setting herself up for a disaster, Joy became furious, then laughed. It was clear that Joy was another addict, but unlike Larry, was not in the least uncomfortable with her behavior. She wanted the world to change! At this point, Jenny told her client that individual therapy hadn't been helpful. If she wanted a group for compulsive spenders, Jenny would find it for her. Joy could not believe that Jenny would terminate her therapy, but the therapist was firm on this score. Only if she joined such a group and went reliably would Jenny see her. And she required that Joy bring her fees up to date within the month. When Joy's tears didn't change Jenny's stance, the client capitulated. It took months more in group and in individual work for Joy to even acknowledge that most of her problems were self-designed and executed.How far she'd go in actually making changes was yet to be determined.

While writing up chart notes on the Robbins case, Jenny reflected on her own life. Now that she had shifted her focus to her marriage, to her life, she and Adam were doing quite well. Adam had come in the night before after registering in the dual master's program at Columbia; he will study international relations and history, and had some idea that after completing these degrees he'd like to teach in a junior college and write. His enthusiasm for this new venture was palpable. Gone was the depressive, irritable roommate always seeking faraway trips. Even the ongoing stressors with Stephen's situation couldn't spoil her moods the way they did in the past, when her home modeled a riptide, peaceful on the surface, but truly dangerous.

Adam and Jenny were headed to the theatre this evening when the phone stopped them at the door. Sara Roth was calling with a new idea to help Stephen: "I think that maybe I can guess why they went after Paul's son." She proceeded to tell Jenny that this idea emerged after a conversation she had with her younger sister, who recalled that Ray Da Silva's wife had a miscarriage right around the time of the investigation of Paul's murder. And Sara is pretty sure he never had children. "Old man Da Silva always spoke of how jealous he was of all his friends who had grandchildren, including your father-in-law."

Jenny responded: "Da Silva supposed intervened with the juror on acase involving his son's friend. So how could it be that he never had children?" but she appreciated Sara's call, and they agreed to keep in touch and even to plan a visit.

During intermission, Jenny left a message for Carole: "does Da Silva have a son? or any natural children for that matter?" She filled Carole in on the information shared by Sara acknowledging it was pretty far-fetched.

The next day, Jenny received her answer: "Ray Da Silva never had children with either of his two wives. His second wife has four children, one of whom is a 35 year old son, now presumed to be working with his step-father." Carole indicated that the information was interesting, but probably not too relevant. Doug was putting the finishing touches on his preparation for trial, and while Carole wouldn't be sitting second chair because she was working part time, she would be happy to be the conduit for any further information Jenny could come up with.

A week later, the Levines got very good news; the NYPD had collared the man who planted the gun in Stephen's condo! The achievement came about after months of dogged police work in which nearly every resident in the development was interviewed. As a result, one young mother reported that "some nice young man who helped me with my packages at the supermarket actually followed me home to return my wallet, which I hadn't even known was missing." Once in the secure community, the "nice young man" found Stephen's apartment and easily got in to plant the gun. Because the witness is an art student and also had two distinct conversations with the man, she was easily able to draw him and then to pick him out of a lineup. Without direct contact with "the boss," the man nevertheless admitted to knowing Frenchie well; he worked for him on this job and others like it. And more important, he was very clear that Frenchie was working directly for Da Silva. Both men had solid alibis for the time of the judge's shooting.

Doug threw himself into trial preparation, which he always savored more than any other part of his job. Evan, second chair for the Da Silva trial, was a solid, experienced guy, not too ambitious so he didn't need to compete with Doug. They fell into an easy comradeship in their assigned roles.

For Doug, for any competent professional, everything is in the preparation. The actual trial is crucial, he says, but without the foundation even the most charismatic prosecutor would generally lose. Juries weren't perfect; in fact they could be dead wrong at times, but good pre-trial work and careful voir dire mostly triumphed. The cases Doug had lost, especially early in his career, were those he rushed to trial before he had a tight case to sell the jury. These days, smarter and more experienced, he took things slower, making sure the pieces fit together, and that there were few surprises.

Carole had loved working with Doug, and had become quite confident trying less prominent cases herself. She was saddened to step down from this role, but with their marital stressors, it couldn't work.

The weekend before the Da Silva trial began, Doug left his office on this, the first Friday in June. He had been practically living with Evan for the past several weeks, which also gave him some needed distance from Carole. In the intervening three weeks, the couple had been superficially friendly, neither of them touching on the elephant still sitting in the center of their lives.

"Carole, maybe we should go back to Fire Island and rent a place for next month. We're running out of time."

"There's no way we're going there. You'd be okay while you're on vacation with us for two weeks. Then, when I'm alone with the kids, with Nick on the prowl, you'd be right back to distrusting me. No go. Would you consider the Outer Banks or the Jersey Shore? I think they're much cheaper anyway."

The Malones were sitting in their living room, the Yankee game on television, when Carole pressed the "mute" and broke through their avoidance: "Since I stopped seeing Marianne months ago, and didn't feel I could go back because money's tighter, I began doing my own therapy.

You never asked me what came out of my talk with my mother, but I'm going to tell you anyway because I think it's important. You know I thought she was having an affair with Aunt Janet…where I got that idea I'll neverknow. When I told her that she was amused, and finally admitted what had really been going on. For nearly twenty years she had been having an affair with one of my father's golf buddies! According to her, they had considered getting divorces and marrying, but it seemed simpler to go on the way they were. So the many trips to help the world were almost always together. And, my mother admitted that she and my father hadn't "slept together" in the last twenty-five years. What he does, she has no clue about, and doesn't care, even now that her affair is over. Her lover moved with his wife to a retirement community in Arizona six years ago and supposedly that ended it."

Continuing, aware that she had Doug's undivided attention, (he even turned off the game), Carole referred to her mother's slightly bitter comment, "your father preferred you anyway." What emerged from that crack was dad's devotion to Carole from the time she became a fine athlete, around age six. He had apparently hoped she would become a tennis pro, while mother openly had contempt for such a career and pushed her toward "the family occupation," medicine; she even told Carole that the girl "didn't have the stomach for such competition even if you have the talent, which is doubtful." Dad attended many of her matches, and selected tennis outfits, which Doug felt from seeing old photos were inappropriately revealing.

"All my boyfriends were athletes, even though I found many of these jocks boring as hell—except between the sheets. I know that to get us back on track, I have to share some pretty distasteful things about myself, but there's no choice. For a while, in high school and in college, I really was quite a player. Men liked me, they proposed to me, I ate it up, then went on my way. I had fun until my junior year when I faced not having a clue what I was going to do with my life. Dad knew the bare bones of my social life and seemed to get a kick out of it. At any rate, he paid the bills for a fabulous wardrobe, bought me a Jag convertible and told me not to worry about my future, some lucky rich guy would take care of me.

"When Leslie started college and declared pre-med right away, I panicked. It was the best thing that could have happened. My advisor urged me to consider graduate school in some area tapping my interests: history, political science, writing and public speaking. I was doing all right in my science courses, but never had real enthusiasm, or I believe any real ability there. So I dumped the athletes, decided to apply to law school and began dating the very ambitious Nick. Along with these changes, naturally I had to cut back on my tennis. Telling Dad was the hardest part; he acted like I died." Until this, Carole had spoken matter-of-factly. Now she choked back tears, breathing irregularly. Doug continued to watch and listen silently.

"When I said goodbye to Nick at graduation, it was over for me, but he kept calling and writing. I felt nothing for him, maybe just annoyancethat he didn't give up and get on with his life. You see how shallow I was?

For me, New Haven was a fresh start away from all the meaninglessness in my life. I was going to be a serious student. In fact, for the most part, I did reinvent myself. Naturally there were some relationships, but nothing like what had gone down before. When I got my law degree, there was none of the shame that I felt leaving Stanford. At graduation, my mother seemed pleased, while my dad was distracted, indifferent. I didn't allow myself to be heartbroken this time. But I nearly fell apart when my normally indifferent brother hugged me, and said he was so proud of me." Carole seemed unaware that tears were literally pouring down her cheeks.

"My God, when we met and even for a couple of years afterward, I thought you had the perfect family. Smart, successful, a beautiful home, the right schools...now I know you and your sister were like orphans. If I wasn't so emotionally involved with you myself, I could almost appreciate your jumping into bed with Nick when you thought we were quits last year.":
Neither of them seemed to know where to go from here. Everything had been said, but there was still so much hurt and mutual distrust. Finally Carole told Doug that she was terrified to count on him staying with her after what she did but she was not going anywhere. And Doug told his wife that he was gun shy about trusting her the way he had, but wanted to try to get past it. They needed time more than any more words.

Carole called Marianne for an appointment, and got in to see her on Monday, June 5th. She brought Danny, having nursed him earlier so he would sleep through the session. She very much wanted her therapist to see the child they had so often talked of. The main focus was Carole's need to be sure that she had done everything she could to preserve her marriage. After listening to Carole's recital of recent events, Marianne could honestly say that she felt Carole to be much more present in her marriage. "I'm so impressed with your growth, much of which you accomplished on your own since we last met." Carole's response was warm, crediting Marianne for starting the healthy process; she thanked the older woman "for letting me lean on you when I most needed it, and letting me go when I had to do that."

Marianne was sad for Doug, though if he had to dump somebody, he made the right choice, holding onto Carole, while getting rid of her.

CHAPTER 36

On July 16th 2001, Doug and Evan of the U.S. Attorney's office and two heavyweight defense attorneys from Dwight and Fairchild sparred off against each other in jury selection. Doug preferred a balanced jury, men and women, white and ethnic, of all ages, working and retired. His tactic was to make a real connection with each person; if that attempt failed, he could and did use a peremptory challenge. The defense attorneys were seeking something else; they preferred older white Italians, preferably male and successful. The plan appeared to be to present their client as a successful businessman who was the object of discrimination just because he's Italian. So his attorneys were also open to including others who might have experienced unfair discrimination, or at least thought they did.

Carole came into court accompanied by her infant son, in good spirits, at around two o'clock. Because this was a very high profile case, both attorney offices were well-represented in the room. The fans were working, but unfortunately not so the air conditioning system on this hot, muggy July day. By four, Carole had to leave, without Doug ever seeing her.

The trial dominated the lives of the families affected and those of the involved professionals for more than two months. Following jury selection, opening arguments were delivered by the two top attorneys, Doug for the prosecution, Lester Fairchild for defense.

Doug brought the jury in on recent events involving the attempted assassination of a sitting judge and the attempted bribery of a sitting juror. He then took them through the setting up of a "weak link," Stephen Roth, via drugs, the juror, and the planted gun. And he then brought in Carole's abduction, with which most jurors had acknowledged familiarity during voir dire. He would prove that the couple abducting Carole worked for Da Silva.

Though history suggested a connection between Da Silva and the old case murder of Paul Roth, the defendant was not being charged inthat murder. They were asked to find Da Silver guilty re the drugs, jury tampering, the attempted murder of the judge, and of the kidnapping of an assistant U.S. Attorney. It was a powerful presentation during which the jury was completely attentive.

Lester Fairchild did his part with charm and intelligence. A small, slim man dressed meticulously, he made excellent eye contact with jurors and never used a word any of them might have trouble understanding. Describing Ray Da Silva as a successful businessman running an interstate trucking company, Fairchild suggested that there had been tremendous rivalry between the Roth and Da Silva fathers; the latter was by far the more financially successful, a pattern to be repeated by their sons Paul and Ray. How Ray had attempted to help Paul out by lending him money when his small business floundered, but Paul turned to selling drugs, and when caught, blamed the Da Silvas, thinking that an Italian family would sell as Mafia to the hungry media. It was indeed sad that Paul Roth died so young, leaving a young family, and it was also a loss to the fathers who had to end their relationship in the wake of the trouble. But Ray had nothing to do with Paul's murder; **IT WAS NEVER PROVED!** Repeating this phrase several times, Rothchild indicated that now Stephen Roth wants to get back at Ray because he irrationally believes he was responsible for ending his father's life. But Stephen Roth never suggested anything like this **until he got in trouble with the law.** Fairly shouting this last, thediminutive defense attorney loomed large. (A couple of jurors nodded; his argument seemed logical.) Now Rothchild turned to Carole's abduction, "assuming it wasn't staged," and the connection between Carole, Frenchie and Marcy Kidd. He would prove that while they did all drive together and were illegally inhabiting a vacant house, "the tryst was consensual, it likely was a ménage-a-tois where one of the parties, namely Carole Lewis, eventually got scared of the repercussions and turned traitor on her friends."

Doug and Carole, in separate parts of the courtroom, were enraged and devastated, respectively. And Jenny, sitting near Carole, felt sick for her. 'Could a jury really be made to believe such a crazy story? Why not, if OJ got away with two murders, juries could be manipulated in any direction.' The court recessed until Tuesday morning, with Doug seeking out Carole amongst the departing public, to no avail. She had left, vowing not to return to this developing circus. But a reassuring call from Doug changed her mood,

117

and they met for dinner later to discuss what had occurred.

"Carole, you're savvy enough to know the more desperate the defense, the crazier the story! Fairchild has to discredit so many pieces of the puzzle, but the hardest one was that couple abducting you. They had absolutely no reason to do this on their own, and Marcy will testify that they were being paid to take you. Frenchie refuses to say who paid, but there is solid evidence that he had been working with Da Silva at the time the abduction occurred. How they're going to deal with Frenchie's hired hand admitting he broke into Roth's place to plant the gun, I can't even begin to guess. His not touching on it in the opening statement means he hasn't figured it out yet either...so you can be sure I'll go after it big time."

"I am concerned about you. Fairchild knows we were living together when you were abducted. I don't have a clue as to why he selected a sexual liaison as the basis for his far-fetched story, but we need to be prepared for anything."

"What are you implying? Will he slander me? Will he go after my character? Oh, my God, I'm not sure if I can cope with this. Doug, maybe I should go stay with Leslie until after the trial."

"That would be a huge mistake. You know that I won't let them go after you willy nilly. But you will have to testify; the other evidence doesn't establish a powerful enough case. I am afraid of Stephen Roth's testimony because he's very weak...but Jenny will be credible when I call on her to identify the diary, and to give background information on what she knew about the Da Silva family. Too bad the old lady can't come up to New York...I can just imagine her impact on this jury."

En route to their home, Carole asked Doug why Jill hasn't been around lately. Was she angry about something? At first hesitant, Doug acknowledged that the astute youngster had picked up "trouble in paradise;" he ended up telling Jill that they were under a lot of strain, but refused to give details. Quoting Jill, "let me know when you get it together."

Doug remarked that his daughter didn't need any more conflict in her life.

"I'm sure, loving you as she does, she can't tolerate the thought that we could be splitting up, but I promised her that you and I were both absolutely committed to fixing this...we are, aren't we?" It was the clearest statement Doug had made so far to Carole of his absolute devotion to their future.

What Doug had not told his wife had to do with a telephone call from Jill's mother. She had read something disturbing about Carole in the tabloids, alluding to sexual misconduct, and told Doug that she did not want her daughter to associate "with that woman". Naturally, he was furious and defended Carole. And, no one could interfere with his access to Jill!

The heart of the Da Silva trial began with police testimony, which was delivered dispassionately by Ivan Brown and his colleague, Matthew Dorn from the NYPD organized crime task force. Doug led them through the events associated with the much earlier drug trial wherein a sitting juror had been approached, and the judge was the object of a failed shooting attempt on his life. Then ballistics evidence was given concerning the retrieved bullets and the ultimately discovered gun, a 9mm Smith & Wesson. Fairchild asked few questions on cross, beyond establishing that at no point was there evidence of the gun being in his client's possession, and the connection with the defendant in the original drug trial was tenuous. In fact, Da Silva had never met that defendant, which Doug's investigation hadn't clarified. So Judge Emily Sanders asked Doug to connect up this testimony; why was it relevant to this defendant?

Da Silva is a good-looking man in his mid-60's, polished, beautifully dressed and well-groomed, with no jewelry or other flashiness which could lead the uninformed to an association with the Mafia. With his graying hair and bright blue eyes, he could be an advertisement for what the "mature" man should look like. One could easily imagine him playing golf, or running a big business. His younger wife sits behind him. Attractive, twelve years his junior, she had come to this second marriage with four children between 12 and 21 years of age, their father having died of lung cancer. The Da Silvas are married for fourteen years, and have been living without a hint of scandal in Old Westbury, L.I and Palm Springs, Ca.

They have a private executive jet which operates between their residences and is also used for his business, located in Delaware and in Texas. Two of Nan Da Silva's four adult children and their spouses are sitting further back in the courtroom, and most planned to be present on and off during the long trial.

By the end of the first week of trial, Doug got a surprise. Carole's name was added to the defense witness list, and a request ordering her to stay out of the courtroom was honored by the judge.

Stephen Roth was brought in from prison to testify about his drug connection with "Frenchie," and that man's coaching of him in seeking to change a juror's vote. He was also able to describe his one visit to a private room in a Manhattan catering hall where Da Silva was hosting a big dinner for friends and family. Doug was pleasantly surprised by the young man's poise on the stand. They had of course discussed his testimony, the need for succinctness, and the importance of his answers not going beyond the question. A quick study, Stephen looked directly at Doug during testimony, spoke clearly, and answered questions precisely. His testimony took up the better part of several days.

Fairchild began his cross examination gently, obviously trying to make Stephen comfortable, and to avoid making himself look like the bad guy to the jury. Stephen admitted using marijuana since junior high, then adding occasional cocaine in high school; he sometimes sold pot to his friends. The attorney didn't challenge Stephen's statement that he wasn't an addict, allowing him to state that he just enjoyed pot for pleasure. "So, Mr. Roth, until you met Mr. Da Silva at that dinner, had you ever heard he was involved in any way in your drug activities? Wasn't it true that the drug transactions were strictly between you and this Frenchie? Stephen had to acknowledge that was the case. "And with respect to the juror, were you in any way made to under stand from Frenchie that you were under orders from Da Silva, was his name used at any point?"

"Never. French referred to his boss, not by any name."

"When Frenchie offered to give you larger quantities of drugs on credit, did you think he was setting you up, as the prosecution claims?"

"I was grateful because of my financial problems. Also I thought at the time that he and I had a long history together, I had always paid promptly, so he trusted me."

"That's a very reasonable assumption, Mr. Roth. I thank you for your honesty. Now to another matter. The very terrible unsolved murder of your father, Paul Roth, twenty years ago. Is it correct that your father's place of business was found to be a front for extensive illegal drugs?"

Objection from Doug, sustained.

"Mr. Roth, I have here a summary, put into evidence, of a police report at that time, listing the various drugs found on the premises of your father's convenience store. Please read the highlighted sections."

After this part of the testimony, wherein Stephen had to acknowledge that his father had gotten deeply involved in selling drugs and then tried to extricate himself, he was asked the most difficult question: "In spite of the police closing the investigation of my client with no findings in the murder of your father, do you still believe him to be the responsible party? Yes or not."

"Yes."

"Would you do everything you could to see him behind bars even if you had to lie to ensure this?"

Objection from Doug, sustained.

On redirect, Doug asked Stephen if he had lied to further his interest in getting Da Silva convicted. "No, never."

But Doug had no doubt that Fairchild had planted a seed in the minds of some of the jurors.

Doug called Marcy Kidd, who, dressed sedately, and did better than expected in not flaring up at Fairchild's hostile cross examination. She established that she and Frenchie were lovers, that they were working for "the boss," and had gotten paid $10,000. cash to abduct Carole Lewis, whom they never met before. The two had been looking over television and still photos of the young attorney and had followed her for just under two weeks before being successful "...in grabbing her." Fairchild followed up on his assertion that the couple was somehow sexually involved with Carole, but bombed with this approach. Doug was enormously relieved, feeling that the defense attorney would be highly unlikely at this juncture to pursue his original hypothesis. However, Fairchild's objections to Marcy's statement that Frenchie had told her they were working for Da Silva were sustained. On cross, Fairchild also got Marcy to acknowledge her pleading guilty on the kidnapping charge, with its potential for a long sentence, and her testimony here, got her a substantially reduced sentence.

Frenchie was brought from prison for his testimony as a hostile prosecution witness. He gave his full name, James Ross, nee Frenchie (because he loved French fries), and address, plus his occupation as salesman for Da Silva Trucking. Beyond this point, the man acknowledged only that he was being held without bail, charged with providing drugs to Stephen Roth in quantities clearly for resale, with jury tampering, with hiring someone to plant the gun in Stephen's condo, and with the abduction of assistant U.S. Attorney Carole Lewis. He then took the Fifth Amendment to all further questions, on advice of present counsel.

By mid-August, both Jenny and Carole were slated to testify, after which the prosecution would rest. Doug began with Jenny, who dressed in her most conservative suit for the occasion. He led her quickly through her participation with Stephen's drug arrest, through her obtaining the diary from her mother-in-law, then backwards in time to her first husband's involvement with the mob around drugs. Fairchild let her testify without much interference until she dealt with the circumstances just prior to Paul's death, the couple's conversations about the mob, and Paul's references "to my contact, Ray Da Silva." Jenny had been extremely patient initially, but became increasingly irritable with the defense attorney's constant objections; so Doug asked for an early lunch recess. Jenny had to get it together, as it was quite possible that she'd be on the stand for days.

Dana, who had been in the courtroom, joined her mother, Doug and Evan for lunch in the office. Doug suggested that they relax, chat aboutanything other than the trial, so they began discussing the Yankees' remarkable season, headed for another world championship. Then Doug noticed that Jenny had dropped out of the conversation and was clearly in her own world. So he shifted back to the present, allowing her to ventilate her rage. It almost seemed that Jenny was emotionally back twenty years, flooded with feelings toward Paul, his father, and the mobsters who had helped ruin her family. Just when Doug was convinced that she might not be in shape to resume testifying, Jenny pulled herself together. "Maybe I needed to do that, to kill them all off; now I can go back and put my brain in charge. Let's do it!" And over the next two days, Jenny did do it.

Doug had deliberated with Evan and his new boss, Barry, about whether to put Carole on the stand first, followed by the mailman who she first asked for help, then the various law enforcement professionals she saw following the abduction…or, if having all the professionals testify first, then winding up with Carole would be best. But opinions were divided, so Carole ultimately made the decision; she wanted to get it over with, knowing that Fairchild might try to crucify her.

Carole is a poised professional on the stand. What she feels inside she does not show, from long practice. Evan takes her through the abduction, from her going alone for a walk around 8:30pm on that Wednesday night in October to her return home, and the circumstances she reported to the Dobbs Ferry police and to the FBI. Signed statements she made at that time were admitted into evidence. Staying completely focused on Evan, Carole manages to avoid eye contact with Doug when the inquiry turns to just why she left the house rather late and alone on that evening.

"I had a fight with my boyfriend, and was further angered when he got involved in a long telephone conversation with a friend, so I left for what I thought would be a walk. Because I hadn't eaten and my favorite Thai restaurant was always open late, I headed over to Broadway. That's where those two started to talk to me."

In response to further inquiry by Evan, who knew what Fairchild might ask on cross, Carole volunteered that the argument was over her pregnancy, and how she and her partner differed in what the outcome should be. Carole acknowledged, with some internal distress, "that I remember being confused, I had thought that he would have wanted me to terminate the pregnancy, and that I wanted to have the child. Instead, when he made it clear that he wanted us to marry and have the baby, I was disturbed. Maybe I was the one who didn't want it. So the walk was partly out of annoyance at him, but largely to clear my head. I definitely wasn't leaving him, I didn't take anything except my pocketbook, not even my cell phone or a warm enough jacket."

After a two hours' lunch break during which time Carole got an atta girl from her husband, had time to nurse her son and visit with his baby sitter, she returned to the stand.

Evan completed his examination by asking Carole what she ultimately decided to do about the pregnancy, knowing that some jurors would judge her harshly if they thought she had terminated it.

"Thank God I came to my senses. We have a wonderful son, Danny, who is now five months old. In fact, he's in the back of the courtroom with his babysitter, Mrs. Cohen."

As Doug had envisioned, the jurors sought out the only infant present, and some nodded and smiled at the plump little boy sitting happily on his sitter's lap. Fairchild smirked, but the deed was done.

At Evan's "Your witness," the judge decided to adjourn until the following day because she needed time for motions on other cases on her future docket. Carole, relieved on one hand, would have preferred to get it over with. Not so Doug and Evan.

Today is Thursday, August 23, 2001, Carole's 31st birthday. What a way to spend it, being grilled by a hostile defense attorney. She had been awakened earlier today by Dog's loving, special gift: a baby charm fashioned from diamonds. And Carole had received calls from her parents and from Leslie as well as numerous cards and good luck calls from friends, especially welcome at this stressful time.

Carole took the stand more confident than was true yesterday. Fairchild may sense this, so he begins in a friendly fashion, not wanting to antagonize the jury. He is also aware that Judge Emily Sanders, very fair to date, could unconsciously identify with this witness, should he be too aggressive. Accepting her story by now that she never knew either of her abductors in a personal or professional relationship, Fairchild asks her about her "flirting with Frenchie." He wanted to know if their relationship developed "after your abduction, did the two of you become friends?"

Carole took her time in responding. "Just as you are trying to be gracious to me in this mutually treacherous situation, Frenchie and I both tried for cordiality. My guess about him is that he didn't want to provoke me and I at least wanted to try to reach him emotionally, so he might let me go, or at least not kill me."

Fairchild was probably not happy being compared to this petty criminal. "You have referred to your "boyfriend" and your "partner," without naming him or saying who he is. Please give the court that information now."

"My partner than is my husband since January 16, 2001, Douglas Malone. He is, as you know, the chief assistant U.S. attorney prosecuting this case."

"Is he the father of your child?"

"Of course!" Carole felt physically ill for just an instant, wondering if the man would pursue anything about her affair... but he changed course.

"Was there anything said during your 3 1/2 days' confinement thatled you at that point to believe that your abduction was in any way connected to the defendant?"

"No...neither of them ever referred to anybody by name, or said why they had taken me. I asked repeatedly but they ignored the question. They were silent around me, and I couldn't hear their conversation, assuming they had any, because each night they gave me sleeping medication."

"So there is no known connection between your abduction and the defendant. So why are we talking? Nothing further with this witness."

Subsequently, the Dobbs Ferry police captain, and two FBI agents testified as to Carole's condition after being released from captivity. Evan then rested the prosecution's case.

From August 27 through the 31st, defense witnesses testified. These included officers in Da Silva Trucking, to prove that the business was legitimate and earned profits commensurate with the family's lifestyle, and others who swore that Frenchie was a low-level employee who barely had access to his boss. Two of his wife's adult children testified as to their step-father's loving, paternal nature and the complete absence of drugs in their family's lives. One of these stepsons acknowledged that he knew the defendant in the earlier drug trial and that the defendant may have had some connections which could have been utilized to influence a juror...that Stephen Roth could have been approached by that man's contacts.

With respect to the gun involved in the judge's shooting, evidence was produced showing it was sold in South Carolina to a reputable farm equipment store owner, and then was stolen, not to reappear until the incident under scrutiny. Nothing in the evidence connected the gun with Da Silva, but there was testimony that Frenchie traveled by car back and forth between New York and Florida.

CHAPTER 37

Judge Emily Sanders excused the jury just prior to the long Labor Day weekend, reminding them that they are still under restriction as far as discussing the case, reading newspaper accounts or viewing television reports of the case. Since this is a high profile prosecution, she certainly understands that only hermits would literally be free of any input, but she nevertheless stressed their sworn obligation.

The Malones were exhausted and could have used a few days away. They had actually been invited to the Hamptons by friends who had a tiny private guest cottage on their property, but Doug felt unable to pull himself completely away from his work. So he and Carole used their free time to go over the case yet again. He was particularly obsessed with two very separate questions: "Who actually shot Judge Reid?" and, "Who had reason to shoot Paul Roth?" Dropping the first query because Doug felt it was likely that Da Silva brought in a shooter from out of state, he asked Carole to "think out of the box; let's imagine the gangsters weren't involved, who else had motive?" They read and reread Stephen Roth's letter, considered some of his father's cronies, and reread their NYPD notes from the long ago work-up following Paul's murder.

On Tuesday, court reconvened at 10am, and now Carole could be in the courtroom to hear her husband's closing argument, as well as that of the defense attorney. Both men did the best they could with the evidence at hand: Doug knew that he had failed to convincingly connect Da Silva with the gun, though he had made a good enough case to support Frenchie's involvement with Da Silva, and thereby lead the jury to a natural assumption that Da Silva for some inexplicable reason had decided to have Carole abducted. The foolishness of such an act was the hole in the argument; why would a savvy guy like Da Silva undertake such a perilous act with so little probability of influencing outcome? Doug tried his best to produce some reasonable hypothesis, but was aware of its limitations. On the other hand, Da Silva's clear involvement with drugs was established; Frenchie certainly couldn't lay his hands on thousands of dollars worth of cocaine and marijuana on his salary, and if all Frenchie did was work sales for the trucking company, why was he earning his relatively high salary? So Doug tied up loose ends, and after asking them for guilty verdicts on all counts, thanked the jurors for their service.

It was Fairchild's turn and he made the most of it, taking the jury through the case step by step, demonstrating each hole in the prosecution's case. He particularly emphasized Stephen Roth's role in "setting up the defendant," bringing in the history, not to indicate his client's guilt in Paul Roth's sad ending, but to give motivation to Stephen's assumptions about Da Silva. turning to the relationship between Frenchie and Roth, and later to Frenchie and Carole Lewis, Rothchild suggested that his client had nothing to do with either relationship; the central figure in each was Frenchie, and he was awaiting his own trial!

Judge Sanders gave instructions to the jury, which would begin deliberations the next day.

The jury deliberated for the balance of the week, reaching a verdict on Monday, September 10th. They found Da Silva guilty on the drug charge, on the abduction of Carole Lewis, and of the attempt to bribe a juror via Stephen Roth. They found him not guilty on the charge that he ordered the hit on the judge. Doug was disappointed, but not surprised.

Though Da Silva was unlikely at his age to ever see freedom, so Doug counted this a victory, there were disturbing unanswered questions, very likely to stay unanswered.

CHAPTER 38

Carole, Doug and Danny left the courthouse midday on Sept. 10th headed north as guests of the Levines. Dana and her family were already there, so the three bedroom cabin would be packed to the rafters. It was a gorgeous sunny day, and in somewhat of a celebratory mood, Doug stopped to let his wife shop the outlets en-route to their destination.

Carole sprinted back to the car after receiving a startling call from Dana "We're uninvited by the Levines! Dana said she wants to meet us somewhere around here…she mentioned the Mohonk Lodge as a place we'd like…she refused to even hint at what's up, but did say we should book her a room as well."

"Let's not even speculate about it. We'll have a great lunch and then call that hotel. Frankly, I'd prefer for us to be alone after the stress of these last few months."

The Malones spent two hours hiking in the gentle hills of the lower Catskills. Doug complained that he was hot and sweaty carrying Danny, he didn't plan for enough water, and he'd prefer driving home tonight instead of spending so much money on this less than elegant hotel. Carole chided him: he hadn't been outdoors in months, had fairly lived in his office, so he badly needed the exercise and the color. and, she had no intention of disappointing her friend.

When Dana, Mel and Amy finally showed up around 6:30pm, the Malones were famished, so they had dinner together without discussing anything of importance. Afterward, the children put to bed, Mel babysitting his daughter in their room, Dana met with Carole and Doug. She only addressed Doug.

"This is the hardest thing I've ever done in my life. I have to do it, but I'm so scared. Mel says I should stay out of it, but my brother and I havedecided that we need your help." Dana rambled, rubbed her eyes, bit her thumbnail, her listeners waiting silently. "Stephen and I have been obsessed recently with finding out more about our father and what happened to him. We've talked endlessly, first about when we were little kids and dad was so rarely around, then those last few years when he took us skating and to ballgames on weekends. We remember him as a great dad, not as a drug dealer. More rarely took us to the store...she seemed almost ashamed of it, or maybe of what daddy did. After all, she was a college graduate, and her friends were social workers, nurses and teachers, and here he was a convenience store owner."

"Stephen and I jumped to memories after daddy's death, like the funeral and sitting shiva, and our grandfather's trouble with the police. For days, we'd email back and forth, with 'do you remember when...' and then either Stephen or I would email mom to ask her to fill in the blanks. Sometimes she'd write back days later, so we were frustrated, but she always was so busy with work, and the trial was taking a lot out of her, so we tried to be understanding. Then, this past weekend, with the trial over, he and I talked about the day daddy died. It's hard to believe, but we never before compared notes on what happened that evening." Dana sipped her water, looked briefly at Carole, before resuming her story.

"It was a Wednesday, and every Wednesday Mom played mah jong, either at home, or at one of her friend's houses. Since Stephen was 13, he had been babysitting me and got paid for it, so Mom often went to a friend's. She always left the name and telephone number, mostly in case we got into a big fight, so I could call to complain. Anyway, that night the game was at Liz Elson's just a few blocks away. Mom left around 7:45 as usual, and told us she'd be back around 10:30. She was always reliable. She typically called us around 9:30 to say goodnight to me, and she did the same that night. I remember because I had begged her to let me stay up to watch a TV program, and she said it was okay as long as I had taken my bath. She also spoke briefly to Stephen."

Carole glanced nervously at Doug. It was beginning to be pretty obvious that they were about to hear something shocking. She didn't want to hear it, but could hardly get up and leave. He was, however, totally engaged with the story.

"Around the time the program ended, I went to bed, about 10:00 pm.

Right afterward the police came, two of them, and asked where our mother was. They wouldn't say anything about why they were here, but my brother guessed that it had to do with our dad. Just as usual, at 10:30, mom came home. Stephen and I both seem to remember that she wasn't so surprised to see the police. They took her into the kitchen to talk, but Stephen sneaked out of his room and heard everything. I was too scared.

Mom didn't even cry. According to Stephen, she said that she'd been expecting this visit for years! Of course, after that we were up all night. Mom got a neighbor to stay with us while she went with the police. She didn't get home 'til the middle of the night; they brought her."

Carole, I don't know if I ever told you what a wild teenager I was.

Stephen and Mom were never home. He was in college and Mom was working and getting her master's. From when I was around fourteen I started to bring friends home, and we'd drink and smoke pot, and I had sex with different guys, some a lot older. Anyway, I know now that I could not stand being alone, in fact I probably still can't. And when I was alone, I used to ransack the house, especially my mother's bedroom, looking for God knows what, but I did keep any spare money I found, and sometimes junk jewelry— my mom didn't have any other kind. Well, one rainy Saturday when I was by myself and searching her closet I found a gun way back behind a plastic chest of drawers. At the time I thought maybe my father had it since he was always worried about us, and that was the end of it. Months later when I went back to look—so I could show my boyfriend—it was gone. I never told Stephen about it until this past weekend."

"Dana, we've been friends for so many years. But you know that Doug and I are a part of the criminal justice system, we're officers of the court. There may be implications in your telling us that aren't true if you told some other friend."

"I'm telling you both precisely because Stephen and I want something done. We are sick about it. We don't know what we actually feel would be right, but we can't live with this anymore." The young woman began sobbing. It was very difficult this time for her to pull herself together.

"Stephen was shocked when I told him the story about the gun. He shouted, "I knew it, I knew it," so the guard came over to find out what was going on. He then added the clincher: when Mrs. Elson had paid a shiva call after daddy's death, he overheard her saying to one of the other mah jong ladies that she had thought Jenny had a boyfriend when she left the game so early that Wednesday saying she had a headache! At the time, Stephen just thought the woman was vicious, but once I told him my gun story, he was convinced mom murdered our father!"

"We left for the Berkshires yesterday immediately after my visit with Stephen. Mel had stayed outside with Amy while Stephen and I had this heavy talk. Then Mel drove. He saw how upset I was but naturally didn't ask me much with Amy in the car. But when she fell asleep, I told him. You know how much he loves my mother? So his immediate reaction was that my brother and I were both crazy; we're looking for any solution and rejecting the obvious, that Da Silva's the guy but no one can prove it. Meanwhile, he refused to hear how Da Silva was in Las Vegas when my dad was murdered, and his men were all at a wedding in Howard Beach because one of their daughters was getting married."

"I agreed with Stephen that we had to confront mom, and since I'm not the one in prison, I'm it. But I couldn't do it last night. Then this morning, I asked her to go for a walk with me alone, and I did it! At first all she did was not deny it. I even gave her an out: did she have a boyfriend who she met that evening? She laughed, saying she wished. Then, with my demanding to know, she told me. How sorry I am that I ever asked!"

Carole started to get up, but Doug restrained her. "It's too late for that."

"My mother told me she took the gun into Brooklyn for her protection in case she didn't find a parking space near the store. It was loaded and she knew how to use it. My father had gotten it for her, not legally, and taught her. When she came to the store, one of his shifty customers was finishing up a buy, so she was already furious when daddy locked up. She took out the gun and supposedly threatened to kill herself; she said he tried to grab it and it went off, killing him. She was terrified, shut the lights off and left. Then she noticed that her shirt had some blood spray so she changed her top in the car, putting on a sweater she had just taken out of the cleaners. She threw away her shirt miles from the store, and then drove directly home because we were expecting her. She said that by then she felt totally calm, like her troubles were over. When she said that, I wanted to kill her."

"That's when we walked back to the cabin and called to tell you guys not to come. Mom told me it was okay for me to tell you, only she didn't want to be there when I did. She knows I'm here with you. If she turns herself in, will she have to go to jail? I want to believe her that it was an accident."

"Dana, all I can tell you is that your mother's confession at this point will certainly open up an investigation. I knew from our perusal of the Brooklyn detectives' investigation of your father's killing that they had not even verified your mother's alibi. They were hot to nail Da Silva for it, after all he was a known mobster and the store was a known drug supplier in their territory. Not all cops are on the take. They also had a fair idea about corruption in their precinct and probably thought they could uncover that as well. But they screwed up. Da Silva didn't really have any reason to kill your father, even if he was getting out of the drug business.

His own father had apparently talked to him, but really it's fiction that anyone leaving the mob gets murdered. Only if they are likely to talk. And why would your father have spilled to the cops? He'd go to jail for sure, so what was in it for him?"

"Do you think mom should go to the police? Will they believe her after all these years?"

"Obviously, Dana, I can't possibly know what will happen once she brings her story to the police. It's very difficult to investigate such a cold case, and clearly they gave up on it many years ago. They might be sympathetic in that she's coming to them when she doesn't have to. But it is opening up the proverbial can of worms, anything can happen."

"Adam wasn't around when mother and I came back. He had been fishing with a neighbor. Mom was more devastated at the thought of telling him than at going to the police. And she thinks you are going to turn her in now that you know Are you?"

"We don't have to do anything. After all, so far all we hear is that two adult children in a lot of emotional pain after this nightmarish year had decided to do their own investigating, and they've come up with some pretty wild interpretation of the facts. That they were young kids when it happened. hat kids, even adults, distort things. So unless your mother decides to go ahead with having the case reopened, we'll do nothing."

"You mean I don't have to tell either? But once Stephen knows, and I must tell him, it's all over. Also, mom definitely has told Adam by now. I can't tolerate thinking that my mother will also go to prison, that Amy…"

Breaking down completely at this point, Dana rushed into the bathroom.

After a few minutes, Carole gently knocked on the door, and once together, the two women spoke for a long time. Then Carole walked Dana to her room, where a worried Mel was awaiting her return.

Carole wanted to talk to Doug, but he refused. "We can't do anything, and I'm beyond exhausted. So are you. Please feed Danny so he'll sleep later tomorrow morning. We'll leave for home around 11. I have every intention of laying around, reading my latest Grisham thriller, and solving nothing more complicated than where we should go for dinner!"

CIRCLE OF STRANGERS:
Part II

CHAPTER 1

Doug and I have been zombies since 9/11, overwhelmed with our feelings and having trouble with the changes at work ensuing from the tragedy. Now my biggest worry is that our moodiness and the frequent absences might be affecting Danny. Doug doesn't seem to be thinking much about us these days, while I'm slowly come back to myself. So I have to watch out for my old demons.

*   *   *

We were on the Thruway headed back to the city, Doug driving, me in the backseat with Danny, when we were stopped cold on the parkway due north of the Tappan Zee Bridge. Naturally, we thought it was the usual thing, a fender-bender knocking out the bridge for twenty minutes.

We heard the requisite sirens, and after a while, witnessed many drivers exiting their cars. As drivers began frantic, even tearful discussions, Doug joined them. Returning to the car, he was ashen; "we can't get to Manhattan, terrorists have bombed the World Trade Center, both towers."

We turned on the car radio, and listened, along with the rest of the country, in disbelief. Doug naturally tried to call our boss, very concerned that some of our colleagues might have been hurt or killed, but he didn't get through. Not being able to access the city, I did telephone my sister in San Francisco, waking her up to this horrific news.

What I remember best after the initial shock was my personal crisis: not being able to get home left me feeling frantic, in spite of my understanding that local police naturally had to facilitate emergency vehicles' access to the bridge while keeping us waiting in place.

The event provided my first opportunity to see Doug handle a real emergency. With all the chaos, he managed to communicate with the lieutenant in charge, identified himself as an assistant federal attorney, and somehow, within hours, got us in contact with the local FBI office.

"Carole, don't count on their doing anything too soon. They have more important issues to deal with than our being stuck here My wanting to get to Manhattan is so we can help, how I can't fathom."

Danny was fine while we waited, sleeping after being nursed, but I couldn't stop my rising panic. Believe me, I'm ashamed, looking back, at my self-involvement. Later, when we got more details about the disaster, I felt even worse. But then all I continued to focus on was when we'd be near a bathroom, and how would we ever get home ?" A middle-aged couple in the car parallel to us also seemed divided on gender lines, she even more frantic than I, and her husband mostly caught up in details of the attacks as we then knew them.

In a weird way, that unending traffic jam turned into an all American picnic. People everywhere got out of their cars, and began intense conversations, and those coming from long holiday weekends shared contents of their coolers. In particular, I remember one striking young guy probably around my age, with a girlfriend who looked like seventeen but was likely somewhat older; they shared a case of cold beer and maybe twenty sandwiches. Doug particularly got a charge out of this fellow, Mike, because of the contrast between how he looked, a little like a slightly upscale derelict, and what he did for a living, corporate accounting. In the meantime, I also got out of the car with Danny because without the air conditioning on, it was stifling. I soon learned that a mother and infant get a lot of attention and offers of help. After a while, Doug and I understood that this was no normal response to being stuck together; we were like displaced soldiers in a war zone, huddling together and trying to find out was happening and how we'd survive."

We had left Mohonk House after breakfast, around 8:45 am, and first learned of the attack closer to 9:30. When we heard that another plane had bombed the Pentagon, that it was on fire, with many dead and wounded, any pretense of calm, and our earlier almost party-like atmosphere vanished as the full implications of this event hit us. Marianne would have described the socializing as a defense against panic. That defense, if that's what it was, couldn't hold up in the face of our very defenders being bombed. "We're at war, where will they hit next?," heard all around us. Doug tried to reassure me, but what had he really thought? He's no fool, so I doubt that he was so sure all would be well, but he absolutely refused to join the doomsayers in predicting widespread sabotage.

After an interminable wait, we were actually identified through FBI channels to NYS highway patrol, and were given a police escort over the bridge. At that point, I was driving so Doug, who was still feeling the effects from the long trial, could nap on the way. I was mostly relieved about being able to go home. The trip took longer than usual because we were constantly forced to pull over for emergency vehicles, fire and police, medical techs and the like, coming from upstate and probably from Massachusetts. Doug tried making calls to our NYPD friends, as he was worried that we'd again run into trouble getting over the Triborough Bridge. Though he never reached anyone we knew, those with whom he did speak reassured him that having gotten our clearance sticker, we would be able to enter Manhattan uneventfully.

It was on the Manhattan side of the bridge that we had our first full confrontation with the life changes brought about by the attack: cops and soldiers everywhere with weapons at the ready. And looking downtown on Second Avenue from our 71st Street exit, we could see a grayish patch hanging over the distant perfectly blue sky. Doug actually suggested that we drive south to see how close we could get to the office, and to the WTC site, but I prevailed, and we went home. From that day 'til this, it was the last time we were in a car together as a family.

My inclination is to go over every detail of that horrendous day; it's obsessive, nonproductive, but I can't help it. Imagine that just the previous day Doug and I had been discussing whether we wanted tile or wood for our new kitchen floor, and granite or Corian for the counter tops. And, though Danny was just a little over five months old, my Doug was hinting that he hoped I wasn't planning to make him an only child, (this from a man I had been sure would never have wanted children.) This was what we'd been discussing when we reached the approach to the Tappan Zee.

Since that day, all our personal conversations last under five minutes, mostly on the telephone; Doug is at work either in the office of at the site, I'm at home or helping Marianne wherever she's working. While this means we rarely argue anymore, it's also true that sex is becoming a distant memory. And our involvement in Jennifer Levine's legal problems, if it comes to that, has ended. I don't even know what she decided to do, as Dana and I have hardly spoken since our last meeting.

CHAPTER 2

"Doug, remember tonight's my first group meeting. Please, please get home by 7. If you can come home earlier, let's eat together. Your son is beginning to call the doorman 'daddy'."

"Very funny! I will be home for dinner, don't tell me you're really cooking! Let's see, for the deprived husband who has been living on pizza and McDonald's, I think that a filet mignon in béarnaise sauce with asparagus and wild mushrooms would suit. Followed by several scoops of chocolate and strawberry Haagan Daz."

"Certainly, my love, coming up! Get your ass home A-sap. I could use a feeding as well, but not of the caloric variety. I complained to Leslie this morning that I was reverting to my virginal state."

Doug, home in time for dinner, looked very thin, older and far more exhausted. "I need a break, it's killing me, but whenever something comes up that might take me away, it feels impossible for me to leave. I know it's irrational, but I feel guilty even thinking about leaving work."

"We have exactly half an hour, can we try to relax, not talk about "it", just enjoy each other? I'm pretty excited about joining the group, but very scared too. What if they ignore me, or if they're miserable about having a new member join? Marianne and the group leader both told me that could happen."

"Carole, they'll love you! And if they don't, why care, they're strangers and don't even know you. Why are you joining the group anyway?
Did you ever tell me?"

"Now I am going to kill you! Of course I told you, several times. I've been feeling like I'm getting dumber, watching TV with Danny, looking around for make-do work, while all my friends are busy with challenging work. Being with Danny means a lot to me, but with you so unavailable...

Anyway, Marianne thought the group could help me with some of this."

"That sounds like a lot of bullshit to me, darling', but if it's what you want...how much is it going to cost ? Look, I'm sorry, I know adjusting to such a drastic change in your life is hard, and my not being around hasn't made it any easier. I've feel plenty guilty about you and Danny."

"I accept your apology but I also resent your feeling that anything Marianne might suggest is bullshit. You're not over hating her yet, are you? Kiss me goodbye, and take good care of our little guy."

CHAPTER 3

On September 12th my plan had been to go into the office, though no one was expected. But instead, I took the subway downtown to Wall Street, pulled toward the site almost against my will. Getting out of that station I was assaulted by a pungent odor which hurt my eyes and burned my throat. My focus on the foul air and smoky sky shifted to the scene: very young armed soldiers everywhere, supplemented by the NYPD. There were few civilians either on the train or in the street....and no private vehicles, quite a contrast from what was normal just yesterday.

Several officers on my route south asked me for identification but even with my badge I was stopped for good by barriers to the still burning site of what had been the twin towers. Firemen were everywhere; dozens of huge bulldozers were parked on the perimeter of the site. Civilians offering bottles of water and food were set up to the east. A number of others, for some reason primarily young women, were mesmerized by the incomprehensible picture. When my eyes and throat begged for relief from the burning, I turned away, walking uptown, not really seeing anything for my tears. Bypassing my office building, I went into a Dunkin Doughnuts on 23rd Street. Hanging with strangers was comforting, as we turned the small place into a parlor where we talked and talked, as if words would somehow mitigate our emotional flooding.

One by one people exited the place, hesitantly, almost against their will.

I know the feeling...going home meant disconnecting somehow from the nourishment of strangers, and facing what was to be.

CHAPTER 4

I dressed very carefully for my first group, making sure that I didn't look too professional or too much the mom, that I didn't put on too much make-up or too little. So largely my anxiety had focused on what to wear; I didn't really think much about what would actually happen in group until I talked to Doug over dinner.

The group has two leaders, Elaine and Gerald, but until tonight I had only met Gerald because Elaine has been working nonstop leading bereavement groups for the Red Cross. She's older than him, and I was told she was more experienced at running groups, and he is a psychoanalyst. Marianne thinks they're both terrific; she's attended workshops they run for very experienced therapists, mostly at national conferences.

When I had asked Gerald who was in the group and what happens there, he asked me what I imagine might occur. So typical of an analyst! On entering tonight, I know nothing and began to wonder how I ever got myself into this.

We're sitting in a circle on cozy chairs in a large, attractive room with floor to ceiling bookcases and huge windows. It's a little too warm in here. Sirens are shockingly loud because the building corners on Broadway and this is a first floor office. There are six other members, half men, half women, so I spoil the balance. They seem attractive enough except for Stephanie, who's in her early 50's, and though slim, has a dowdy, depressed look. Gerald introduces me to Elaine and to the other members, but only Elaine acknowledges me. Soon I notice that they also ignore her, looking at Gerald, and addressing only him even when she speaks.

Gerald comments on the group ignoring Elaine; maybe they have feelings about her being away so often in the past three months. Stacy, an extremely attractive, elegantly dressed 40 plus year old radiologist, scoffs at his comment. "We just prefer you. After all, you're smarter, better trained." I was shocked and felt like saying something, but kept my mouth shut. A few of the other members talk about their lives, naturally I have no way of really following what they refer to…then a very charming man named Bill turned to me: "and what brings you into this dangerous cell?"

Such a question was exactly what kept me up nights right after I agreed to join two months ago.

"You're Bill, right ? I'm a little flustered from nervousness. But I'm okay about you asking, even relieved! I'm home with my first child since he was born 7 1/2 months ago, except for some part time work about two days a week. My husband is hardly home anymore since 9/11 and I've had a hard time. Even before 9/11 I was wondering who I am if I'm not working at what I love doing."

Peter, who seems the silent type, at least at this juncture, asks me what work I do and some other questions that I could answer comfortably.

Then Stacy told him that he was out of line, and that she resented him giving me the floor when others who were here a long time had work to do on their stuff! Just at that moment, with me feeling shaky, a violently barking dog was heard outside, followed by a verbal brawl between two screaming men. Laura, a petite blond physical therapist, around my age, single I gathered, ignored the wild interruption, and turning to Bill, smiled seductively, "I was the one working with you last week. Are you so fickle to give all your attention to the newest lady here?" Though the leaders certainly said things from time to time, all I can remember thinking after the first group was that at least two of the women would have liked to see me dead at their feet. The men were either attentive or neutral. And the leaders clearly didn't see their role to include protecting me. Well, coming from my family, that's familiar!

The best thing that happened after group was my getting Doug up from a sound sleep to make love, a first in weeks!

CHAPTER 5

It's Thursday exactly a week before Thanksgiving and I'm at the family support group run by Project Liberty social workers and psychologists. The office is sending attorneys down to offer whatever help we can, to answer legal questions concerning how families can get death certificates or file for emergency financial help. But in reality, the people I speak to mostly just want to talk about the people they lost and how they are managing. The upcoming holidays definitely make things worse.

How odd that I can now come downtown and face the empty site of what was the World Trade Center without feeling that sick tightening that I can remember from those first days here. From mourning the physical power of the buildings and the anonymous murder of thousands, my thinking these days is about particular young people whose families I've gotten to know working here.

Ethan and Jane came right over to me this morning, asking to talk to me in particular. They don't want to join the group today. Ethan tells me that they're having a rough time. Maybe their marriage won't survive this. Jane is acting like he killed their son because the 26 year old young man had wanted to leave his bond trader job to follow his first love, music, and his father discouraged him. From Jane's "if it wasn't for you, he'd be alive," to poor Ethan's own guilty, "don't you think I know it ?," the couple gave me a show and tell performance of what was going on in their lives at home. I urged them to see a marriage counselor, but Jane absolutely refused, and I didn't know where to go from there. Probably I shouldn't have said this, but I did tell them that my having that kind of help saved my marriage. I practically begged them to speak to Marianne after she ended the group today, but I'm not sure whether they did.

Marianne strongly prefers to have a co-leader in these groups in case any one attending needs urgent, private attention. Because this afternoon there's no other mental health professional available, she asked me to co-lead. "Please don't be too inhibited; the only mistake you are likely to make is to stay silent, arousing their anxiety." Marianne has such a wonderful way of making me feel good enough. This group consists of eight mostly young women whose husbands were murdered in the WTC disaster. They know each other from prior meetings with Marianne as well as from other groups, so there's an immediate discernible closeness.

These wives speak under pressure with intense emotion, describing their devastated children and grieving in-laws. Seeing them, and thinking of Doug and of my own baby, I feel tears coming, and wonder how Marianne keeps her composure. She is able to listen with tenderness. Then I was startled to hear her say that she too had suffered a terrible loss, that of her first infant daughter many years ago. It seems silly to admit this, but I hadn't actually thought of her as having a real life, with her own serious family problems.

While I was willing to be a liaison with some of the WTC companies on issues where I could be of help, after my next (and last) group I told Marianne that I wouldn't co-lead again. In that group of parents, mostly in their sixties and seventies, all of whom had lost adult sons, there were two sets of parents who had lost two sons each. Listening to their stories, I found myself disappearing, mentally putting myself far from this place, thinking about my Danny and whether Mrs. Cohen has checked his temperature as I had asked. I guess law is the profession for me...I could never, ever do this emotionally draining work.

CHAPTER 6

Carole is much more sympathetic to what we're doing here since she's gotten involved with the 9/11 work." Now speaking to U.S. Attorney Barry Golden, Doug was aware of how much more personal their relationship had become since this shift in emphasis. It felt very similar to just after the first WTC bombing in 1993, when staff working on the case rarely left the office, so that they became like a caring, if enmeshed family. Barry reverted to more formality after their resounding successful prosecution.

Barry told Doug that he's going to authorize more hours for Carole.

"These aren't normal times. We have funding to get more attorneys on board, but I can't use inexperienced people, so as much time as she can give me, I'll take. She can either follow up on some of the criminal cases we've been putting on hold, or she can help you with the special work."

"I think Carole might like to return to the criminal cases, but can you ask her, Barry? I could be wrong, but I don't think dealing with the WTC investigation would be her choice."

Barry, Doug and the rest of the staff had all attended many funerals and memorial services for friends and colleagues. One of the most painful losses was that of Doug's friend Ivan with whom he had worked on the Roth case. The young, very smart and talented detective had been a part of the early response team when the first plane hit, and he perished along with many from his unit. As no remains were found, his family finally decided to go ahead with a memorial service in their Rockville Centre, L.I. community. Carole had also known and respected Ivan, so Doug asked her to join him. When he called her at home, Doug told his wife that he could really use her support, "so come for me." He smiled to himself, noticing that it wasn't even hard for him to ask.

The memorial service took place in a Catholic Church, crowded with friends and family, and with scores of Ivan's brothers from the NYPD.

Doug, both from his own Catholic heritage and from the many services he had attended, expected this turnout, but Carole seemed shocked. She had to bring Danny with her, and both parents worried about whether he would tolerate being held; he had just begun to walk holding on, and at times fought against any attempt to restrain him. But somehow his presence seemed to mitigate against the sadness of this event, not only for his parents, but for those close by as well.

CHAPTER 7

Bill Warren left his therapy group this evening and headed straight for his favorite watering hole. It's an upscale bar in an Italian restaurant in the East 70's, within walking distance of his Park Avenue duplex. He thought of calling Ann to join him, then remembered that she was meeting their married daughter to pick out wallpaper. Actually, Bill prefers to go out alone anyway; he usually meets interesting people and doesn't have Ann leaning on him to leave early. Her mantra: "we have to get up for work tomorrow, let's go!" Everyone knows Bill at this place, beginning with Mario, the boss, who's an effusive master of ceremonies orchestrating everything that happens here, including who gets to feel welcome. Then there's Bill's favorite bartender, Shari, a warm and funny gal in her late 20's; she makes a mean drink, and shares honors with her man, Jeff. Naturally in such a place there's never trouble and everyone seems to know each other.

Most of the crowd is over forty, and though presumably married, few are inclined to drink with their spouses..

Bill drinks too much on a regular basis, but he denies to anyone who'd ask that he's an alcoholic. His father had been a "real alcoholic," drinking to unconsciousness. But a "great guy,' a very successful CEO of a machine tool company. Early in his parents' marriage they drank together, but after her first facelift at age 50, she cut it out completely. Later, his father found other drinking buddies until he dropped dead prematurely at age 61 following his first coronary. Bill expects to die young too; fifty-five now, he figures he has a good ten years and intends to enjoy them.

Tonight Bill's evening takes an unexpected turn when 30 year old Laura, a phenomenally-built physical therapist and member of his group, shows up. Both know the golden rule: no socializing outside of the group; if you meet by accident, keep it short and superficial, and then tell the group at the next meeting. As far as Bill knew, it was an unplanned meeting, but Laura knew otherwise.

Laura was the only group member who grew up in Manhattan, and the only "blueblood' as her ancestors went back to the Mayflower. Both she and sister Bonnie, 34, attended the best private schools, had English nannies, and didn't have dinner with their parents regularly until they were in grade school. The girls went separate ways, both devastating their traditional, decent parents. Bonnie is a lesbian, living in a committed relationship with a much older woman, a high school principal. Laura, who might have pleased them by her early clear-cut interest in men, threw her parents into angry panic by openly smoking pot, and by announcing at age 14 that she wasn't a virgin. Her parents reacted by sending both girls away to schools, and by the time Laura was in college, the parents moved to Barcelona where they had always had a home.

"Hey, Laura, I was just about to go home. Nobody interesting to talk to tonight. I never saw you here before; you're a little on the young side for this place."

"I felt in the mood for company, and remembered you had said in group that your favorite bar is a real good place to talk to interesting people. There's no law against me being here, is there ?"

"No, of course not. Listen, I haven't eaten since a late business lunch; let's grab a pizza next door, okay ?"

"What's wrong with this place ? The food sucks, or you're not inclined to be seen eating with me ?"

"The truth ? My wife and I eat here a couple of times a week, so it's not such a good idea. Besides, I actually prefer the pizza joint. The food's better, at a tenth the tariff".

The two went next door, ordered their pizza, and settled in for what proved to be a long chat, feeling like old friends who know a lot about each other, but are curious about what they don't know.

"So Bill, how about we have a nightcap at my place ? It's just a few blocks from here, so we can walk. I moved in only three weeks ago; Mom and Dad finally sprung for it."

"I don't think so…aren't we already on thin ice with the group ? What are we supposed to tell Elaine and Gerald about this little entrenous ?"

"Tell them?—nothing of course. What's their business ? Are they Gestapo ? Didn't you learn from twelve on to keep your mouth shut when you wanted to do something that was nobody's business anyway ?"

"Listen, Laura, I have two girls, and I wouldn't want them to have that attitude. Now they're women, of course, and I'm no angel, but you're over the top. I'll stop by your place, but just for a few minutes.

"Don't do me any favors! Guys usually are pretty happy for an invite, so I'm not exactly desperate." Laura then went into the bathroom to make herself throw up.

On the way to her place, Bill and Laura must have met up with a a dozen dog walkers, with Laura stopping to pat every animal, from the tiniest Maltese twins to an enormous mastiff. Frozen by the time they arrived at the luxurious building on Fifth Avenue and 64th Street, Bill wondered why at his age he would elect to walk so far on a bitterly cold, windy night.

Laura poured them some good merlot, then put on a remarkable CD, Lowell Greer on horn playing Beethoven. Within minutes, Bill found himself very aroused, which he must have telegraphed because Laura reached over, pulling him toward her. Holding his face, looking into his eyes with her subtle smile, ('I have him!'), she kissed him long and deeply.

He gently pushed her away for a second to come up for air, at which time she began stroking him, his face, his neck, then gradually down his torso to below his belt. Undoing his trousers, and pushing him down on the couch, Laura negotiated his pants over his engorged penis, and took it in her mouth. Before he could come, she motioned to him to return the favor. He explored her wetness with his mouth and tongue, till she came.

Bill then mounted her, moving slowly at first to get her going again, sucked her full, young breasts. He then came violently, and afterward masturbated her to a second climax.

"I'm exhausted, babe, but that was pretty terrific." Bill was already up and dressing, apparently anxious for a quick getaway. I've got to go, the wife will have a fit with me coming home at this hour."

"You really care all of a sudden ? Let's have some more wine." But Bill wanted to head home.

The doorman got lucky, so Bill was able to use the cab ride home to consider what he was going to tell Ann about why he was so late. 'Midnight, for Christ's sake!' The whole ride took five minutes, and with no believable excuse for his quite intelligent wife, he decided on a version of the truth. Ann was asleep, probably since ten, so Bill didn't have to deal with her 'til morning, when she was one hell of a furious woman.

"You are getting to be insufferable! Catting around without any respect for me. Don't you dare tell me some bullshit lie. This is your own Waterloo. I'm seeing a divorce attorney this week."

"You can't do that...I love you. Whatever I've done, they've all meant absolutely nothing to me. Think about all we've been to each other, think about our daughters, our grandchildren when we have them. Ann, please, be reasonable!"

"You have a nerve, asking me to think about our family, when you have serviced the tri-state area for years. Don't you think that I've known just who you are, what you're up to ? I've had no self-respect 'til now, but it's been growing. Somehow becoming fifty has actually had a wonderful freeing impact on me. I don't give a damn what you think anymore, you've lost the right to have me care."

Bill headed for the office, skipping breakfast. 'Ann will certainly change her mind, she's just angry, as well she should be. I've screwed around once too often, and with who, a bunch of nobodies I couldn't care less about, who I don't even remember. To throw away my wife...oh, my God, the girls will definitely support their mother! What if they even refuse to see me ?' Going around in circles, telling himself that Ann would definitely change her mind, then shifting to believing that she really means it, Bill did something he never did; he went into a seedy bar on Second Avenue near his office, and downed a double scotch—at 10 am. After chewing a dozen cinnamon mints he dared to go into the office, praying he wouldn't meet anyone. He needed to call his friend Joe, a corporate attorney representing the firm in some merger prospects, to get advice on just how to handle this calamity.

Elaine, a petite, dark-haired dynamo in her early 50's led the group alone on this early December evening. Two members were missing: Laura, who hadn't even called, and Stephanie, out by plan visiting her married sister in Virginia. Peter, normally the last one to speak, surprised everyone by asking for the group's help; he has wanted to change jobs, feeling overworked and underpaid, but his fears kept him stuck. His wife is beyond frustrated, since he has been saying the same thing for two years, and doing nothing about it.

"So, Peter, what can we say to you that's so different that you might be inclined to take a risk ?" When Peter naturally couldn't come up with an answer to her question, Elaine suggested a role play, with of all people, the very successful dentist, Roger, playing Peter, and the most terrifying possible boss, Stacy, being the interviewer. What a remarkable cast! The "audience" to this drama got into the act with their own observations, while Peter, who was asked what he had felt watching, kept quiet.

Carole then turned to Peter: "you're letting all of us run away with things here. Let's shut up and wait for you to talk!" Though Stacy glared at her, Carole stood her ground and was proud of it. The group followed her lead, resulting in a long, uncharacteristic silence.

"Carole, I like you, so I know you're putting me on the spot to help me. I bet you wouldn't have any trouble going for an interview." When Carole didn't respond to Peter's attempt to put the ball in her court, he had little choice. "I felt like running away watching Stacy, and I was disgusted with myself, watching Roger play me as such a weak sister."

Elaine invited Peter to consider whether he had experienced other relationships in his life where he couldn't deal, to which he replied, "You know, with my mother. She screamed from morning 'til night, for no particular reason, and hit my little brother viciously, but we didn't stop her.

Putting his head down and his hands over his eyes to conceal what were obviously tears, Peter eventually went on. "We were afraid to tell our dad when he came home every night, and we just planned to run away. I can remember making all kinds of plans with my brothers on the walks home from school, but we never did anything. Then she died in a car crash." Group members listened and were silent, leaving Peter space to continue, but he couldn't. So Elaine intervened again: "When your mother died, what did you feel?"

"We boys had to go to the funeral and to two wakes. Everyone was crying, saying how sad we must be, how bad it is for such young children to lose their mother. How young she was. It's funny, I never thought of her as young, but she actually was only 32 years old with three sons, 10, 8 and 5." Turning to Carole, Peter said that when she shared a recent recurring dream about her childhood, he had an urge to tell her about his.

"I'd like to hear your dream, Peter, but you didn't answer Elaine's question about how you felt when you heard your mother was killed."

Stacy remarked to Carole that she was pleased that Carole could be tough, like the prosecuting attorney she was...so that Stacy wouldn't be the only "tough broad in this group."

In the midst of all this action, Elaine had noticed that the normally active and jovial Bill was not only silent, but seemed depressed. It was close to the end of the session, so she was very reluctant to let Bill leave without speaking. But Elaine also didn't want to interrupt the rarely voluble Peter. She missed her co-leader just then, to whom she might have turned with the dilemma:

"how can we take care of both Peter, who is doing so well tonight by talking about real stuff, and of Bill, who clearly needs us now ?" Her decision made, Elaine posed that exact question to the group, who until then, hadn't seemed to notice Bill's pain. But she was wrong in that assumption, as all the others, outside of Peter, threw in comments indicating that they had, in fact, taken in Bill's sad demeanor.

Peter turned to Bill: "It's okay with me for you to have the floor. I know after tonight that I can talk to you guys. What's up with you ?"

"My wife's seeing a divorce lawyer. She's hell bent on filing. Not that I don't deserve it. You know I've been unfaithful for years, well, the jig's up. She's had it…Believe me, I don't blame her. If she had pulled what I did, I'd have been out of there twenty years ago. But I never thought she'd leave. And now I'm sick about it."

In response to caring inquiry from several group members, Bill admitted that he had been thinking of suicide. Stacy's response, "No spouse is worth that much" seemed to irritate others, but Roger took a pragmatic view: "she'll take you for plenty. But you know you're an attractive guy, women really go for you, you'll be fine after the first shock wears off."

Elaine was not so sure. She told the group that ideas about suicide need to be taken seriously, and that she insists on seeing Bill alone after group.

Carole was more than shaken up by Bill's acknowledgement that he felt like killing himself, so when Doug told her that Jill's dance recital is set for next Wednesday night at 8, she was relieved to have an excuse to miss group. After all, if the leaders can miss, and other members don't always even call when they can't come, why shouldn't she ?

CHAPTER 8

On 9/11 Dana knew she'd have trouble getting back to Long Island, so instead she drove back up to the Berkshires with her husband and daughter. Naturally, Jenny and Adam had made no plans to leave, having listened nonstop to CNN coverage of the bombings in New York City and the Pentagon. So in fact, Jenny had never had the conversation with Adam about her first husband's death, and the more time elapsed since her talk with Dana, the more uncertain she was of actually telling him.

With Jenny so focused on Amy, probably using her for protection, Dana could hardly address the issue...and seeing Adam 'normal' around Jenny, Dana was convinced that he knew nothing. It wasn't until Amy's bedtime that Dana finally grabbed her mother, taking her into the guest bedroom. "Did you tell Adam anything at all ?" was followed by silence, and then by acknowledgement that Jenny was no longer sure what she wanted to do. "I told Carole and Doug everything! They said it's up to you, so unless Stephen insists on reporting you, I think you should keep quiet about it. Whatever happened was so long ago, and it was an accident, wasn't it ? So let sleeping dogs lie." The two women held on to each other, both tearful, whispering their love for each other, and their need to be together. "Don't leave us, mom. I couldn't handle that, please!"

"Adam, I have to talk to you, though I don't want to." He looked up in surprise and waited for her to continue. "Stephen and Dana discovered the truth about Paul's death, namely that I shot him and got rid of the gun. The police never really suspected me, so nothing in the way of a thorough investigation ever took place, they were so sure that the gangsters did it.

Ask me anything you like. You deserve to know who you're married to."

"You're kidding, aren't you ? This can't be happening! You are either off your rocker now, or the best liar ever, all those stories you told me, to everyone including in the courtroom were lies ? How could you ?

What's gonna happen now ? Why are you telling me this ?"

"I just told you, Stephen has been suspicious for years, not of me, of course, but of just why the police never learned who killed Paul. Once in jail, with all the resources coming out of his own experience, he gradually became convinced that Marco Da Silva didn't kill his father. During the months awaiting trial, he and Dana communicated regularly, and often sent me questions via email after their visits or telephone calls. Dana then remembered finding a gun in my closet three years after her father's death.

When Stephen learned this, he recalled that the friend I was supposedly playing mah jong with had mentioned that I left the game early that night.

So he put two and two together... insisted to Dana that I did it, and that she had to interrogate me because if he did it on my visit to him in jail, he'd carry on and get in trouble. Well, Dana did ask me plenty. That's the real reason the Malones didn't show up for our dinner Monday night. I told you they cancelled out, but that wasn't true. I asked Dana to meet them at a hotel, to tell them everything and get some advice. She did, and from what she tells me, Douglas Malone says it's completely up to me what I do. He won't turn me in... but he thinks I better confer with Stephen, because if my son tells the cops, I have no leverage. So if Stephen insists that I must confess, I will do that on my own."

Adam sat down, listening to the television in the background going over the horrors of this day. Somehow the public disaster paled in significance to what was happening in his own life with Jenny. "What do you want me to do? Or to say? I'd love to pretend I'm dreaming, or that you're making this up, but I know different. You want me to tell you what to do? Well I can't!"

The Levines were trapped in their cabin and in their own private thoughts, even more so because the disaster meant they couldn't get to Manhattan, where they probably could have gone their separate ways.

Forced into each other's company for at least a day or two, Adam read nonstop while Jenny visited neighbors.

In the middle of this dark night, Jenny woke her husband up, demanding that he listen to her story of why she killed Paul. "You never asked me anything after I told you that I killed him. What's wrong with you, don't you even want to know ?" This said to a bleary-eyed Adam, who had been in the midst of dreaming.

"Jenny, maybe you're better off from a legal standpoint not telling me.

Then I can't possibly answer any of their questions, if it comes to that."

"We're married, so they can't make you tell them anything. I know that from the cop shows. I haven't been able to sleep at all. Let's make some cocoa, and talk." Against his will, Adam found himself being propelled downstairs to the tiny kitchen.

Jenny told her husband essentially the same story she had told her daughter, that she had taken a gun on a visit to Paul's store one Wednesday evening because at times the surrounding neighborhood was dangerous. Then she caught Paul in the midst of a drug deal, became enraged once the "customer" left, and took out the loaded gun threatening to kill herself. When Paul failed to get her to hand it over or put it down, he grabbed it, the gun went off and killed him. Naturally she panicked, and ran out of the store, first turning off the lights. She then changed her shirt, and went home to the children. The police were already there, having been notified of the crime by Paul's neighbors who occupied the upstairs apartment over his store. They hadn't seen anyone since the departure of the customer, whom they couldn't identify. Since the cops found a large amount of cash, along with stashes of marijuana and cocaine, they had reason to believe that the killing was drug-related. Jenny didn't disabuse them of this notion. She admitted to Adam that her first husband's death felt almost like freedom, after two years when she was terrified daily of his business acquaintances. Even her serious financial problems and the children's pain over the loss of their father didn't diminish her relief that it was over. "So now, what should I do ? Should I turn myself in, or hope that Stephen will let this go ?"

Adam had never had anything remotely like this to deal with. His kids, a now forty year old daughter and thirty-six year old son, never presented any legal problems. He himself had been totally on the straight and narrow. His parents as well. In fact, Adam never even had a friend in any trouble with the law, as far as he knew. Instead of responding to Jenny's unanswerable question, his thoughts shifted to whether he could tolerate staying with her now.

"Adam, I think you wish you'd never met me, now that you know. If you feel this way in the morning, you're free to go. I'll stay in the apartment in the city, because of my practice, and you can stay up here. We'll split everything down the middle, no hard feelings. I don't want to live with you if you're going to look at me the way you are at this moment."

"Listen, I just heard all this, what do you expect ? Give me time…"

CHAPTER 9

Carole was sitting peacefully alone in Starbuck's, having emerged from the Chambers Street subway station on the way to her office. Quite annoyed at the ringing of her cell phone, she saw immediately that it was from the one person she knew out in Suffolk County, friend Dana, and at such an early hour. The two women hadn't seen each other since 9/11, and Carole couldn't be sure whether that was because they were both working so hard, or if their last painful meeting made each of them seek some temporary distance.

The coffeehouse was crowded with students from Manhattan Community College, casually dressed and laden down with backpacks. 'How much easier life was back then.' Feeling she couldn't possibly speak to Dana here, Carole walked out drinking her black coffee, into the crazy quilt of young students, nannies pushing strollers, and well-dressed lawyer types headed in her direction. Passing City Hall with its dozens of steps clearly not welcoming the handicapped, Carole for the millionth time admired the view toward the Brooklyn Bridge, then walked under the archway and through the pretty park at the end of which was her destination. She had an early appointment with boss/husband Douglas Malone, but learned from his secretary, Barbara, that he'd be delayed. He and their big boss Barry were still meeting with the mayor. Telling Barbara that she is expecting her three new supervisees at 10, Carole picked up mail and messages, and reluctantly dialed Dana's number.

"I appreciate your calling me back, Carole. We probably have been avoiding each other, or at least every time I thought to call you, I forgot!

But I do feel you and Doug deserve to know that my mother has decided to go to the Brooklyn NYPD. She can't live with herself now that we—she explained that before it was out in the open, she actually never thought of the killing as having anything to do with her. She believed her lies, can you imagine ?"

"What I can imagine is what you're going through, Dana. With all the trouble I've had with my mother, if she were to be in that place...wow. I will tell Doug. Frankly, we're swamped here, so I can't have a decent conversation with you from the office, but I will call and hopefully we will get together very soon."

Carole finished the call by telling her friend of her new assignment; she had just agreed to work one extra day, had renegotiated her pay scale so that her babysitter wasn't earning more than she was, and she was taking on three litigators from 'downstairs' and would begin today supervising them on more complex cases. It was striking to Carole that neither young woman made reference to the terrorist attack, or to its impact on their lives. Maybe for Dana it wasn't even on the radar.

Two women and a man came into Carole's office, where she had prepared coffee and folders with information they would need to function in this much higher-powered environment. They spent the next hour together discussing what experience each of them had prior to coming to the US Attorney's office, and something about the cases they carried since their arrival. It was clear to Carole that at least one of them had very strong previous experience, and one was probably going to need more handholding. She would use the individual meetings to discuss the cases subsequently assigned to them, and go over the preliminary complex work required for each case. The three seemed excited at the opportunity to be bounced up in responsibility. One of them was also intimidated, and not only by the complexity of cases; their work would get greater scrutiny.

Carole would take responsibility for protecting them from too much media attention, but some interest was inevitable when a case was high profile.

Following the meetings, Carole joined Doug for a late lunch, and launched into a personal problem: "You know I'm sharing Leona Dell's office, so I naturally need some drawer space, and to leave some of my stuff around. I never knew her very well, but she's certainly my senior and always was cordial. Well, she clearly resents me using her office even when she's not there. My stuff disappears...it's thrown all around, most everywhere; Barbara found it on her desk last week, and this morning it took me forever to unearth my day planner. Any suggestions?"

Doug had already heard from Leona, who was furious that she had to allow anyone to use her office. Even knowing that Carole was Doug's wife didn't stop her from complaining bitterly, and asking him, "can't you find someplace to stash her ?" Since he was responsible for both staff, and certainly didn't want to favor Carole, Doug was in a bind that even with her problem, Carole could appreciate. So after ventilating, she told her relieved husband, "I'll handle it, ignore my bitching".

From there they discussed two of the most serious cases, which Doug insisted Carole supervise very closely. He had no other senior attorney available to tackle them, so her "babies" would have to manage under her guidance. "The first case seems simple on its face; thousands of cases of Russian vodka were smuggled into this country by ship, the manifest listing furniture. The FBI was brought into the mix because the designated recipient of the shipment was a high-up known member of the Russian mob. They allowed the man, known as Leo "Rocky" Asinov to   send his men to pick up the shipment, and then arrested them. The group works out of Brighton Beach, Brooklyn, referred to as "Odessa by the Sea,' because of the thousands of Russian immigrants living there.

The FBI is continuing the investigation, as obviously they wanted to nail Asinov, who had been charged before in other operations, but never convicted in the United States. By now Asinov is a citizen, so he obviously can't be deported, but others working for him have not yet become citizens and are more vulnerable. We'd like to use this to get them to give us something, but we're not particularly optimistic.

"Carole, let two of your kids work on this case together, and keep on top of it. If it goes the way I expect it to, I will prosecute personally, and we'll see, maybe you can sit second chair. It's highly unlikely that one of your people will actively assist me at trial, but we'll see how that plays out."

"They all want that kind of trial experience. I don't see why you wouldn't want to consider that from the outset. Two of these lawyers are very experienced litigators from their years at excellent private firms. The third needs much more help, so I wouldn't give her this case. What else do you have?"

"A case maybe too close for comfort for you, involving drugs and kidnapping. On the surface, we have a white middle class couple from the Soho area kidnapping an infant whose mother left her outside a pizza joint, supposedly for ten minutes. Do you remind Melissa regularly to never, ever, ever leave Danny unsupervised for one second ?" At his wife's grimace, Doug continued. "Naturally, FBI was involved immediately, only to discover that this couple has a record of adopting babies from other countries, like

Columbia and China, bringing them here, and then selling them. They've used several alias...have never been caught up to now, and were only suspected this time because of a tip to the NYPD by a neighbor, whose suspicions had been raised when she saw other babies, supposedly belonging to the couple's friends."

Sometime after 6, Doug left the office to meet friend Max, an FBI agent who headed up the Command Center down at the WTC site where Doug and many other assistant US attorneys had worked periodically even before 9/11; a few of them were almost killed that awful Tuesday.

Doug still feels guilty that he had been away, and safe. He is very aware of being an outsider as these six colleagues, now intimate friends, get together regularly to revisit their memories of that horrific day.

"Max, I've assigned Carole to work with you, along with two of our less experienced attorneys, on the Asinov case. Part of their learning will undoubtedly come from you, I picked your case with that in mind."

"Oh, great, so now I'm a babysitter! Just kidding, you know I love to work with Carole, and I'm sure with all you have on your plate, you have pull in the troops. Let's look at what you have for me."

The two friends then shifted focus on what had come to light about the nineteen terrorists who had flown the hijacked planes on that horrible day. Doug remarked on his needing to find a way of clearing his calendar to concentrate on this case, very like what happened in '93. "But I'd like to get your take on what would appear to be a garden variety criminal who NYPD picked up last month on a drug sting."

"Jerome Miller, a 49 year old ex-con originally from New Mexico, was caught by customs ten years ago with a shit load of weapons, along with explosives, and detonators. Alcohol & Firearms identified the material in their lab as likely coming from the former Soviet Union, but further investigation didn't get much more out of Miller. He served his sentence, and on discharge disappeared from our radar. Then, on August 5th this year he was arrested by NYPD when he inadvertently was caught in their surveillance of a local Hispanic gang. They speculated that he was their drug supplier, found not only with a quarter of a million bucks worth of pills and thousands of dollars, but also with a gun on him, which was later identified as having been used in a local homicide. The Bronx DA was not at all inclined to let us in, believe me, but FBI fought the good fight, and insisted that Miller be charged by us. The case was presented to the Grand Jury, and an indictment handed down; Miller is now awaiting a trial date. But, after 9/11 and our reevaluating what we hand on hand, in my looking over this case, something stunk! Would you agree to use some man hours to follow up ? Believe me, this guy is no ordinary drug supplier; his earlier involvement with a huge weapons cache makes him different. As does the no work and tons of money, even given his involvement with drugs. Did I tell you his bank accounts, some here, others offshore, have hundreds of thousands of dollars?"

Max agreed to handle this case for further investigation, and took on the second one involving a recent immigrant from Bosnia. By the time the men were finished, it was after 9, and they hadn't eaten. They went their separate ways, home to wives who knew better than to wait dinner.

CHAPTER 10

Jenny Levine walked into Brooklyn's Sheepshead Bay NYPD, asked to speak to a lieutenant, and with her lawyer present, told her long secret story about husband Paul's death in 1980. The officer was astounded, and found himself wondering if she was imagining her guilt or what else was propelling her at this time. But after two hours, he took her signed statement and called Brooklyn's District Attorney's office. It turned out to be an all day process, interrupted many times by outside influences, lunchtime, her attorney's calls to his office, and Jenny's own emotionality.

She was finally advised that the NYPD would have to reopen the case with a new investigation of the facts before any plea bargain could be offered. Though her attorney had tried to prepare her for this eventuality, Jenny was nevertheless shaken by the result.

Returning home, Jenny opened a mailing from Medicare; she had requested the form which, when submitted, would allow her to see patients in another jurisdiction. When she saw questions about legal judgments, Jenny lost it. It hit her that she could lose everything, her marriage, her profession, her freedom...worst of all, her son, whose rage at her might be understandable, but left her bleeding. Putting the application aside, Jenny picked up stationery to write to Stephen, but not a word came to her.

Douglas was at home on Sunday watching Danny while Carole ran errands and met a friend for lunch. Their little boy seemed remarkably athletic, as he scooted across the living room on his knees, propelling himself swiftly, then pulling himself up, and managing to walk holding onto furniture. His dad was impressed, also alert to possible dangers, but the whole place had been childproofed. Doug was considering diapering his smelly little toddler when the doorman rang through to let him know that Mel, of all people, was downstairs.

During their other visits together this handsome, well-built young man was warmly friendly, lively, and pleasantly talkative. Today Mel was unshaven, his clothing wrinkled and slightly stained, and he seemed to be having trouble making eye contact. Though he noticed Danny, who was now in his highchair eating pretzels, Mel was preoccupied. He did accept a Beck's, and at Doug's suggestion, detailed what brought him.

"I've been in Manhattan since 11 o'clock last night. With no sleep to speak of, unless you count the couple of hours I slept in my car. Even to me I don't sound coherent. Dana went to see her brother upstate early yesterday, as she does every month, only this time she didn't come home.

Normally she takes the bus from Port Authority, about a 3 1/2 hour ride and then takes the LIRR to Ronkonkoma where I pick her up around 5pm.

When I didn't hear from her, I just met that train, but she wasn't on it.

So I went home, thinking she may have missed it. But why wouldn't she have called, and why didn't she answer her cell phone ? So I was pretty irritated when she finally called around 7 o'clock, saying she was in NYC and was buying concert tickets at Madison Square Garden! She sounded funny— I couldn't put my finger on it—but she did say she'd make the 7:40 train and I agreed to pick her up. Well, I got my mom to watch Amy, and did another pointless run to the train."

Doug, listening intently, began to feel impatient, as was his style, but held back, aware that Mel had to do it his way.

"Two hours later I got a call from Bellevue Hospital. Dana had walked in front of a bus. The spokesperson wouldn't say anything else, except that I was being asked to meet with the psychiatrist on her case.

I thought Dana could come home, but the resident said he considered her to be suicidal! She begged me to take her home. She's always telling me that I'm too much of a pushover for everyone, including her. Well, that was in my mind listening to her begging me. So I told her absolutely not., but I would take her to another hospital, Mt. Sinai, straight from here if she agreed to sign herself in. Because the psychiatrist told me privately that he couldn't actually keep her against her will; she wasn't psychotic, and was denying that she would hurt herself, or even that she had tried to...

She had been drinking heavily before the incident. And Dana barely ever drinks at all, so I knew something was very wrong. She had 4-5 drinks at a crummy bar opposite Penn Station."

Mel went to the bathroom, and on his return seemed somewhat more composed. Accepting a refill, he resumed more fluently.

"Anyway, I'm a lousy story-teller, so cut to the chase, Dana was admitted to the psych unit at Sinai, and she's still there. She's crying a lot, her doctor says she's very depressed, big surprise, and is strongly recommending that Dana stay for a while for evaluation, and maybe medication.

Dana can't handle what's going on with her mother. She's very upset with Stephen, but she's more guilty about her own part in this. Believe me, I knew this would happen, and I begged her to stay out of it, not to push her mother to answer questions about her father's death. But it seems that Stephen was brainwashing her. Now it's a disaster, a runaway train that nobody can stop."

"So I take it Jenny did go to the police ?"

"Yeah, the day before yesterday, Friday, and it's opening up an investigation just as you said it would. Dana said that you hinted that her mom wouldn't have to do anything even after she confessed to Dana; she knew why you couldn't actually say it straight out."

"So how can I help now? Or were you hoping to find Carole at home?"

"Actually, Dana asked me to speak to Carole. She doesn't want anyone else to know she's here, none of her friends, not anyone at work, not even her mother. She trusts Carole, and we both trust you."

* * *

Built in the early 60's, Mt. Sinai Hospital's Klingenstein Clinical Center houses the in-patient psychiatric services and the psychiatric day centers. Dana's admission followed a fairly typical route, through emergency where she was evaluated by a resident psychiatrist, who felt her to be too depressed to be treated as an outpatient.

Carole took a cab across the park and uptown on a bitterly cold December evening, feeling anxious about her friend and what she might expect of her. This was not her first visit to a psychiatric unit; when she was a Stanford freshman one of the girls on her floor made a serious suicide attempt, taking loads of pills. Carole and her roommate had visited her twice before she was transferred to a facility near her Chicago home.

"Dana, how are you?," hugging her. "I never would have predicted that our next meeting would be here, my friend," Carole joked.

"Your levity is lost on me, Carole. I feel like shit, worse. But don't worry, I'm not going to kill myself. I'd never do that to Amy. Come in the lounge; I want to speak to you privately without the nosy staff overhearing us." The two women walked past the nurses' station where a couple of residents were writing chart notes, and entered a rather attractive room done up in cheerful primary colors. Motioning to Carole to be seated, Dana began speaking in a voice barely above a whisper. "I have to stay here for a few days so they discharge me rather than say I left against medical advice. When I do go, I'm getting Amy and leaving New York.

I have some money saved up, a few thousand dollars that I was planning to use for Amy's day camp. Well, I'm taking her where no one will ever find us, we'll change our names, and get new social security numbers.

I know I can manage. But I need your help."

"Dana, what about Mel? He's Amy's father, and he adores her. She loves him. He'll definitely go to the police, he'll never just give up his child.

Why are you thinking of this? I thought things were going well with you and Mel."

"It's not about Mel. I can't live with the reality that my brother and my mother are felons! And I won't tolerate this for my daughter! You can be smug, with two doctors for parents, a surgeon brother, and a husband on the right side of the law. No matter how much you dislike your mother, at least she hasn't committed a crime. Maybe you just can't understand. Why did I ever think you'd help me?"

"What do you have in mind?"

"You know a lot of shady characters from your work. I need documents with a new name, you know, a driver's license, passports for Amy and me, and probably a copy of my college degree in my new name. Can you find somebody to help me?"

"You can't be serious! First of all, I don't know any such person, but if I did, do you think I'd risk everything, my family, my profession, to help you with this crazy scheme? Dana, I love you as a friend, but…"

Dana interrupted Carole, in a rage: "Go…get out of here. I do not need fair weather friends, goody-goodies who can't think out of the box. Go home to your perfect life. Get out!"

While Carole tried to argue Dana out of this insane idea, it quickly became clear that the latter was getting more agitated, more enraged, so Carole left, devastated. Once out of the building, Carole began to call her husband but thought better of it, so instead just took a cab home. She found Doug stretched out on the sofa in front of '60 Minutes'.

"Doug, I want you to promise me that you won't tell anyone what I'm about to tell you in confidence."

"You have my attention…you're not about to confess to a murder, are you?"

"Please be serious! I'm no shrink, but I really think that Dana is in the throes of a nervous breakdown. She's completely irrational, even paranoid, and has come up with a very dangerous plan. How can I be her friend, and yet stop her from doing this crazy thing.?" Getting a troubling response from her husband, Carole rejected it: "I totally disagree with you that we should tell Mel. How can I violate Dana's trust? Did he seem to suspect anything when he talked to you?" Then, Carole thought of a somewhat farfetched plan, which might just work. Before the night was over, she made two important calls to set this plan in motion, but never said a word to Doug about it.

CHAPTER 11

Jenny entered the dimly lit, worn lobby of her small Manhattan building. The block itself was pretty, with well-kept brownstones now decorated for Christmas, and its location near the park was normally a source of joy, for Jenny loves to walk. But today, she is distracted, still able to notice that her own apartment is without charm, and has not gotten the attention that might have transformed it into a home.

Adam is not here. Though this would not normally be a time he would have elected to stay in the Berkshires alone, he is in fact there, and much to his surprise, his children have been attentive. He had broken down and told his daughter, unable to maintain silence in the face of what was to come.

Jenny did not miss Adam. It seemed just now that having to pay attention to a husband, to a marriage, was impossible. Her energies needed to focus on her legal vulnerability, and on addressing this catastrophe with her patients. Today she had several client appointments, beginning with Larry.

"Larry, our meeting today is going to be very different from any we've had, and I won't be charging for it." The 46 year old slightly overweight man expressed surprise, but unlike his past self, waited patiently for Jenny to continue. "You will this very day be reading in the local papers about a terrible tragedy in my life that happened 21 years ago. My then husband had been for some time, mostly unbeknownst to me, involved with the mob around drugs. I will not go into detail or answer any questions about the event, as there are legal implications here. But I will say that there was an accident with a gun while I was holding it, and my husband was killed. I only just went to the police, and they are in the process of opening an investigation. Clearly, this affects our work. It means that I may well be distracted, or actually called away. It certainly means some notoriety; all of these issues cloud our relationship. So, I'd like to hear from you about your ideas as to next steps."

Putting both hands over his mouth momentarily, and giving himself a good half minute to digest what he had heard, Larry spoke softly: "I'm so sorry for your trouble. I won't ask you why you've opened this all up after so many years, naturally I'm curious. But if you're going to be at all available, and are willing for us to continue, I'd like to keep going. The prospect of breaking up this good team is unsettling. Can we keep our meetings? I promise to be flexible!"

To her surprise, several of her clients had very similar responses.

Her last appointment would be an exception. Joy Robbins, 63, blond, tiny, stunning and struggling to overcome destructive over-spending and promiscuity, was immediately irritated at Jenny's taking charge of the session. After her inquiry, "can't this wait?," and Jenny's explanation of just why it couldn't, Joy smirked: "So I'm not the only one who does self-destructive things. Why in hell would you confess after getting away with murder twenty-odd years ago?"

"Joy, nobody's talking about murder, but of course you have every right to your own questions and conclusions. I cannot discuss the case, obviously. But I do want you to direct your attention to your needs now, and for us to set a plan in motion."

"Frankly, Jenny, you're worthless to me as a therapist now. You'll be totally preoccupied with trials and may go to jail. So I have to start with someone else. I think under the circumstances you should reimburse me for therapy appointments for 2001."

"You'd like to have me pay you back for a year's therapy, that's approximately 45 sessions, because this just came up? You're saying that all our work together, and you have made solid progress this year, is for naught because of this trouble?"

"I have to start with someone new. I may regress because of your abandonment. So, yes, I think that's entirely possible."

Though Jenny had not expected the caring sympathy other clients conveyed, Joy's nearly vicious position shocked her. She made it very clear that moneys would not be returned, and that she was very willing to help Joy find a good therapist with whom she could process this change.

Jenny would assume financial responsibility for four transition sessions. But Joy walked out in twenty minutes. "You'll hear from my lawyer."

The phone had been ringing all day while Jenny was seeing clients, and now messages had to be addressed. The most important one was from Mel: "Mom, it's urgent that you call me as soon as you get this. Oh, it's not about

Amy, so don't worry." He was always thoughtful. Returning Mel's call, Jenny was relieved to have him answer on the first ring. "Mom, thank God you called. I'm frantic with worry. I'm right across the park, so I'll come over if it's okay…"

Jenny and Mel had had a warm relationship from the first, with each responding to the genuineness and similar self-deprecating humor. Both in fact drew people to them, in contrast to Dana, who was smarter and more aggressive, so put some people off. Today's conversation was all about Dana.

"Mom, Dana's on the psych unit at Mt. Sinai. I brought her there after she got drunk and stepped in front of a bus. She's not hurt. But she's very depressed, and frankly, sounds weird. I just came from a meeting with her doctor and the social worker, with Dana there, of course. They want her to stay, but they can't force her because it seems she's not really suicidal, thank God. But she's not with it…you know, thinking clearly. I'm afraid to take her home. She wants to go home and says she'll see Dr. Marcus for meds. What do you think?"

"I'll go talk to her. Without seeing her, I have no way of guessing what would be best. Another something I have to be guilty about."

Mel had gone to Jenny even though his wife had strictly forbidden him from telling her; he was too frightened to handle it alone. He had also called Carole again, heard her plan, and shared it with Jenny, whose reaction was non-committal. But Jenny did say she would absolutely go to visit her daughter, and if Dana refused to see her, so be it.

The other calls included another therapist making a referral, which Jenny could not accept under the circumstances, and the district attorney's office, asking her to call for an appointment this week. Others, from friends, would wait. 'How can I possibly go over all this with everyone I know?'

Afterward, Jenny walked eastbound across the park and uptown covering the four blocks to the hospital. Taking the elevator to 7South, she found herself confronted immediately by Dana, who blew up at her, then burst into tears. A young plump staff nurse dressed in street clothes but with an identifying tag came over to help, and the three women went into a small private office on the unit. Once it was clear to the nurse that mother and daughter would be all right, she left them alone.

"Mom, I love you," tearful, rubbing her eyes, fingering her ponytail very like her as a child. "I can't take what we did to you! I feel so guilty for my part in it. And now you'll go to jail."

"Dana, I forgive you and Stephen. Something like this can't stay a secret forever. And I think that as much as I pushed it deep down, it must have done its damage to me as well. So this could actually be freeing."

Rapidly shifting from her loving and low-key state, Dana turned on Jenny with fury: "I despise when you're a Pollyanna! This whole thing is a disaster, and you'll acting like it's for the best. What's wrong with you that you turn things around? You did this when we were both kids, and that's how come you never faced what each of us kids was up to."

Dana walked out onto the unit, leaving Jenny stunned. Gone was the reassuring mother, and in her place, Jenny found herself terrified.

'I feel what Dana must be feeling...' She sat there for a long time, until a resident needed to use the office and seemed surprised to see her there.

On exiting the hospital, Jenny called Marianne, and asked for her help. "I'm in terrible trouble, and I trust you more than anyone." Hearing the desperation in her friend's voice, knowing how hard it is for Jenny to reach out for herself, Marianne told her to come over. Appointments would have to be cancelled, so be it.

Jenny and Marianne spent hours together talking, laughing and crying, retelling their shared histories, and going back into their younger more private selves. The constraints each had felt even in this strong and wonderful friendship were thrown overboard. At the end, nothing was so called "solved," but both felt richer, more peaceful, even safer in her very complex life. From Marianne, "I'm so grateful to have you in my life," to Jenny's, "Your being there for me is the most precious gift.".

CHAPTER 12

Carole entered her group tonight, the last before the Christmas holidays, and immediately sought Bill out. He was sitting there in his usual chair, surprisingly gregarious, with no sign of the depression which had characterized his demeanor two weeks before.

Members engaged in superficial chatting until the leaders entered, at which point all was silent. The leaders almost never broke the silence. At this stage in the experienced group it was rare for a member to use a joke to end it, so the wait continued. But Stephanie, there for two years, continued to be superficial: "I guess I'll tell you about my trip south. My sister has a business in Virginia Beach, and a room for me in her house if I want it. When I was with her, I thought it was a good idea, but since being back, I'm not so sure."

The group and its leaders had heard this, or a version of it, many, many times. No one said a word until Roger cracked: "why not spend half a year there, and half here—that should take care of your chronic ambivalence!" Peter and Carole ventured comments to Roger on his own chronic behavior, in his case sarcasm. Just then Stacy came into group late. Normally group members are aggravated by her periodic lateness, but tonight they acted relieved. She interrupted the dead, boring quality of tonight's meeting by her comment: "It looks like I haven't missed much tonight, huh?"

Carole addressed Stacy: "Stephanie is continuing to struggle with her conflict about making a decision. I know how that feels. When I'm at work and loving it, completely captivated by the excitement even when it's draining, I don't want to be anywhere else. Then when I'm home with Danny and he tries something new, this week he's experimenting with letting go, I think of leaving him and am devastated. Doug is bored stiff hearing me complain, but last night he said something helpful: 'Lucky you, you love everything you do!' "He's so right...I am fortunate, while he's buried in work and says he misses us terribly."

Stephanie seemed to wake up when Carole spoke, nodding at Doug's helpful comment. "My sister says the same thing to me sometimes, maybe a little differently. She told me that options are terrific and I have them, including people who love me in both places. So maybe Roger is right, even if he was a little hostile."

The leaders took turns in helping Stephanie, Carole, then Peter explore the feelings underlying difficult decision-making. Then Bill came into the mix: "Just a couple of weeks ago I was ready to blow my brains out thinking of Ann leaving me. Well, I decided that I'd be fine. I'd keep the apartment since it is my inheritance, and I know how to meet people. Maybe all my womanizing as Elaine calls it really means my marriage hasn't been good for years. So I'm looking at this as a chance to try it alone, to see how I can manage. I even went on a diet and lost twelve pounds."

Carole couldn't get over the rapid mood shifts evidenced by Bill, and on the way home began to think of her own old tendency to be enthusiastic, then bored with possessions and with people. 'With Bill it seems characterological and chemically-induced, but with me, it used to be my running from anxiety. I just realized that it hasn't happened in ages.' Stacy had not told the group much about her own serious and very recent troubles. Her daughter, now eleven, had been found drinking at a boy's house, and performed fellatio on him, caught by the housekeeper.

She didn't want to discuss this in group, but felt the need for help, so set a private time to meet with Elaine to address it.

Part of the group's deadness had to do with secrets. For some reason, not yet unearthed, the atmosphere had turned unsafe for most.

It wasn't until after the holidays that Gerald put his finger on it: several of them, including the leaders, were terrified that some attack would occur around Christmas. They had feared the World Series at the Stadium, then the tickertape parade given for the World Champion New York Yankees, and then the Macy's Thanksgiving Day Parade. When nothing happened, instead of relief there was widespread but largely unspoken anxiety, when will it occur? Gerald, this time not "analytic," stated that he had been experiencing stress since 9/11 associated with fearing another attack. Elaine was pleasantly surprised at her co-leader's realness tonight.

Laura was lost to the group, and had not returned calls from either of the group's leaders. And Bill had not opened up about his secret; at the time, he was too preoccupied with his marital situation, and afterward he almost forgot about the woman and the event. Because both group leaders had been so concerned about Bill, they had not seriously pursued the question of his special relationship with Laura, and his feelings about her absence. Others had spoken about it, some sad, some mad, but Bill was then immersed in his own pain.

Elaine pursued the question once the group got back on track: "what are your fantasies about Laura and her disappearance?" Peter, Carole, Stephanie, then Stacy all shared their thoughts, but Bill was too silent. Gerald turned to him: "You have a secret from us that's getting in your way." When Bill continued silence, shrugging, Gerald continued: "You are used to keeping secrets and feeling ashamed. Can you possibly do something different with us here?"

Looking only at Gerald, Bill replied, "Laura followed me into my favorite bar, and enticed me to go home with her. We had sex, then I literally raced home. She was very upset when I left, and you know how my wife felt the next day. So I trashed two women in one evening. What else can I feel but shame about myself? Maybe I should leave the group too. You probably are repelled by me."

Group members assured Bill that he belonged here, but must deal with these issues. From Carole: "I tried sex for years to cope with my insecurities, and almost destroyed my relationship with Doug before we were married. I slept with an old boyfriend after Doug and I had a fight…just thinking of how I handled myself, and how stressed I was later waiting for him to find out, then how devastated I was when he did…Believe me, giving up that behavior was a huge relief."

"Carole, I'm not sure that I'm up to that. For one thing, I can't stay alone for more than a few hours at a time. I love superficial relationships, you know, meet someone attractive at a bar, talk intimately for hours, then get laid and never see them again. Normally I don't feel guilty. They're no kids either and get something out of it for themselves. But I knew Laura was a depressed kid and I screwed the group, so I feel terrible this time."

Elaine asked the group what they expected the leaders to do or say when a member clearly violated a basic group code of ethics. Roger got angry with her: "You're acting like you want our okay on throwing him out, well you're not getting it from me!" Peter surprised Elaine the most when he spoke to Bill: "It's actually good that you screwed us the way you screw everyone on the outside because now we can work with you on it, instead of listening to your fascinating stories and just giving you another rapt audience for your adventures."

There was widespread agreement that Bill's 'penance' was complete honesty with the group. "I'll try my best."

CHAPTER 13

Midway into her meeting with Sam and Robin on the Asinov case, Carole took an emergency phone call from Mel. Dana had left the hospital shortly after her mother's visit, had gone to Amy's nursery school, picked the child up without incident, and left the area. No one seems to know where she is, including Stephen and Jenny, whom Mel had contacted.

Concentrating on helping her supervisees explicate next steps in the case was difficult what with the devastating news about Dana, but Carole had no choice, and unfortunately, had nothing to offer her friend at this juncture. FBI agent Max Brand arrived to join their small group, to bring them up to date on the investigation's progress following Asinov's indictment for racketeering, smuggling and tax evasion. Max was delighted that for once Asinov could be tied directly to the crimes, making for a solid case when it would ultimately come to trial.

The second case was far more troubling. Evidence was emerging that the Evans' had established a far flung network involving the buying of central American and Asian infants which they then sold on the black market all over this country. Nancy and Ralph Evans, 43 and 49 years old respectively, were both college graduates, born in New York City, married for fourteen years, both teachers in the same private high school. They had no record, but probably have been involved in criminal activity before, and in this particular activity at least since 1998. That means dozens of infants had been placed for adoption. Carole was not alone in being horrified at the disruption in the lives of innocent people which would inevitably follow the fuller FBI investigation. Max was anxious that Carole and her team begin to interview the Evans', who of course were already represented by counsel, and being held without bail because of their potential to leave the country, given their many international contacts.

At midday Carole sought Doug out to bring him on board with the information on both cases, and to share the troubling news about Dana.

She was invited to join Barry and Doug who had been meeting for hours.

"Sit down, Carole. We won't be discussing cases here today, something much more urgent has come up involving us all." Barry, normally quite composed, continued standing behind his desk as Carole took the offered chair. Doug hadn't said a word. His demeanor was so disturbing that Carole seemed to absorb his anxiety.

"We've been alerted by Justice that a special training is being set up for Doug and two other assistant U.S. Attorneys from the Southern District.

They're will be heading up our prosecution team on the terrorism case. I don't know much more than this right now."

"I'm stunned! Does this mean that we'll all have to leave New York, and spend a lot of time in Washington? For how long?"

Doug answered her: "Families are not included in the 'invitation,' and there was no time frame specified. I can, of course, decline, but Barry here pointed out that we are federal employees, and can be tapped for such work, especially during wartime. There's a lot of speculation that this effort reflects the widespread acknowledgement that poor communication between FBI, CIA, border patrols, and the FAA lead to this debacle."

"I don't know what to say. Let me go finish up for today." Carole started to walk out of her boss' office when Barry stopped her.

"Look, Carole, Doug and the others will go and do us proud. Of course you and he can fly back and forth on weekends, and we certainly hope that your family won't be disrupted for too long by this crisis. Let's face it, in wartime women were always left to manage the home front."

"Please don't think I don't understand that. And I know Doug will go, and that we'll survive this. It's just that…it's all so shocking." With that, Carole began to leave, but Doug stopped her; they'd go home together.

The Malones needed a peaceful dinner hour, but Danny was very fussy tonight, so they did little talking until he was in bed for the night.

"Carole, we're in for a lot of stress, long hours, not a lot of family time. When we went through this before, we worked 18 hour days, seven days a week, to put the case together. We'll have to manage."

"Will you be allowed to tell me about what you're doing if I don't work on the cases? We've always loved sharing our work."

"Justice will be in charge of our training, with FBI/CIA doing the actual training. They're planning to bring together vetted federal employees from law and law enforcement, whose specialties have been in identifying potential terrorist plots and prosecuting participants. In our unit, the three of us have worked domestic terrorism cases for many years.

You know that our office handled the first WTC prosecution, and that we along with the New York FBI field office get any cases associated with Usama Bin Laden. Barry has asked me to head up our little group, and to be responsible for devising a mini-training for the balance of our staff once we're back here."

The telephone rang and neither Carole nor Doug jumped to answer it, until listening to the caller. Of all people, it was Wendy, Jill's mom, who had to talk urgently to Doug: "I've just be given a fabulous opportunity by my firm. They want us to open an office in Prague, and expect us to exit New York by the end of next month. Richard is heading up the project, as senior partner he's critical to its success. So, you finally get your wish; Jill can stay with you beginning just before we leave. Do you have any problem with that ? She'll come over to stay with us for part of the summer, and go to camp as a C.I.T. for the other half."

"Of course Jill can stay here. I am delighted, thrilled, and Carole will be too. How did Jill take the news?"

"She's excited for us...and I must admit, looking forward to spending more time with you and the baby. I hear he's adorable."

"He is, though not particularly tonight! Anyway, keep us posted if there's any change in your timetable. Good night."

Carole had overheard Doug's part of the conversation, and was anxious for him to get off the phone. "You didn't tell her that Jill would be under my care, that you'd be in Washington!"

"It's not necessary. I don't want anything to spoil this. I've always wanted Jill to live with me, and now Wendy has a reason why it's good for her. You'll be here, Jill loves you, her school won't be disrupted, and I'll be home weekends."

"You can't be sure of that and you know it. What if one of the big shots calls a weekend meeting, what if you're invited to Camp David by the President, you're going to turn him down?"

"I'm going to make it my business to be here or in Washington with my family. You don't seem to believe me."

"It's not that I don't believe you. You don't have a clue as to what's in store for you, so you shouldn't really commit to anything. Once you know, that's different. Meanwhile, Doug, we certainly shouldn't consider another baby now, don't you agree?"

"No, I don't agree. We just decided to go ahead with this, it's still what we want, and I'm not getting any younger. Let's go for it...we might as well try while we're still together fulltime. How about tonight?!"

CHAPTER 14

With Christmas two days away, Jenny had no choice but to honor her commitment to lead several FDNY family groups. These groups meet in schools and community centers in the various Long Island communities, or in local fire houses.

Dana's and Amy's disappearance had left Jenny frantic and made her own problems seem minor. Since working always helped Jenny to feel useful and capable, especially when she's at her most impotent, she was grateful to have this truly gratifying work.

Adam had been in regular touch with Jenny, and they had seen each other several times during December, including at the Chanukah party hosted by his daughter. But they had not slept under the same roof once this whole month, though neither had stated that this was their plan.

Tonight's meeting is in the Freeport Firehouse just off Sunrise Highway. The community, heavily minority, increasingly has seen white families move into the southern end near the waterfront. Businesses are thriving, restaurants opening, homes being refurbished. Jenny knows every nook and cranny of this south shore village, and feels a special camaraderie with the mostly male volunteer fire department. The work she is doing is under the auspices of the American Group Psychotherapy Association and the Counseling Department of the FDNY. There have been groups set up all over New York City and its suburbs, but many of them have been under-attended, especially by the firemen themselves.

The Chief greeted Jenny: "I hope you're not getting discouraged.

The guys hide from you therapists, but you're doing great things with the families. I think two of the men are actually trying to show up tonight!"

"I'm okay with whoever comes, Jeff. This isn't for me, you know.

When they can, they will. But you were going to check to see if any of the men were having trouble with alcohol, or obvious depression."

"Yeah, but the problem is I think most all of them are drinking more than they should, not on the job, of course, but they go out together. And they seem to be taking on the families of the lost firefighters, maybe even neglecting their own."

Jenny sat down alone in the too large area. Nothing cozy or offering privacy here. Such a departure from how she traditionally works, but it would have to do. Slowly five women in their 30's and 40's came into the room, and two greeted Jenny, having been in this group before. They brought their friends, which was just as she had suggested. Here again, nothing like therapy groups, where privacy rules. This group also never seemed to start on time, and typically began with a social period, where the ladies would ask about the children's soccer matches, or remind each other of upcoming church functions. Tonight for the very first time two men sheepishly came in and sat down. From Jenny's, "we're delighted to have you join us," to each young man's, "hi, I'm Mike," or "I'm Jimmy," the group took hold.

"I sense how hard it's been for you men to join these groups, and I so respect you for taking the leap. And I'm delighted to see new faces among the women as well. Let's have a go-around with names, and then we can talk about what this group is for."

After introductions, Jenny told the seven adults present that "the purpose of the group is to prevent the escalation of unhealthy responses to the trauma of the WTC disaster. Everyone present is in fact traumatized, which means that both the mind and the body hold onto memory of the horror, and can replay it in dream or awake states. That's normal. What we want to do is discuss how everyone is managing, how you are dealing with yourselves and your children."

The "old" members broke the ice, describing how their husbands were at the scene and survived, but feel guilty about those who died. In one case, Angie described her husband spending all his free time either at the firehouse or with his dead buddy's family, going to those children's games, and neglecting their two sons. Another speaker lost her husband; she is alone with four young children, two pre-schoolers, but has great help from an impressive extended family. However, one of the children, a boy 8, is very depressed and has begun to avoid school. Jenny offers to see this woman, Julie, alone after the group, and will follow up with a referral for evaluation of the child.

Jimmy spoke about the morning of 9/11. "I actually am a city fireman, but I do volunteer work here 'cause I live in the community.

That morning, working out of my Brooklyn house, we were at the scene very early, within minutes. There was chaos, everyone trying to help, very little effective communication even amongst the firemen. People were rushing down the stairs which were filling up with smoke, while we were headed up to help, if we could. Of course the cops and paramedics were also there. All of us operating independently. Then we saw people jumping out of the buildings above where the planes hit. This was when we would come out briefly with a civilian, only to reenter the building. It had a surreal feeling. Afterward I realized that seven of our guys were not back. They died that day, one of them a new kid, around 23. He had just become a father."

Mike stayed out of the conversation until one of the women who knew him actively tried to engage him. "I'm not much for talking, especially in a group. Except maybe in a bar. My wife and kids and I were upstate on a camping vacation, we left on Saturday for our first vacation in years.

We were fishing when someone near us who had a portable radio told us what happened. I felt like sh…horrible about not being there to help.

Even my 12 year old son said, 'dad, let's go back, we need to help' and we did. But by the time we got to the city, it was all over, except of course for the weeks of digging. We really thought we'd find people alive. In fact, when our captain told us that was unlikely, we were pissed."

After an hour in which each person was encouraged to share their stories, Jenny actively asked how each was handling their grief. Not at all surprising to her was that the women acknowledged sadness and fear, while the men spoke of anger, of wishes to hurt back. Jimmy, in particular, would have liked to rejoin his Marine unit to "kill those fucking bastards."

The groups were gratifying but emotionally exhausting for Jenny.

Normally she hung around the firehouse, making herself available for anyone who wanted private time. Tonight she saw Julie for fifteen minutes, and then was preparing to leave when Mike approached her. He didn't want to sit down to talk, but instead asked if they could go outside so he'd be able to smoke. "The Chief said you asked him if anyone was drinking a lot, or depressed. Well, I'm a classic case. Not so depressed, but let me tell you, the wife and I are really at one another. I can't stay home for an hour at a time. I can't go to the movies, or sit and read like I used to. Even going to a ballgame is tough…and I have been drinking every night. Just a few beers, well maybe a six pack. But my Dad and my uncle are both alcoholics, so I guess that's not so good."

"Mike, it's important that you're asking yourself some key questions.

They are, 'am I in trouble with alcohol, and why can't I resume my normal life?' Let's talk about that second question; we already know the answer to the first one." Therapist and fireman spoke for an hour, and made plans to meet again. Before he left, Mike told Jenny that he wouldn't drink this coming week, "to see if I can stop," and that he'd try to do the deep breathing exercise she showed him to see if he could stay home more.

On her return home, Jenny made some notes for herself on tonight's group, prepared herself a fast snack, and settled down to watch 'Law and Order.' Around eleven o'clock, Mel called. He had heard from Dana, thank God, and was allowed to speak to his little girl. Dana had told her daughter that they were on a long vacation, but told Mel that she had no intention of returning, perhaps forever. "Don't try to find me…I'll let you know from time to time how we are, and I'll let Amy send you cards, so you'll know she's fine. I need to wait to see how mom's case comes out.

Maybe if she's not prosecuted, I can come home. But I'm not sure." Dana hung up before Mel could say much of anything.

Jenny couldn't stay asleep, though exhausted. She'd catnap, then wake up in a panic. Her dreams or fragments of dreams involved awful scenes of running from unknown terrors, or falling off cliffs. Around 5am she gave up, made coffee, and started to consider just where Dana might go, given the young woman's background and interests. She had gone to school at the University of Colorado, at Boulder, but this was many years ago; she had traveled through Arizona and New Mexico, loving the landscape and climate, and the terrific New Mexico skiing. And, she had several friends in California, from her days of tennis competition.

Up until now, Jenny had begged Mel not to contact the police to report Dana as having kidnapped their daughter. The family had enough trouble with Stephen and Jenny both involved with the criminal justice system. But now, Jenny wasn't so sure.

"Carole, it's Jenny Levine. Mel told he that he alerted you and your husband about Dana's disappearance. I need advice about whether to bring in the police at this point. We did hear from Dana, so we know she and Amy are fine, but she has no intention of returning home."

"I'm certain that Dana would never do anything to harm Amy or her self. She seemed more angry than depressed, frankly, though I'm far from an expert in that area. Jenny, right now I can't involve Doug in this, so you'll have to settle for my best advice. She's only gone a few days, she's already called and may well contact Mel or you again shortly. I'd give it a little more time before pulling in the police. After all, in a 'kidnapping' the FBI has to get involved, she's clearly crossed state borders, so we're talking federal involvement all the way. Let it for now be seen as a loving mother taking her child on a trip just to temporarily escape from the terrible stresses of the past year. What do you think ? And would Mel go along with this for now?"

"I will try to persuade him. He was frantic before she called, but now might be more amenable to a waiting period if it's not too long. In the meantime, I plan to do some sleuthing of my own. Thanks, Carole."

CHAPTER 15

Nancy and Ralph Evans were being held without bail on multiple charges associated with buying and selling infants, defrauding adoptive parents, kidnapping, and income tax evasion. The case would take a long time to put together, as it involved several countries and agencies within those countries, as well as finding those families with whom babies had been placed. This daunting assignment was given to Carole's supervisees, Marie and Robin, who were also being supported by a very experienced paralegal and investigative staff.

The two young attorneys, both in their early 30's, had become fast friends in the short time they were working together. Marie was from the Boston area, and had gone away for the first time when she attended law school at William and Mary. She had been married shortly after graduation, and elected to come to New York for a clerkship, following which she and her husband both accepted jobs here. They had no children and were both very ambitious. Robin, slightly her friend's junior, had come from Westchester where she grew up in a very affluent family. She stayed in New York City for both undergraduate and law school at Columbia University, and lived very comfortably in a co-op purchased by her parents as a graduation present. At this time, Robin didn't seem to be dating anyone in particular; she was a little overwhelmed by the work, and therefore hesitant to add outside pressures just now. Both young women were fond of Sam, and a little in awe of him. Several years their senior and with more trial work for his high-powered private law firm behind him, Sam seemed without worry. He was tapped for the Asinov case, with its potential for more media exposure. Sam was married, separated from his wife of ten years; the couple has one son, 7 years old, who attends a special school for autistic children.

Marie and Robin each took one of the couples who were known to have adopted babies via the Evans', and contacted these families, who both lived in the Midwestern U.S. It was an emotionally daunting task for each young woman to drop a bombshell on the telephone; this would be followed by the couples being interviewed in person by their local FBI staff. If the case ever went to court, these couples would have to testify.

At this time, no one was ready to speculate as to whether the supposedly legal adoptions, which thus far had been identified in fourteen states, would be overturned. The potential for this was devastating to the families.

Carole had suggested that local community mental health or adoption agencies be tapped to do in-home evaluations of these families. In each case, the local social service entity had done one pre-adoption screening, but it was worthless, as the couples had been prepped to distort the circumstances under which the adoption had originally been initiated.

The FBI had frozen all the Evans' assets, which were considerable; more than $2,000,000 was located thus far.

Doug was working on the Miller case, involved closely with his FBI friend Max, and an NYPD rep from the Joint Terrorism Task Force, as well as Evan, with whom he had worked successfully on the Roth case. The assistant U.S. attorneys met with Jerome Miller, a 49 year old tough guy, overtly hostile and contemptuous, rejecting any suggestion that he plead guilty to the current charges to diminish his sentence. So neither of the attorneys was optimistic that they could get anything useful out of Miller on the 1991 weapons smuggling.

Doug and Evan were sitting in the jail cell with Miller, with Doug, as usual, playing the hardliner, and Evan the softer touch. Max had been with them, but walked out in disgust, indicating that "this loser could have the book thrown at him, so why are we wasting our time?" The two attorneys actually had the same thought, when out of the blue, Miller, contemptuous, asked: "You'll have to give me plenty to get me to talk on the weapons deal." He went on to say that in exchange for information about that, "I want to walk on the current charges." When Doug told Miller that the prisoner would have to tell him just what he had to offer before any agreement, Miller said, "No deal. You commit first, or I'm not playing. All I can say is that if you guys had known more about how this went down, you might have been smarter in catching Bush's pal, Bin Laden."

After the interview, Doug conferred with the FBI supervisor on the case, with Max present, and later on that day, with his own boss. Barry was not inclined to believe that Miller had any information from 1991 which could possibly be of value today. Doug wasn't so sure. "You know, the plan for 9/11 took years to develop, during which they attacked our interests abroad and sought opportunities to finish what they started in '93. They were very disappointed then that they didn't bring down the World Trade Center and kill thousands instead of the six. It wouldn't surprise me a bit if plenty of weapons had been smuggled into this country for many years before as part of planning for 9/11. You know, to disrupt our economy, to stir up anxiety, to make us feel vulnerable. In a way, it's surprising that more hasn't been done on our soil, like car bombings, subways and buses, etc. How dare we be so self-confident that we hadn't made any significant attempt to control illegal immigration, or to follow up on people who come on visitors' or students' visa, and then disappear! Any why shouldn't they ? No one seriously looks for them!"

"Doug, more has been going on under the radar than either of us knows about. For all the talk of lousy cooperation between FBI and CIA, it did get better in the past five years or so, and even the NYPD has said that FBI has been more respectful, not so heavy-handed. The joint taskforces are making collaboration real, as opposed to what was on paper.

After Congress scrutinizes the various agencies' role in missing the preparations for 9/11, collaboration overall will improve." Barry told Doug to confer with the NYC ADA about a potential deal with Miller.

Since it was Thursday and therefore Carole's night to get her nails done and go out with her friends, Doug took himself shopping for last-minute Christmas gifts, for his mother, Jill, Carole, and secretary Barbara.

The stores were jammed, and the shopping difficult, but in contrast to real stress, it was actually pleasurable to be involved in such mundane tasks.

Afterward, he watched the skaters briefly in the Rockefeller Center rink, noticing the celebratory crowds, and seeing *danger* instead of pleasure.

On his return home, Mrs. Cohen told Doug that he had gotten an urgent call from Washington, that she had tried to reach him on his cell. In the mob scene, he hadn't heard the phone.

Kissing his sleeping son, Doug paid Mrs. Cohen and placed his call.

He had been given an identifying code, and was passed to several people before reaching Jack Marsdon in Justice. "Mr. Malone, we'd appreciate you paying us a visit tomorrow; please take the 8am shuttle from LaGuardia, and we'll pick you up at Dulles at 9 in time for a 9:45 meeting.

Plan to stay overnight. We have a few other people for you to meet and they're unfortunately not able to be around tomorrow."

"I have a full day at the office because it's my last day at work before the holiday. How about Wednesday, the day after Christmas?"

"Not possible, sir. Our situation here doesn't really call for much attention to holidays or days off. But out of respect for your family, we will get you back home Saturday night, and not expect you here again 'til after the New Year." As Doug hung up, he had a sick feeling in anticipation of telling Carole what was in store for them. He then put in a call to Barry, and another to Max, to fill them in and to see if either knew any more about the assignment than he did.

Carole also got a call while in her nail salon, this from Sam, who was excited about something the NYPD detective on the Asinov case had unearthed. After apologizing for possibly disturbing her, Sam asked if she might meet with him in the morning to go over the new information, and sign off on an approach on the basis of it. Because she was not going to be in the office at all until after Christmas, Carole invited him to join her and some friends in a local cocktail lounge.

"Carole, the NYPD has gotten forensics back on the shipment they confiscated. Guess what? It showed some evidence of being near explosives. They're speculating that the vodka and the explosives were separated for shipment to the States. Naturally with this information the joint taskforce is on top of Azinov. This is considered a national security issue, so this guy isn't going to be handled like a common racketeer."

We need to alert Doug to this, Sam. It's his area, and we can't go with it on our own. I'm certain he's going to want to talk to everyone involved. Sit tight. You and I are probably not going to run with this particular ball, so don't be too disappointed. It's out of our league."

CHAPTER 16

Dana was sitting at the reception desk in this Sedona spa, pleased at her good fortune in finding her job, where she will be able to bring Amy any time her daughter isn't in school. After playing around with the idea of going to Boulder, Colorado, Dana had had second thoughts, as she believed her mother would surely think of that town first. She then considered Vail, perhaps teaching skiing to little kids, which she had done on school vacations. However, Vail is such an expensive town, and the pay is lousy, so she ended up here where she knew no one.

Looking out at the gorgeous red rocky landscape, Dana felt calmer; she could stay here indefinitely. Her daughter, at present watching TV, had other ideas: "Mommy, when can we talk to Daddy again? I miss him and I want to go home. I want to go back to my school and my friends."

Such regularly spoken pleadings were getting to Dana. Maybe she should send Amy home. 'I shouldn't even let myself think of her as Amy.

She's Nicole!' Returning to her computer work, Dana had a difficult time concentrating.

On the way back to their neat and very inexpensive one bedroom apartment, 'Nicole' was at it again, and this time Dana said they'd call Mel.

She totally forgot about the time difference between Arizona and New York, thus ended up awakening him at 1 am New York time.

"Mel, I'm sending Amy home to you via Southwest Airlines this Sunday. She misses you and her life at home. Please don't try to find me just yet. I promise I'll keep in touch, and when I'm ready, I'll return."

Mel was barely able to take down the details concerning the flights when his wife hung up. But he had gotten a caller identification system, so had Dana's number. He decided not to use it for now.

"Amy, you're going to be a very big girl and fly on two planes to New

York, where Daddy will meet you. The airplane has someone special to help little children who go alone, so you'll be fine."

"But, Mommy, I want you to go too. Why aren't you coming with me?"

"I need to stay here a little longer, sweetheart, but I'll be home soon. Please don't mention the name of the town we live in here, okay, because, you remember, this is a grown-up hide and seek game. Promise?"

"Okay. but I'm sad and mad. Will I see grandma too?"

"Yes, of course. I'm sure she'll come to the airport with Daddy."

Mother and daughter went to bed, but Dana had a terrible time falling asleep. Finally, she had a dream. She was in a cave, dressed in shorts and a CU polo shirt, freezing in the wintry weather. All around her were stalactites, sharp and dangerous. She kept going, thinking she was about to find the exit, but never did. Awakening barely able to catch her breath, Dana washed her face and went into the kitchen. It was 4 am, 7am in New York. So Dana called her mom, and nearly hysterical, told her where she was, about her dream. She was so very confused.

"Dana, you need to calm yourself to think clearly. Your dream says you want to come home but you deny that. You can't do this to your daughter, or in fact to Mel and me. We love you, we know this past year has been a horror for you. It will get better. Please come home and see a therapist."

"Mom, you're always sending everyone into therapy. I do feel so trapped in my life, pulled toward Mel and you, and then wanting to run from you both. You both have let me down, but I'm not as angry as I was, just stressed by my own confusion. I might go get help here."

At 9am Jenny called Adam, who was staying with his son in that young family's beautiful Bedford home. After bringing him up to date on Dana's situation and her own, Jenny told her husband that she wanted him to come home. "We made a very deep commitment to each other, Adam, and this mess has played havoc with it. I understand that it's all my fault, and I'm prepared to eat crow. But I don't want to lose you. Please, please come home."

"I was hoping you'd call because I do want to try to talk things out. But I'm not sure how I can go through the next few months when you're still so involved with police and the district attorney's office. How about we meet after Christmas in town, somewhere private. I promised my kids that I'd hang out with them over the holiday. Anyway, if it's all right with you, let's meet at Adolpho's on the 26th at 5 o'clock.

CHAPTER 17

Carole was stunned by Doug's news, but offered him her support: "I'm sure their calling you to Washington on such short notice must mean they have something special in mind for you. They haven't invited the others from our office, have they?"

"No. I'm not sure I want to be special. Do you realize the implications? I hope they don't expect me to stay in Washington!"

"Of course not. You're needed here to run the team prosecuting those bastards. Why would you think otherwise?"

When Doug returned after his quick trip, the couple barely had time to talk before they had to get ready for their Christmas party. Nearly fifty friends were expected; the catering service provided a bartender and a waitress. Danny and King were to stay with Mrs. Cohen for the night.

Every year the Malones looked forward to this party, but this year felt so different. 'How are we going to get through this,? Doug wondered. But once their guests began pouring in, the music playing, delicious food and good drink, they both relaxed and found themselves actually having a good time.

Carole had bought an emerald green velvet tight-fitting dress, the color accentuating her eyes. She had her normally straight long hair piled in an upsweep, with dangling curls held by 'diamond' clips. Doug, not characteristically concerned about his clothing, wore an outfit Carole treated him to, a black cashmere sweater with matching slacks.

After the party and the cleanup, the Malones collapsed, barely wishing each other Merry Christmas. In the morning, Carole woke her husband, arms holding him, kissing him with tenderness, whispering in his ear: "Doug, can I entice you to wake up? I want us to make love, are you with me?" Moving herself on top of her willing partner, Carole touched him knowingly. Interested, aroused, Doug responded, first putting his hands under her hair, pulling her to him, kissing her passionately. His lips moved to her taut nipples, while positioning her body on his erect penis. She held him tightly with powerful young muscles, then relaxed for them to breathe, resuming long, intense kisses. Climaxing together, feeling so close, Doug put his hand over her flat belly, and ran his fingers through her dark pubic hair.

"It's very difficult for me to think about being away from you."

"I can take care of whatever comes up while you're away, if it's not too long. Your working is for us, to make us safer. Jill and I are both proud of you; you're a patriot, and we can be a little patriotic too by supporting what you do. Of course, I did make Jill swear that she'd be an exemplary teenager, since I have no clue as to how to mother one. After all, my mother never was around when I was that age."

"You sound so sure that you'll be fine. I hope that doesn't mean you won't miss me! At any rate, I have to be there Monday, the 7th.

Carole persuaded Doug to take the whole family down to Naples to visit his mother, in spite of the exorbitant air fares over the holiday.

He was unlikely to be able to go once in his new job, and she knew that Mary Malone wasn't healthy enough to fly up north during the winter.

The Malones flew Jet Blue into Ft. Myers, rented a sharp red SUV, and drove to a motel on Bonita Beach. They spent a couple of hours at the beach, though the water was much too cold for their taste. Only Jill ventured in briefly, before huddling under a terry robe. Around five, by now cleaned up, they picked up Mary and all went out to dinner at a local steakhouse. Mary had seen Danny right after his birth, and couldn't get over the lively nine month old he'd become. Carole later remarked that she was unprepared for how awake and good-spirited their young son was this evening, way past his normal bedtime. He even flirted with some nearby diners, and totally captivated their receptive young waitress.

Carole and Doug flew to Freeport in the Bahamas for an overnight, leaving their kids with his mom and aunt. There they gambled a little, danced in a gorgeous waterside setting, made love, and slept late. This would obviously be the last time they'd feel so free for months to come.

Carole didn't even allow Doug to contact his office or access messages during their two day vacation.

Flying back to New York on Tuesday, January 1st, Doug would have a scant five days before going to Washington.

CHAPTER 18

Elaine and Gerald welcomed the group back after the long holiday break. For a change, everyone was present on time, and seemed happy to be back.

Stacy, normally aloof and caustic, better at asking others unnerving questions than in sharing her own life, told the group she needed to talk.

"The vacation was hell. Not because I missed you guys. My daughter got into serious trouble. I rarely spoke to you about her because I fear for her privacy, but also I feel so guilty. She's 11 years old going on thirty, involved with a 16 year old boy sexually, though she denied having intercourse. They 'only' have oral sex! Well, they also use pot, and in fact stole his mother's Zanex, which she reported to me. I also never told you that Joanna is not my husband's daughter, though he adopted her shortly after we were married. Her biological father doesn't know about her...we had a one night stand, and I wasn't about to get him involved. I had to tell Joanna when she was about 7 or 8, and she didn't even seem that interested. But now, she called me a 'whore' and wants to meet him."

Several group members were sympathetic to Stacy, but only Bill asked what Stacy needed from us. To everyone's surprise, Peter turned on Bill: "She just needs us to listen, she never asks anything of us for herself, so we should just listen as long as she wants to talk."

Stacy went on to tell the group other 'secrets,' namely that this was her third marriage, the first two ending after the briefest time together. And, her biggest shame: "I'm on lithium, my psychiatrist is pretty sure I'm bi-polar.

Because of this and my own insane adolescence, I'm terrified that Joanna just might have inherited it from me. I talked to Elaine about her, and she recommended a child psychiatrist to evaluate Jo, but I'm having a helluva time getting that kid to go."

From Roger, "If you mean business, she'll go. Don't give her a choice. Don't let your shame over this cloud your judgment. I just got tough with my 17 year old son. He's still pissed about the divorce, the fact that I initiated it, and he doesn't want to see me. But he does want me to buy him a car, foot bills for sports equipment, ski trips and next year, for the expensive college he has in mind. So I told him there's a catch: he expects certain things from me, and vice versa. He made a nasty crack about me suddenly wanting to play father, but I don't get any more arguments about our seeing each other."

Gerald remarked that his son needed affirmation from Roger that he really cared...and that Roger was right, Joanna needed her mother to take charge. Parents don't have it easy, and need to get past needing to be liked.

Carole had been quiet tonight, still feeling the effects of Doug's leaving two days before. But she did respond to Elaine's invitation to participate. "I reassured Doug that I'd be fine because I know he needs that from me. But here I'm not so sure. Days are always all right, what with work, Danny and the activities I do with him keeping me so busy.

But after I put him to bed, Jill's not with me until the end of next week, I feel so alone. Imagine, I've just slept alone two nights, and already feel...

I had a dream, but I only remember a fragment. In it, I was back at my parents' house, there was no Danny, and I was sunbathing. It was a very pleasant scene, yet I woke up disturbed."

Stephanie, who had seemed reluctant to acknowledge that she had had a nice holiday trip with a friend, responded to the dream: "I've had that same dream repeatedly over the years. Usually when I want to run away from my life. Which is always!" She gave a rare chuckle.

Peter and Bill both agreed they also want to run away from their lives. Both their wives are pursuing divorces, and in Peter's case, he is devastated by the anticipated separation from his young son. Bill admitted that he already has a girlfriend: "You know I can't stand to be alone for long. We met at the carwash, if you can believe that, and have been seeing each other every night. She's separated, no kids, so she's free to travel with me, and we were in Barbados for the holidays."

Gerald reflected on different styles of running away; he half joked that he hasn't heard a good one yet. But Roger got serious: "Since 9/11 it's pretty frightening to be here in New York; I keep expecting another attack, and would leave the east coast if it weren't for my kids."

A new member had been invited to join the group, and actually came the following week, as anticipated. A tall, statuesque 60 year old civil engineer,

Natalie was happily married and still employed as a safety engineer on city construction. She had no prior psychiatric history, but had been very depressed since 9/11, and had attended both group and individual therapy to cope. After her group ended, Natalie asked her therapist, Marianne, to find her therapy group, and she recommended this one. Although Carole and Natalie had never actually met, they had seen each other on site of the Project Liberty program in lower Manhattan, and of course, both had Marianne as their individual therapist.

Roger cracked: "Our leaders must have brought Natalie into the group to get us talking about the attacks. I notice that every time one of us says anything about them, no one picks up on it."

Peter shared a dream. He thought it was related to the terrorism. "I dreamt that my office building was gone when I went to work one day. It wasn't bombed or anything like that, it just never existed. In its place was a perfectly lovely park, with fountains and everything. People were there with their dogs, eating lunch, it was sunny. I asked a couple of people if they knew what happened, and they totally denied that it had ever been any different. So I felt crazy, very anxious. The way I felt, it was such a contrast to the peaceful scene."

In keeping with the group's mores, other members shared their personal associations to Peter's dream. Stephanie felt that she couldn't handle what happened, and certainly can't face what could happen here.

"I want to run away from the idea of it. In fact, these days I don't watch television, but only rent old Hollywood musicals. She turned to Carole: "How can your husband tolerate being enmeshed in all this terrorism stuff, and what about you? You probably know more than the rest of us from your husband's insiders' position."

"Doug has secret clearance and I do not, so he tells me only what you could read in the papers or see on television. Our conversations are personal, about us, the kids, people we care about. Oh, and he did describe in excruciating detail some of the more peculiar-looking characters he's already met in D.C.!"

Bill acknowledged that he's been drinking even more since 9/11. He isn't sure whether it's that, or his wife proceeding with the divorce when he doesn't really want it. "She still doesn't believe I love her and would give up my screwing around if she'd take me back." Then Bill returned to Peter's dream: "It's like nothing is solid, we can't count on anything, and the park is like us covering up our real sadness with imitation stuff, like my finding a 27 year old, or the bottle, when I really want my wife."

Stacy began to cry, startling everyone, including the leaders. "All I can think of is that everyone who ever meant anything to me left me, or I dumped them without even knowing it'd hurt." Rejecting the tissues offered by Roger, Stacy further shocked the group by walking out of the room.

Elaine followed her, understanding that a shamed, vulnerable Stacy might not return to group without her therapist's support.

Gerald asked the group to respond to what had just occurred, and several did. Some, like Bill, were angry with Stacy: "how dare she act out like that in here, after two years of group? We've all cried here!" Others were more sympathetic: Stephanie remarked that "Stacy is really opening up with us for the first time, so she's scared to death. Even here she's been 'the doctor' or 'the stunning woman,' so why are you so hard on her, Bill?"

The group ended without Stacy or Elaine returning, but before the good nights, Gerald turned to the newest member, Natalie, and asked her if she could say what this had been like for her. "Probably Stacy wasn't happy to have a new member join the group, especially a female. I didn't mind her walking out, but I do wonder why Elaine would run after her, it's just indulging theatricality."

What Carole didn't share was her irritation with the group's always-present fascination with Doug, and with his work. Intellectually she could grasp why, after all they saw him on television, and now he's off to do the special work. But everyone always wanted to know about him. What about her work, her interests? The men used to hang on her every word, but of late, turned their attention elsewhere. She was hurt.

CHAPTER 19

Jenny and Adam came from separate directions for this early dinner meeting at their favorite haunt. The crowds in Manhattan were nearly overwhelming, what with the stores all having after-Christmas sales. And, the freezing rain did nothing to improve either of their spirits. Jenny was nervous and admitted it to herself. Adam had already had a couple of beers in Grand Central Station, so was rather calm as he approached the dramatically decorated Italian restaurant. Later on he reflected on his focus before their meeting: Adolpho's fabulous osso bucco.

Until the owner's greetings were done with, and the cabernet sauvignon was poured and sampled, there was no real conversation. But as usual, it would be Jenny who would begin difficult topics.

"I wish I could tell you that everything's all better, that the D.A. gave me a pass on Paul's death, that my kids are doing just fine. I know you can't handle all this stuff."

"Guess what, Jenny, I don't want to handle it. I could, I guess, but who in their right mind would elect to pour mud over their head? Was this the retirement that I dreamed of?"

"I want to suggest something and hope you'll consider it. What if, once I am cleared legally, I sign on for your version of things, that is cut back on how involved I've been in all my kids' troubles? I've already begun the process." And she proceeded to tell him about Dana's situation.

If Jenny thought her describing what occurred with Dana, and telling of her resolve to keep out of it, would be relieving for Adam, she was very sadly mistaken! How could she, so in tune with her clients, be so far off the mark with her husband? After they parted, of course Jenny asked herself this, between fighting off her tears as she boarded the cross town bus.

She was even more thrown by the others on her bus, generally happy-looking family types mixed in with young people holding hands.

Adam returned to Grand Central, heading back to his son's house.

He felt lighter somehow, and it took the whole trip to Bedford for him to understand why. He would be able to take back his life if he divorced Jenny. 'I'm not made for all this stress and drama. I need peace, fun. And I shouldn't be ashamed of it, like she wants me to be. Jenny's always molding people, but this person doesn't want to be molded.' On Jenny's return to her apartment, she had to see two clients, and was grateful that she couldn't focus on her own life. Amazingly enough, she had two good sessions, where she was able to be engaged, and so decided to put off her thinking too much until another day.

On Adam's return to his son's home, he found the kids involved with video games and the adults playing bridge. He accepted their invitation to be a fifth, and demonstrated his excellence at the game. After coffee and cake, Adam went into the stunningly decorated guestroom with its private bath, and slept like a baby 'til late morning.

When Mel called Jenny to invite her to join him in picking up Amy, he was surprised by her response: she would "pass this time," as her work schedule was tightening up. Then she added "I've decided to try to pick up more work, after all, who knows when I'll get a clear legal decision, so why not commit to what I love." Seemingly as an afterthought, Jenny told her son-in-law that she and Adam would be getting divorced in the new year. And she's not afraid any more, after all, if she had been able to survive Paul's death and her children's troubles, she's certain to move on. Though Mel didn't completely believe this, he wasn't about to contradict her.

Adam told his daughter-in-law that he would be contacting a matrimonial attorney in the next few weeks, asking her if she knew anyone.

The young woman was surprised, but encouraging, and gave him names of two attorneys who practiced in her office. When she remarked on how much more relaxed he appeared, and that she was very surprised at his demeanor, Adam told her that he's a very passive guy. "I would never have left Jenny even though I probably wasn't happy for two years, and not only because of the legal mess. She's very lovable, but we have no intellectual interests in common, she's pushed me to do all sorts of things that she enjoys but I tolerate, and I went along with it all. Probably I also was ashamed about strike two, another divorce. But I know that the real shame is my going along with whatever, then blaming her for everything."

CHAPTER 20

They had asked me to report on Monday, January 7th at 10am, but when I arrived at the hotel at 9am, a message cancelled the day. So I spent the morning in the Holocaust Museum, just blocks from the Capital, and then hung out at the pool and sauna. There were plenty of people around, but I didn't see anyone I knew until I went to the bar around 4...I had started to feel lousy, almost depressed. I don't think it was just being away from the family and not knowing just where this is going.

Being here somehow makes it more real how serious the country's problems are, and how dangerous our failure could be.

During the next week I attended at least a dozen meetings led by almost as many people from numerous government departments. Though we were welcomed at every one of them, and told how important our work would be, each speaker left us with a different take on just what that work would be. There was plenty of uncomfortable talk amongst us...

Thanks to Carole, I looked like a fashion plate for my first entry into Washington's scene. She probably thought I'd bump into Bush or Chaney.

Up to now I hadn't met one "famous" person, but today was to be different.

Ted Jax took charge of the meeting, and gave us some picture of what we'd be doing. The seventy of us, primarily men and mostly from criminal law, law enforcement, and accounting/tracking backgrounds would join with the FBI, CIA and Alcohol and Firearms, immigration and customs, FAA, and counterterrorism committee chiefs from NYPD, to examine how communication can be facilitated, and what changes in the law will be required to effect this. After the charge, we were split up into five groups to consider the questions posed.

Jax referred to all of us as being part of a greater army of American patriots fighting against the global enemy. He then invited a few questions, but evaded answering most on grounds of national security. He left us clear, however, that we would be in and out of Washington as needed, sometimes on very short notice. I walked out of the hall quite worried about how this would play out with my family, and noticed that this was a big topic in the hallway headed for the working lunch.

My group consists of seventeen individuals ranging in age from 34 to 72, men and women, most strangers to each other at the outset.

The leaders suggested full introductions, and in this way we quickly learned very interesting facts about each other: two are former detectives, one is an MD/attorney, there are several attorneys specializing in tracking assets, two of the younger attorneys are of Arabic descent, and are fluent in Arabic. The others have impressive experience as prosecutors handling racketeering, terrorism and other major crimes. Most of these people headed up some program or other in their home offices, so the trick will be how to forge a working group, to minimize unhealthy competition. But I noticed that we all listened pretty carefully to each other.

While lunch was being served, we chatted informally, gradually relaxing. Then each group was given the same complex mock case.

After joking with us about how we were being graded, Jax revealed his apparently well-know addiction to duplicate bridge when he remarked:
"This is similar to duplicate bridge, where each team gets to play the same hand, then compare notes later on how they did. Go over the case, then present to the larger group when we reconvene. This approach should help us make the best use of our different talents, and to learn from each other."

Afternoon spilled into evening, and I found himself energized by the group's interaction. Certain people were standouts: the woman of Jordanian parentage who had been working on homegrown terrorist networks; the oldest man present, whose tremendous experience was supported by his calm, respectful demeanor, and articulate presentation.

And another man, he from Miami and of Cuban background, a linguist, rather quiet, from a tax/accounting/legal background, someone who didn't say much, but when he did, made a real contribution. At the end of our long day, I considered myself fortunate to be part of such a dynamic group and energized by the prospective work ahead.

CHAPTER 21

"The baby snatchers," as the federal attorneys called them, weren't saying much, but the evidence was piling up daily. It was one of those cases where investigators all over the country were only too happy to cooperate, so disgusted were they by the scope of the tragedy. The two identified families were naturally devastated: one, a young black professional couple living in Ann Arbor and working at the University of Michigan, had adopted twin boys, now three, and had just learned that the adoption was illegal. The couple had suffered several miscarriages, and because of an ectopic pregnancy the woman had to have a hysterectomy before her 30th birthday. A legal guardian had been appointed for the boys, and had agreed to make his adoptive parents his foster family until such time as his birth mother was located. Because the rules for foster placement were fairly rigid requiring a fulltime person at home, the foster/adoptive mother had to give up her teaching position at the University, even knowing that she might lose the boys at any time.

The second case involved a five year old girl with cerebral palsy.

This child had been lovingly cared for by her adoptive parents in Shaker Heights, Ohio. There the lawyer appointed to protect the child's rights had elected to place her in a specialized program for physically handicapped children. The child was reported to be seriously depressed, not eating, soiling, and refusing to speak. Though anxious to right this additional wrong, the New York federal attorney's office would not consider intervening with the state of Ohio in a fight over jurisdiction over this decision.

Nancy and Ralph Evans had never had direct contact with any one of the families. Instead, in the mid-western United States they used an intermediary, who then hired a local attorney specializing in adoptions. As Robin and Marie collected evidence, it became clear that the attorneys were ignorant of any criminal component. For example, in Ohio and in Michigan, the attorneys had been contacted by Purnima Jain, a heavyset Indian woman in her early 30's purporting to be in her last trimester, and seeking to give up the child or children for adoption. She had all the proper documentation, claimed that she could not identify the father in either case, and collected money from the families for herself, and for the Evans'. Each family paid Purnima $30,000. The investigators had had a very difficult time locating Ms. Jain, but finally did so in March 2002; she was working as a bank teller in a small Kansas farm town. Interviewers reported that she had been living there only six months, having lived for the previous five years in four Midwestern states. Her impressively large bank balance was far greater than her earnings could explain and initially she refused to provide the FBI with any reasonable explanation.

Ms. Purnima proved a worthy opponent for her interrogators, who of course wanted her to give up the Evans'. She finally broke when they located her extensive family, and threatened to pull them in to the criminal investigation. Her parents are American citizens, born in India, who came to Jackson Heights, Queens, in 1980 with their two children, a son now 37, a pediatric neurologist, married with two children, living on Long Island, and their daughter Purnima, now 34, single, a Queens College graduate with an accounting/business degree. The family had been living within a close knit Indian community, and it was expected that their daughter would marry within the group, as had the son. However, Purnima had rarely shown interest in dating. She rejected the still practiced custom of parents arranging a marriage for their young adult children and shocked her traditional parents by leaving their home at age 27, though for a time she lived nearby and worked as an accountant for a local bank. Purnima, with little advanced warning, left the area, telling her parents that she wanted to take a master's degree, and would do so at Purdue University, in Indiana.

She did, in fact, complete an MBA there, and while in the area apparently met the Evans' at a conference in nearby Chicago. The couple had been attending another conference in the same hotel, and befriended the obviously isolated, rather physically unattractive younger woman.

Purnima stated that the couple initially asked her to do 'small tasks' for them, utilizing her business background; they paid her modestly for her time. After about a year, with the young Indian-American extremely lonely in her new Iowa location, the Evans' promoted her to junior partner in their adoption schemes. She bought into their claim that they were doing good if technically illegal work in that they provided desperate couples with the chance to become parents. The FBI agent remarked that Ms. Jain was either the best liar he ever met, or the most naive.

However, once caught, she literally flooded the room with information, vomiting out precise details even before they were asked of her. One FBI agent experienced her as reveling in the attention, but others agreed that she was 'not the criminal type,' and therefore was discharging some of her guilt with this confession. Ms. Jain had refused counsel, though her parents and brother had urged her to be represented.

Carole came into court to watch as Nancy and Ralph Evans pleaded guilty and had to spell out details of their criminal behavior in compliance with their sentencing agreement. Robin and Marie led the couple through their sordid story, and Carole, on behalf of the U.S. Attorney, accepted the agreement. The Evans' attorney had pushed hard to include any other illegal adoptions facilitated by his clients, but this was not at all acceptable to the office. The couple would be serving a long prison sentence, which would undoubtedly be extended when other cases were prosecuted.

The Miller case was temporarily transferred to Carole in Doug's absence. Until his return, Carole and Evan would work together, with Max coordinating FBI information; they had also taken over the Azinov case. Carole's supervisee, Sam, would assist. Both cases required a tremendous amount of coordination with police in several jurisdictions and with the FBI and AFT. Miller was in jail on gun possession and drug trafficking, while Azinov was out on $2,000,000 bail.

After a long conversation with Doug late in March, Barry called Carole into his office. He had been mostly out of the office since 9/11, regularly consulting with Mayor Blumberg and Governor Pataki.

"I need you to think long and hard about what I'm about to offer you. Doug knows about this, and wanted me to do what I'd normally do, without reflecting on what I know of your personal life." Carole, listening intently, was mystified, but a little worried, as her boss continued. "We have holes in this unit for obvious reasons, and anticipate that much of our staff will be involved with the terrorism cases for the long term. I'll be bringing in more staff to do the regular criminal work. I'd like to offer you a promotion to acting supervisor. Before you turn it down, let me assure you that I will be very available to support you, as will the other supervisors."

Carole was stunned. She had never thought of herself as being in her husband's league. And, she had not been professionally ambitious, so why would Barry want her? In response to her boss' inquiry, Carole reestablished contact with him. "I'm tremendously flattered by your offer.

And I understand that you don't want an answer today. This is not something I can respond to hastily."

She ran into nemesis Leona Dell, and had a delightful fantasy that her first official act as supervising attorney would be to move Leona to the smallest office in the complex, while taking over Doug's office for herself.

CHAPTER 22

S am was the point person to coordinate the various law enforcement agencies' relationships with the U.S. Attorney's office on both the Miller and Azinov cases. As such, he met regularly with FBI supervising   agent, Max Brand, and they had begun something of a friendship. So it was not completely inappropriate for them to share something of their personal lives.

Max had described his wife's frustration at his long hours and not infrequent absences from social events she considered to be important.

He also spoke of his own irritation with his teenage daughter, of whom he saw less and less because of her vast social network. But overall, it was clear that Max was a happy family man.

Not so with Sam. He and his wife Margo had been separated for two years, and were recently divorced. Their marriage had suffered from the terrible strain of having to co-parent a severely emotionally handicapped autistic child. Since their separation, the couple had renewed their friendship, but faced the inevitability of their divorcing. Sam had become so invested in his new job that he rarely dated.

"Sam, I think I better talk to you about something I've been noticing.

You're probably not going to be happy about my putting in my two cents.

Am I wrong that you've fallen for Carole? Please tell me if I'm way off base."

"Nothing has happened, if that what you mean. We spend a lot of time together on the days she works, naturally, since we're working on the same cases. At times we end up eating together. I'd have to be pretty crazy…believe me, it's been on the up and up."

"I do believe you, but I've also noticed how you look at her. You're all my friends, and the last thing I want is to see anyone hurt. Are you denying that you're emotionally, shall we say, involved?"

"I'm crazy about her, and if I'd met her first…she doesn't have a clue about how I feel, and we'll leave it that way. I'm no home wrecker, and she thinks her husband walks on water, anyway, so I'd lose all the way around."

The two men returned to their work discussion, both relieved at the shift and determined not to take this up again.

When Sam and Carole met later that afternoon, he felt uncomfortable and transparent, so kept things very case-focused. When Carole asked about his son, Sam answered in monosyllables, an obvious shift from his normally responsive demeanor. She may have wondered if he was upset over something, but had her own private concerns, so let it go.

Marie and Robin both noticed the special friendship developing between Sam and Carole, and gossiped about whether it was romantic.

Marie in particular was a little jealous, being accustomed to admiration from her superiors.

CHAPTER 23

Jenny was parked outside the Brooklyn District Attorney's office expecting her lawyer to join her shortly. Normally a healthy person, today Jenny felt she might be having a heart attack; shortness of breath, some pain—was it rotating down the left arm—she wasn't sure, and intense heat, even worse than her hot flashes associated with menopause. When her physical pain didn't increase, Jenny decided that like her many patients, she was having a panic attack. She opened the windows of her car, responding with pleasure to the stiff chilly breeze on this early April morning.

Jacob Nathan joined his client, startling her with his quiet approach.

The two sat in her car for fifteen minutes or so, discussing their response to the various possibilities. "I'm sure you won't go to jail, but they might put you on probation, pretty silly, don't you think, after so many years? There's no chance that they're going to trial, after all, who could they get as witness to this so-called crime?"

They were in downtown Brooklyn where the traffic was daunting; the multi-ethnic mix of people seemed to be rushing somewhere, remarkably missing each other by inches. Jacob held Jenny's arm as they walked to the district attorney's office. The D.A. had a reputation for being tough—thus far, they had only met with his assistants. Though Jenny might have liked to meet the famous DA, her more knowledge able attorney feared sparking the big guy's interest. They were ushered into a small conference room where eventually an assistant district attorney and a legal secretary joined them.

"I'm Laurence Bradley, ADA in charge of this investigation. This is Mrs. Elaine Raider, who will be taking some notes as we go along. Please feel free to interrupt me with questions or comments. As you know, Mrs.

Levine, we have had the NYPD look into the circumstances of your first husband's death. As part of their investigation, they did interviews with over twenty people, including with your former mother-in-law, currently residing in Wilmington, North Carolina, and with your husband's probable associates in the drug business, Obviously, after so many years, 22 to be exact, some people are deceased or have not been located. We went over your discussions with the police at the time of the death, and were able to interview your mah jong friends, two incidentally still live in the area. What we think occurred is the following: that you actually went to your husband's place of business armed with the intent of threatening him, at minimum, and planned the mah jong game as cover should questions be asked. You purposely parked a distance away to avoid your car being identified; a neighbor renting the apartment above the convenience store reported there was plentiful parking at that hour when most businesses were closed for the night. So you lied to the police about why you took the gun, supposedly for your protection in walking a distance to the store.

"To continue, you undoubtedly expected to find your husband doing business, having regularly overheard numerous conversations; you told the police and us as much. So you knew that afterward, the police would find a large sum of money, as well as other illegal drugs on the premises, and you hoped they would conclude that it was a drug buy gone wrong.

And you were fortunate, they did believe you, without even checking your alibi. Because they had known of the connection between your husband and Da Silva, they bought into the gangster murder scenario, allowing you time to dispose of the weapon.

"You're wrong…"

"Let me finish, and you then can make a statement, assuming your attorney agrees. Had the NYPD pursued proper investigative strategies at that time, you might have been convicted on murder one; do you know what that is? It's premeditated murder, which is suggested by the facts just recited. Given the time lapse, and the fact that you have never come to the attention of the criminal justice system since that date, we are open to offering you a plea bargain. You may plead to man one, which has a 12-20 year prison sentence. If you refuse this plea, we are prepared to go to the Grand Jury for an indictment on the more serious charge.

Jenny fainted for the first time in her life. When the RN was called, she discovered that Jenny's blood pressure was 180 over 96, her skin was clammy, breathing irregular. She was transported by ambulance to Maimonides Hospital.

Jacob Nathan had accompanied Jenny to the hospital, and tried unsuccessfully to contact a family member once there. It was most un fortunate that her family, friends, clients and colleagues learned of her heart attack from reading about it in Newsday or the New York Times.

Both papers were obviously intrigued by the 'cold case' investigation, paralleling television programs on the same subject.

Mel and Adam both came to see Jenny immediately, but Marianne was unavailable, attending a Spring conference/vacation in San Diego.

Mel also called Dana, discovering that she had left her job in Sedona, leaving no forwarding address.

The two men were similar in some ways; both could be described as likeable, but un-ambitious and too easy-going. Neither could figure out what they should have done differently, but shared a vague sense of guilt that they must have done something wrong. Both men had loved their wives, but couldn't really be equal to them in assertiveness or professional success. And now the women were in trouble, but neither man could imagine just how they might help matters.

When visiting hours were over, after making sure that Jenny would be all right, Mel and Adam went their separate ways. Mel had a daughter to pick up at his parents' and Adam was headed back to Massachusetts.

CHAPTER 24

Doug was slated to return to New York, but at the last minute the group was told that their training had ben extended through Saturday morning, and would resume Monday.

Arriving at the hotel mid- Saturday afternoon, Carole approached Doug, who was standing with two men in intense dialogue. After introductions, the strangers left, and Carole followed her husband into the hotel coffee shop. Neither had eaten since breakfast.

"Doug, we really need to figure out how we're handling all these changes. How much you're going to be down here, whether I should consider taking Barry up on this unbelievable offer. Thank God with all this, I'm not pregnant!"

"You're seriously entertaining taking it? I told Barry that I wouldn't stop him from offering it to you, but I never really considered that you would take it because of Danny. I can see how it'd be tempting…but how can we both have crazy work commitments and still be there for the kids?"

Doug was aware of a beginning anger, but kept himself in check.

"I know that I can't do your job; the hours are impossible, there's no way I would leave Danny for sixty hours a week even if I could handle the responsibilities. But you see how flattered I am, and how tempted I am… how it feels like I'll never have another opportunity like this?"

"Carole, I've never understood why you underestimate yourself. Do you really believe that if you pass this up that you'll never be offered another opportunity? That's ridiculous!"

On the elevator up to Doug's room, the Malones didn't look at each other or exchange a word. Observers couldn't have known that they're a couple. After a brief nap and a call to check on Danny, they taxied over to a very upscale and noisy French restaurant. Luckily for them, it was very difficult to talk, so they concentrated on the excellent cuisine. Then, reacting to Doug's ordering his third martini, Carole abruptly stood up: "Do you need that? How are we supposed to have a conversation with you plastered?" Not waiting for the already ordered dessert, Carole left the restaurant. Just before her leaving, she had tried without success to pursue her objective: "Doug, I want you to tell me what you think I should do about the job offer."

"You're an adult, you know what's right to do, so why are you insisting that I play bad guy? You want me to tell you to go ahead...well that's not going to happen!"

When Doug dropped Carole off at the Delta Connection, he felt crummy and Carole was furious.

I would have loved some alone time when I arrived home, but of course Danny was awake and needing some mommy time, so until his bedtime we were a twosome. Then I unpacked, put away his toys, and read the NY Times magazine and book review sections. A friend of mine who just had a book published was desperate for a review, but didn't get it.

I almost called my parents or my sister, but I didn't want my mother's usual advice (work comes first) or my sister's (you're a mother and should stay home), and I couldn't call Doug because it was past midnight and he was so exhausted. So instead, I went on line, checked my emails, then sent Doug one: "So sad that we had a rough time together. We're both so tense and have so little time together. I'm sorry to have put so much on you because I don't like feeling guilty. I LOVE YOU! Carole"

Just before signing off, I was instant messaged by my friend Dana, who I hadn't heard from in ages. Even though I'm very irritated with her, and think she's unbelievably selfish, I was grateful to talk to anyone, so I immediately wrote back.

"Dana, where are you, how are you? Of course your husband and mother have both called me to find out if I'd heard from you."

"I'm fine, I have a decent job, and I have a new name. Because of that, I'm not calling too often, though Amy's always in my thoughts. I've come close to flying home several times, but truthfully, for now this is the best I can do."

"You are only thinking of yourself, Dana...your daughter needs you.

And Mel is distraught. Your mom has so much on her mind, she probably isn't focused on you the way she'd normally be. Did you know that Adam has filed for divorce? According to Mel, who's in contact with him, Adam says over and over that he loves your mother, but can't go through her chaotic life anymore."

"Tell me about you…surely your life is not so dramatic?"

"Doug's in Washington, training for anti-terrorism work, and we're here in New York. Need I say more? It may not be dramatic, but it is very disruptive. And I'm working many more hours than I'd like."

Signing off, I reflected on the stories that were flooding my brain…determined to hold on to what was most important. In the morning, I emailed my husband: "I will definitely not take the job here unless Barry will allow me to do the supervision in three days, essentially taking me out of the loop for my own cases. Please forgive my selfishness in not showing support to you…As ever, Carole"

When I returned from work Monday evening, I read Doug's email: "You're not being selfish; the change is daunting, chaotic for both of us I fear for the children. We'll figure this out together. It may mean one or both of us will back out if it's too much to manage. Much love, Doug"

Barry agreed to my proposal, though he didn't love it. I could tell because instead of his usual invitation for coffee, and low-key style, he was totally matter of fact, almost formal. He even said that 'we all need to consider how the domestic attacks have changed our lives, and altered our freedom to be cavalier about choices.' It infuriated me that he was intimating that Doug and I are 'cavalier' when we care so much, and want so much to do the right thing. I nearly told him off, but then remembered that he's my boss, and he's almost incredibly stressed by the added demands on him, so I let it go.

I want back to my group with every plan to tell them goodbye, but just being there made me feel that I needed this support. Bill put it very well: "You can't really expect Doug to do it all, even loving you, you know. Why do women always think we can be lovers and great dads, bring home all the money, in short be perfect? No wonder he got drunk it's exactly what I would have done!"

Though I was annoyed and said as much, later I gave a lot of thought to what Bill said. He's essentially right. I want Doug to be my lover and my perfect father…and he actually had been excellent at both until this latest pressure.

It was actually good for me to hear others 'real' problems, Stacy having terrible mood swings as she tries to cope with a very disturbed adolescent with next to no support from her husband, and Peter's serious depression to the point where he can barely make it into the office since his wife filed for divorce. Not that I am happy for their troubles, only that it's possible to put mine in perspective. Plus I haven't really known how to support another adult and put myself aside...that's what the group actually confronted me with. Not easy to hear, but probably true.

The very next day, I remember it was a Thursday, when I got to the office to my surprise Max was already there, deep in conversation with Sam. The FBI had leaned on the Bronx DA to grant Miller full immunity on the recent drug charge to get his full cooperation on the more important old weapons deal.

Max filled me in on what FBI interrogation got so far. "Miller was the middleman between the Russian mafia who supplied the weapons and their customers, who were in three locations here: South Carolina, Montana, and northern Michigan. They paid Miller $100,000. up front to take charge of the shipment, which had come into the country in California because they had felt New York was getting too hot. Also Miller had been living in Arizona, so he preferred a west coast arrangement. Things seemed to be progressing smoothly. He had lined up a tractor-trailer to take charge of the shipment, and was to rendezvous with other smaller truckers in southern New Mexico, to set up the three deliveries. Afterward Miller was to receive another payment of $150,000. Of course, it never happened, and Miller now claims the mob wrote him off as unreliable."

"What do we know about who the recipients were to be?"

"That's the most important part, naturally, since it involves our own wonderful citizens. You know that we've discovered that there are groups in arms training all over the country, some preparing for what they think is the inevitable war against the Muslim world, others who hate our government and our way of life, and still others who are just crazy.

Well, initially Miller claimed not to know just who these three groups were specifically, but we really pushed, and are beginning to get some solid information. He claims that the Montana group is the largest and most dangerous, and the one with whom he had the most pre-shipment contact. He gave us names and dates...never had addresses, but did have telephone contacts with all the groups. Wait'll you hear this! And I put in a call to Doug before six this morning. Azinov was named as the Russian contact here in the U.S who connected Miller to the weapons guys! Now, we never had made this connection ourselves, so no one ever mentioned Azinov...As we speak, the guy is being interrogated."

"For all this, what's with Miller's crack about Bin Laden? Does he have anything which suggests a connection there?"

"So far, nothing. My guess is that he just tried to seduce us with that high profile name. But what we do know is that the Russian mob is arming terrorists all over the world. The Mossad has given us hard data to support this, and are looking into whether that includes nuclear weapons."

"Oh, my God. Max, I'm not sure how much I want to be involved in this...how can we have children, and dream about their future, in such a frightening world?"

"Guess what, Carole, if we don't face reality, and intercept these animals, we might as well throw in the towel on our future. Our knowing whatever we can has already paid tremendous dividends and kept us from even more attacks. Don't think your hiding is the way to go."

"Doug just called on my cell, he's coming into town, didn't even hint about any of this, but obviously this is why." (I had hoped it was missing us.) Hours later, Doug, Max and Sam went down to the prison where Miller's interrogation was continuing, watching from a one way mirror.

Simultaneously, Carole and Evan observed Azinov's interrogation by FBI and AFT case officers. Carole and Evan were quite struck by Azinov's calm demeanor and stonewalling: "I have nothing to hide, I love this country, why would I want to hurt it? A little booze, that's one thing, that you got me with, I love money, but terrorism, absolutely not!"

Azinov, who had already pleaded guilty to racketeering, smuggling and tax evasion, (which he claimed was his primary motivation), denied any connection to arms smuggling. And at present, there was nothing solid to link him to this, beyond Miller's assertion.

Toward the end of the work week, Doug got a call from Max. The continuing interrogations of Miller and Azinov were making progress. "Doug, it's possible that Azinov, besides connecting our homegrown criminals with the Russian mob is also helping them launder money, using his legitimate businesses here. You'd better stay with this case, it's a beaut!"

CHAPTER 25

Jenny sat in her attorney's office within several days of her discharge from Maimonides Hospital. Though Jacob Nathan handled some criminal cases, he had just informed Jenny that she should add to their team with someone more experienced with major crimes.

"You don't seem to believe me anymore, Jacob. I did not go to Paul's store intending to kill him! But when I found him there right after an obvious drug deal, I did go crazy. He had promised me that he was finished with all that…our kids' futures were at stake…"

"So are you saying that you shot him intentionally? Remember, what we say here is confidential."

"I'm not completely sure, but it's possible. I do know that he never did go for the gun, though he begged me to put it away, and at one point seemed sure it was unloaded."

"How good a shot were you? Had you much practice with firearms? I noticed in the earlier transcript that you reported that Paul had provided you with the gun for protection, and had taught you how to use it."

"He did, but I hadn't actually touched it for at least a couple of years. When I took it that night, I planned to check up on him; I didn't trust his promises because he still was getting so many nighttime calls. So I also thought I'd scare him. I didn't want him to see me pull up to the place, so that's why I didn't park in front of the store. Do you believe me?"

"Look, they haven't indicted you yet, so maybe they're not so sure they have the evidence to support a manslaughter charge. With all that they do have, if my partner who has more experience with this agrees, I think we should offer to plead to the lesser manslaughter offense, which does have jail time, but you could be out in four years."

"You want me to go to jail for four years? I'd rather be dead! I prefer to go

213

to trial, just let them try to convict me, someone on the jury will be sympathetic to me. I'll testify."

"Jenny, you're being foolish. There's no way of knowing what will come out of a trial. This ADA is shrewd, he'll never go in without solid witness testimony. What do you think your old mah jong friends know?"

"Nothing! I never told a soul about Paul and his so-called business.

The night of Paul's death I did leave early on some trumped up excuse, and I had never done that before. Our charming hostess asked me up front if I was meeting a lover!"

Jacob's partner, Emily Fox, joined them for the last part of the meeting, getting details from Jenny that Jacob hadn't thought to elicit. Of particular concern was Jenny's going to the vault early on the morning in question to take out bullets for the gun she used to shoot Paul. That fact was unknown to the ADA, but was likely to come out if Jenny testified. So Emily told their client that she could never take the stand if she went to trial. She agreed with Jacob :"accept a plea on man,,, two."

When Jenny arrived at her apartment, she had back-to-back shocks: two officers from NYPD were there to arrest her, charging her with manslaughter; and, daughter Dana was sitting in her living room. The officers were very gracious, allowing Jenny to take some personal items, and to briefly talk with Dana, who did not appear to be shocked at this turn of events. They told the two women that an indictment had been handed down by the grand jury this morning, and that Jenny would be arraigned tomorrow, and of course, they read her rights. Asking Dana to call Jacob, Jenny went off without a struggle.

"Mel, it's Dana. I'm staying at Mom's place. She was just taken away by two detectives, charged with killing my father. I'm dying to see Amy.

Can you bring her here? I have to be in court tomorrow when Mom is arraigned, so can you come tonight?"

"You expect me to jump to your whim after disappearing for months?

There's no way I'm driving into Manhattan tonight, but after the arraignment you should come home to see your daughter. You want to know what you did to her? She's always scared about where I am if I'm ten minutes late. She tries to watch the news, sure you are dead, though of course I've told her otherwise. And she asks me over and over, 'doesn't mommy love us anymore?" Hearing Dana sob at this last, Mel softened a bit.

"We'll have a helluva time ever trusting you again, but at least Amy wants to give you a chance."

CHAPTER 26

Ray Kelly had taken over for his second stint as NYPD Commissioner, and he was really shaping things up. Feeling that the feds had badly let New York City down, he was setting up his own powerful counterterrorism bureau, and staffing it with skilled people from many different backgrounds. Amongst them was David Cohen, formerly CIA's station chief in New York, now appointed NYPD's deputy Commissioner for Intelligence.

Doug had returned to New York, and settled into his new office further downtown. Speaking to former colleague and friend, Emily Fox, Doug said that "things almost seem .back to normal. But of course, now normal means looking south to the barren wasteland that was once the twin towers, and constantly seeing small groups of mourners, among the always present FDNY and NYPD at the site. And, we're all wondering when and where the next attack will occur."

Emily had arranged a lunch date with Doug at Jennifer Levine's request. Her client wanted Emily to consult with Doug because Jenny felt strongly that she would not accept a plea involving jail time. She wants to go to trial. "You know how crazy that is, Doug. The woman actually believes that with all her lies to the police she can convince a jury, or someone on a jury, that she's essentially innocent!"

"Well, Emily, having seen Mrs. Levine on the stand, and remembering how I believed all her lies, maybe she's right!"

"I'm not too happy with your joking like that. She'll hang herself, and you know it!"

"I do not want to get involved in this. Somehow that family, just because Dana and my wife went on tennis competitions together and became casual friends, has entered our lives with all their shit. I want out! So you'll have to tell Mrs. Levine that my general advice is for clients to follow their lawyers' advice or get new lawyers."

When Doug went home that evening and filled Carole in on his conversation with Emily, he was surprised that she totally supported him.

"I really thought you'd be annoyed…how can we get these people out of our lives? They're attractive, smart people, but somehow they're always in trouble, and seeing us as, what, rescuing them?"

"I pretty much told Dana the same thing, that I've given her my best and most caring advice, but she never follows it, so I'm through. It's as if she feels our long ago fun together justifies her asking for my blood!"

Changing the subject, Carole, feeding Danny and simultaneously wiping up the new tiled floor, reported more important news: "I'm pregnant. Two months, if Dr. Cherry is on target. And guess what? I'm so excited about it!" Getting a bear hug from Doug, Carole giggled like a young teenager. "What ever happened to my usual conflict over everything important? Who is this 'sure of herself lady' I've become?!"

In late March, right after Danny's second birthday, the Malones learned that Jenny Levine's trial was on the summer docket, and on the very same day, Doug headed up a large team prosecuting Azinov. It was striking that both defendants who faced overwhelming solid evidence of guilt elected to go to trial, both defying their experienced attorneys' best advice.

The courtroom would be closed to spectators on the Azinov case because the pre-trial motions had garnered such intense and chaotic public response. The defense had been unsuccessful in getting evidence thrown out on civil rights grounds; they claimed that evidence obtained under the Patriot Act's special provisions, should be disallowed.

In speaking to Max, Doug had expressed his own reservations:
"We may be throwing out the proverbial baby with the bath water under this Patriot Act. Some of the stuff you boys collected would be illegal by almost any standards! Are we so sure that what we're up to is kosher?"

"Hey, when those bastards committed mass murder here, they woke up the sleeping giant, now they're gonna pay, big time. What would you have us do, advise them of their rights, pussyfoot around them and make nice? They want to destroy us, any way they can."

"What if we lost what's so special about our lives here in the service of wiping them out? What will we be if not more like them?"

"Bush and Chaney have the right idea…we've gotta go after them, and use every tool we have. What are you, getting soft about this? I'm surprised at you, Doug, you were always a tough bastard! It's part of what I admired about you."

"And how come we're undermining the U.N., almost pushing to go it alone in Iraq, now that Afghanistan is going so well. If we do go, we could turn the place into an inferno, and make the Muslims hate us even more by occupying their territory. Then what? Create a huge training ground for more terrorists? I just hope to God they know what they're doing."

The larger than usual team of assistant U.S. attorneys had been debating these issues, interspersing differing positions throughout their preparation for this very public trial. What they could all agree on was how different the work atmosphere had become, what with the split along political lines, and the emerging subtle distrust of one another. The absence of the esprit de corps that normally permeated their work made the long hours they spent together tense and at times confrontational.

When Doug walked into a pretty volatile pre-trial conference of his top litigators, he felt like yelling at them. Instead, "hey my children, kiss and make up, daddy's here!" Handing out red white and blue lollipops and pints of chocolate milk to his staff's "what are you nuts?", or "give me one, give me one!", the laughter diffused what might have become ugly. Then, via telephone, Max dropped a bombshell in Doug's lap.

"Doug, I hope you're sitting, you won't believe this! Remember the Da Silva case you prosecuted last year, well, the guy requested via his lawyer that we meet with him. I'm coming in to see you, just to see your face when I tell you what he said!"

Before Max arrived, Doug considered many possibilities, but he couldn't have guessed what he ultimately heard.

"Da Silva decided to be a patriot, according to him. Of course, if we can switch him to a more convenient prison, he wouldn't mind the quid pro quo, but no strings."

"Get on with it, Max, you're killing me!"

"Miller had contracted with Da Silva Trucking to transport the 1991 shipment to the three sites. And, guess what? There had been two prior deliveries to other sites, both in 1990. When Miller was intercepted by Alcohol & Firearms, someone alerted the trucking company, so the tractor trailer, and of course, the smaller trucks were immediately cancelled, and Da Silva claims not to know the name of the guy who alerted them. Now's the corker: guess who set Da Silva up with Miller? The wildest guess you can fathom, come on, go for it!"

"Azinov?"

"Jesus, Doug, you're too damn smart! I thought I had you for a minute. Yup…And Da Silva can nail him. So I suggest you ask for a continuance to put it all together."

CHAPTER 27

"It's been very difficult for me to get up the courage to actually make this my last group tonight. You've become so important to me." Looking around, Carole found herself tearing. Peter handed her a tissue, and Bill broke the rules, again, by patting her gently on her knee. "Because of our lives these days, and especially with our work hours, being out still another night doesn't compute for me. And, I'm feeling terrific…have been for months. If I stayed in group, it would be for you guys, and because this once 'quick change artist' now has trouble leaving people who matter.

The group meeting went on, with others touching on their stuff.

Then, halfway through their time, the door opened and shut loudly. In walked Laura! "Hello everyone, I'm back!" Even the leaders were astonished and remained silent. After "What the hell!" from Bill, and a surprisingly warm "Welcome back!" from Stacy, Elaine turned to her coleader, suggesting that they discuss just how to manage this surprise.

They agreed to "wait it out and let the group deal with it"; then Laura filled them in.

"I was on heavy drugs when I was here before, and doing stupid things I never told you. After Bill and I did our thing—I'm sure you know all about that—I went into a drug program. I'm clean for the first time since I was twelve years old. So I'm back to really be in therapy. OK?"

Carole entered her apartment anxious to talk to Doug about how she felt, but found him on a long conference call. She was about to walk out of his 'office' when he motioned her to sit down, and wrote a note: "We got the continuance on Azinov, and now they're talking like they are open to pleading. But not now, we don't know enough!"

At midnight, Doug was ready to talk, but Carole was exhausted, and in bed. Doug asked his wife if she was upset with him that he couldn't talk to her when she clearly wanted to…"Doug, you know we're not there anymore. That's long passed. You probably also have a lot to tell me, but I'm wiped out. We have tomorrow."

Doug, restless though exhausted, went on line. Still another surprise, a helluva lot less important than Azinov: Jenny Levine was acquitted!

THE END

Printed in the United States
51368LVS00004B/31